# Carpe Diem

Caroline,

A piece of my heart lives between the pages of this book.

## Also by Dawn Ramos

*Storybook Romance: the Ultimate 10-Step Guide to Loving Yourself and Improving Your Relationships*

*Christmas in Winchester: A Holiday Love Story*

# *Carpe Diem*

## A BEACH READ LOVE STORY

**DAWN RAMOS**

*Carpe Diem: A Beach Read Love Story*

Copyright © 2022 Dawn Ramos

All rights reserved under International and Pan-American Copyright Conventions. No part of this book may be used or reproduced in any manner whatsoever without written permission from the publisher, except in the case of brief quotations used in critical articles and reviews.

ISBN: 9798421556695 (print)

Edited by Lynne Pearson

Cover and book design by Sue Campbell Book Design

Contact the author: dawnramos.com/contact-us

*This book is dedicated to the loving memory
of my father Allen R. Lane*

While writing Carpe Diem ... I lost my job, sold my house, and lost both my father and father-in-law within a six-month span. Do you need more proof that there is no time like the present to *seize the day*?

### Not Just Another Day
*I woke up this morning and imagine my surprise
when the sky was blue, the sun was shining, and the
birds were chirping.*

*Has no one told them?
People frantically rushed, anxious, overwhelmed, and
exhausted from the pressures of their daily lives, completely
missing the beauty surrounding them.
I watched in disbelief …
Did they not know how precious each day was?*

*Life …
How can something so relentless and cold also be
so delicate and magnificent?
Here one day and gone the next… giving no
promises of tomorrow.*

*Is it possible that when one life is over the others must go on?
Has no one told them my father is gone?*

## CHAPTER ONE

Bella sat on the beach in a cross-legged posture, eyes closed, back tall, shoulders relaxed, while her hands rested gently in her lap. When her best friend Amber told her the ancient practice helped people with everything from stress management to anxiety, she knew she had to try it, but Amber didn't divulge how ridiculous she'd feel sitting there doing absolutely nothing. Bella inhaled a deep breath and attempted to focus more on the breath itself rather than the chaos in her mind.

Despite her best effort, she couldn't stop her mind from wandering. Meditation was supposed to clear her thoughts, yet it made her think twice as much. She thought about everything from generating more sales to a passing bird pooping on her head. She cracked her left eye the tiniest bit to ensure her safety from flying predators.

Like a gift from God, the sun's golden warmth shone down, making her feel like the only person on earth. Providing her the comfort and reassurance she needed, somehow everything would be alright.

Bella sat for a few more minutes, admiring the beauty of the Pacific Ocean. The crystal blue water mesmerized her, and the steady ebb and flow of the waves stole her heart. Most people would spend months or even years considering a cross country move to a place they'd only heard about, but not Bella. It took a piece of paper and a few hours. She was head over heels in love with Coronado, California and wanted to shout it from the beach.

A glance at her phone revealed she'd been meditating for thirty-five minutes straight. Her best stretch to date, she did a little dance to celebrate.

She dusted the sand from her legs, grabbed her eco-friendly canvas bag, and headed for the nearby palm tree where her beach cruiser waited.

A year ago, she would have laughed at the idea of a bicycle as her primary source of transportation, but somehow, she made it her new reality with little effort. She took pride in simplicity, and her Tiffany Blue bike with an attached basket reminded her of that.

Cruising down Orange Ave, the crisp breeze kissed her face and danced through her dark brown hair. Riding her bike felt like therapy because all the thoughts swimming through her mind during meditation seemed to drift away.

The strand was peaceful this time of day, with only a couple of early morning joggers and a few dog walkers. Thanks to scorching temperatures predicted for this afternoon, soon, it would be flooded with stay-at-home moms, and college students headed to the beach. The average temperature year-round on Coronado Island was an ideal seventy degrees, so when there was an expected ninety-degree day, the locals went straight to the ocean. Those fresh faces were the clientele she needed to walk through the door.

Just over the horizon, she could see Carpe Diem. Sandwiched between the Ex-Squeeze Me Juice Bar and Jack's Brews and BBQs. She was proud of the little boutique that changed her life. Freedom to make her own choices, freedom from her parents, and the chance to design a life with an exciting future.

The angelic sound of chimes welcomed her as she opened the door. She jammed a wooden wedge below to prop it open and flipped the sign to welcome. Being functional and practical, her bike looked like a piece of vintage art when she parked it in the far corner of the store. The bike complemented a powder pink beach towels display while providing a suitable place to store it.

The store had a specific vibe: boho, hippy, with a dash of beach goddess. Featuring high-quality clothing, accessories, and fun odds and ends like the sign above the door. It read, "Whatever is good for your soul, do that." A reminder to never return to her old life.

After a full sweep of the floor, she noticed a couple of wrinkled garments. Bella grabbed her new steamer and got to work, making light-duty of the task utilizing her favorite business investment to date. She smiled, considering and rejecting the idea of taking home the antique white dress she worked on.

Most people only saw the color white but not Bella; she saw the entire palette of possibilities from eggshell to cream. In her childhood dreams, she was a fashion designer, often creating one-of-a-kind pieces using old sheets and a dynamite hand stitch her nona taught her. Designing dresses kept her busy, locked away in her room for a month or more. Her dreams came to a screeching halt when her mother discovered she had destroyed the new Egyptian cotton sheets intended for the guest room.

One last glance around the store convinced Bella that today sales would start to improve. The crowd made their way to the beach, and she was ready for them. She even promised a pair of beaded chandelier earrings that she'd find them a loving home today if it was the last thing she did. Bella loved every piece of jewelry in her store. She obtained a unique selection of handmade accessories, all crafted in California. She spent time getting to know designers by their reputation for quality materials and customer satisfaction. She only selected the very best from ethical companies whose designs complemented the boutique's style.

In her twenties, she'd spent most of her free time in boutiques like Carpe Diem. Learning about different designers and spending way too much money on her apparel. Bella considered herself to be put together. She always wore something gorgeous and accented with unique accessories but never over the top. She believed true beauty didn't need to be overdone.

The store featured vibrant colors, funky patterns, on-trend clothing, an easily accessible location, yet Carpe Diem struggled. She tried everything: fliers, banners, even an ad in a local magazine, but nothing seemed to work. Last month, a persistent sales guy explained the value of printed marketing for over an hour. He could get an advertisement for her store into the mailboxes of thousands of Coronado residents, and she was ready to make a one-year commitment until he revealed it would cost her over a thousand bucks a month.

It was like Carpe Diem was hidden from the world by an invisible cloak. Why were people going into neighboring businesses and skipping hers altogether?

Amber whooshed in like a breath of fresh air, looking fabulous in her mint green yoga pants with coordinating sports bra. She had the body of an athlete thanks to her rigorous schedule and tenacity. Bella admired Amber's determination but embraced the goddess curves she had thanks to a combination of genetics and a love of carbs.

Proudly displaying the juice of the day, Amber let out an enthusiastic, "OMG – Oh My Ginger. This one has apple, lemon, and lots of ginger; you're gonna love it." Only she could get this excited about juice. "It's like spicy lemonade."

Amber had a sassy pixie cut with pale blonde hair and the most beautiful hazel eyes that shifted color with her mood and clothing selection. Helping people live a vibrant, healthy lifestyle was her first mission in life. The second was more complex. She wanted to fall in love, get married, and have kids before her thirty-fifth birthday.

"You're up and at it this morning," said Bella.

"I have a busy day. I opened the juice bar at six, I have yoga classes at 9:00 and 11:00, then back here for a couple of Reiki sessions." Amber had more income streams than any one person should ever consider. She loved living in Coronado and worked hard to afford the swanky lifestyle she'd grown accustomed to. She made balancing three jobs, dating consistently, running an average of three miles per day while still having the desire to hang out with her bestie look easy. At the end of a long day, Bella barely had enough gas left in the tank to grab takeout and wash the makeup from her face.

"Do you want to come over later?" Bella asked. "There is a new rom-com on Netflix."

Amber laughed out loud. "Are you asking me to Netflix and chill?"

With a raised brow, Bella replied, "I guess I am."

"Sweet, I'll be there, but I'm bringing my table. You need a session."

"A Reiki session?" *Damn.* She dodged that bullet the last time Amber offered. Nothing personal against Reiki; it sounded like more mumbo jumbo malarkey. She'd already given in to Amber's plea for her to drink juice and begin a meditation practice. Now she wanted her to do Reiki too?

"Yes, don't even try to say no. If I have to watch a rom-com with you, then you're going to drink some wine and open your heart chakra."

As a skeptical girl from Ohio, she was hesitant about the new age hoopla Amber peddled. Bella huffed and puffed before she finally agreed. "Deal, I mean, how bad can it be anyway?"

Amber threw a triumphant fist into the air before heading to the door. "See you later."

Bella frequently skipped breakfast, and being a thoughtful person, Amber always brought her a juice to help get her morning started on the right foot. Not always loving the juice, she appreciated Amber's kindness and even started to look forward to the juice of the day. Bella cracked the seal on the cool bottle dripping condensation along the sides and verbalized an enthusiastic *OMG* before gulping the spicy lemonade. She raised her brow and nodded in agreement. "Not too bad," she confessed to herself.

The store was kept in immaculate condition, and most mornings, she'd either fold shirts or rearrange the window display. She decided to take another crack at the window display, convinced if she made it impressive enough, she'd attract new customers. She moved items back and forth while her favorite nineties grunge mix played overhead.

Entranced by the ocean air and blue skies with fluffy white clouds, she reflected on how different life in California felt. It wasn't only the weather; everything seemed different, the trees, people, even she felt different. No longer the same girl she left behind in the Midwest, she felt independent and stronger than ever before.

Confident this display showcased her best work to date, she checked another item off her mental to-do list. Only one task remained. She filled her arms with the boxes from yesterday's shipments and thrust her hip at the metal bar to release the back door. The big blue recycle bins were approximately fifty yards away, giving her enough time to be there and back in three minutes if she hustled. Tucked away behind a tall picket fence, she blindly hurled the boxes into the air toward the dumpster. Above the thud of the boxes dropping into the container, she heard people arguing. Not able to make out the words from the heated conversation, she peeked from behind the enclosure and saw her neighbors from the restaurant.

Bella needed to get back to the store because she'd left the front door wide open, and if manifestations actually worked, she was expecting a swarm of customers today. Determined not to interrupt their squabble, she decided it would be best to wait for a couple of minutes. Hoping to hear some gossip to share with Amber, she remained still.

"Damn it, Jack, I'm tired of the lies. You need to come up with the cash, or you can forget about it." Chelsea was obviously furious over a financial issue, but Bella needed more information.

"I told you I'm trying. I don't understand why you're being so unreasonable." Jack responded in a steady low tone like he could soothe her into submission.

"You better get your shit together soon. I'm done with California, I'm done with your empty promises, and I'm done with you," Chelsea fired back, then stormed off, leaving Jack behind.

This wasn't the first time Chelsea displayed a hot temper. On two separate occasions, she'd yelled at Amber for parking in an area that she deemed for customers only and even threatened to have Amber's car towed away.

Hearing a loud bang, Bella peeked back around the corner. Jack kicked the side of a small storage unit several times while he rambled on about something she couldn't make out. He looked up and made direct eye contact. She had been discovered, and the expression on Jack's face informed her that she was not welcome.

He looked to the sky and shook his head before stomping off toward the back door of his restaurant.

Bella wasn't oblivious to his rich chocolate brown eyes or how attractive he looked sporting a five o'clock shadow. His style made him look carefree, but his rock-hard biceps and plethora of tattoos told a different story. No matter how hot Jack appeared, he screamed trouble. More than likely, he and Chelsea were a perfect match.

Her three-minute trip to the dumpster left Bella a bit frazzled and more confused than ever about her hot angry neighbor and his irate, beautiful fiancée. She didn't know much about them except what she'd gathered from her observations. Jack practically lived at the restaurant; he was the first to arrive and the last to leave. They were difficult to work for, judging by their tempers and the steady stream of new employees. Last but not least, one of them was responsible for the smell of hickory-smoked ribs that lingered in the air, reminding her of the Berea National Rib Cook-Off and making her stomach grumble in the afternoons.

Eager to get back to the comfort of her space, she darted across the lot and through the back door of Carpe Diem. She had been gone for a good ten minutes, and anything could have happened during that time. She glanced around the store to ensure everything remained as she left it and was surprised to find Mr. Douglas waiting for her.

He cleared his throat. "Good morning, Bella."

Startled, she wondered how long he'd been standing there.

Wearing his staple three-piece grey suit and carrying his leather briefcase, her accountant, Mr. Douglas, was somewhat of an odd duck. Shorter than the average man, he had brown hair he kept combed over to the right, was clean-shaven, and was pleasingly plump in the midsection. Bella found his quirks to be rather endearing because they reminded her of her dad's brother Phil. Like Mr. Douglas, Phil had sweaty palms and a need to blink more times per minute than any human should.

After interviewing more than twenty accountants, Bella had chosen Sunshine Tax Pros to help her with her business and financial needs. Mr. Douglas lived in Southern California his whole life and had many connections within the community. He presented her with a comprehensive financial plan that included everything from a recommended POS system to individuals who would assist her with getting things established. She didn't need to worry about anything, including obtaining her business license, build-out, insurance, advertising, and of course, her finances. Absolutely everything she needed was carefully outlined in the red binder he'd made for her.

She welcomed him with a smile, "Hello. What brings you in today?"

"Did I disturb you?" He inquired with a raised brow and a look of concern.

"You're always welcome, Mr. Douglas. What's up?"

"I'm afraid I have some rather unpleasant news." He straightened out his bold-framed glasses and looked to the ceiling before making eye contact. He said, "I know you've been working tirelessly to improve your sales, but things are much worse than I anticipated."

"Worse?" Her stomach in knots, she gulped and braced for the new information.

"I'm afraid so." He shifted his weight from one foot to the other. "Last night, I reviewed the numbers, and if you're lucky, you'll have enough capital to get you through the next six months."

Her stomach felt like someone punched her in the gut. Barely able to gather her thoughts, she replied, "Six months. How's that possible? Last month when we spoke, you said I'd have enough for at least another year." He'd explained things weren't progressing as well as he'd hoped, and she'd need to tighten her belt a little more if sales didn't increase rapidly. She kept the binder behind the register and stuck by the plan to the letter. There were precise instructions for her personal budget and the store's expenses. She tried her best to follow his advice, but it seemed that it still wasn't enough despite her best efforts.

"You've been doing great sticking to the budget, but I told you the store wasn't earning enough to sustain itself. I recommended you diversify your portfolio to cover the deficit, and with your permission, I moved a sizeable amount of assets over to a high yield investment. That investment didn't perform as expected, and unfortunately, we took a big hit. It's all in here." He handed her a report that he said included spreadsheets, graphs, financial statements, and banking information. "I'm so sorry, Bella, but I need you to look this over and make some decisions."

Bella had tremendous respect for Mr. Douglas; not only had he been her first friend in California, he'd walked her through this journey side by side, a trusted advisor who did an excellent job helping her understand the unknown aspects of her new world. "I don't understand how this is possible."

He rested his hand on her shoulder and lowered his head. "Please review the report and consider your options. I feel terrible about this."

"You have no control over the market. I should have researched the stock better before I agreed to move assets."

He sighed heavily, looking somber. "Let me know what you decide."

Bella clutched the report, still home to the sweaty fingerprints of Mr. Douglas. He was her most trusted advisor, and according to him, she was screwed.

She couldn't deal with this right now; she had a store to run and since crawling into her bed wasn't an option, the coping skill she would embrace to get through the rest of the day had to be denial. She placed the report in a manila envelope behind the counter and continued reworking the window display like she hadn't received the second worst news of her life. If she couldn't control the financial state of the store, at least she could control the physical state.

# CHAPTER TWO

Salted caramel popcorn and white wine sounded like a perfectly acceptable dinner until Amber arrived. "Where's the food in this place?" she demanded, holding both refrigerator doors open as if the electric bill weren't high enough.

"I worked later than I thought, and I didn't have time to stop on the way home." Bella didn't have the heart to tell Amber that she was preoccupied with an all-consuming pity party caused by her financial woes.

"Unacceptable, Bella, this isn't dinner, this is … poison, filled with GMOs." She plopped down on the plush white bean bag chair.

Bella needed her best friend by her side to keep her company, despite her apparent disapproval of the evening's dinner selection.

For the first time in her life, Bella felt happy, and now because of one foolish decision, she could lose it all. She loved Carpe Diem, her friends, and even the tiny apartment she called home. Her teenage years were spent at open houses, preparing offers, and following up with title companies. She wanted to attend The Fashion Institute of Technology in New York, but her mother refused to indulge her childhood fantasies, insisting real estate was the logical option. When Nona gave her the gift of opportunity, she jumped on it. Finally able to taste a mouthwatering bite of her dream, it was about to crash to the floor.

Bella extended the bowl of popcorn toward Amber like a second-rate peace offering. Amber reluctantly accepted, "We're doing your Reiki session before the movie."

"Okay, but why are we doing this again?"

Amber threw her hands into the air. "Because your heart's blocked, that's the reason you haven't been able to accept love into your life."

"I *can* accept love. Right now, I have a lot on my plate, and I'm not looking for anything serious."

Amber said in a condescending tone, "I know, that's because your heart chakra is closed, and we need to open it."

"Touché," replied Bella. She didn't intentionally block her heart, but who could blame her after Andrew broke things off. He politely explained that he tried his best to make things work, but his lack of attraction to her led to their ultimate demise. Not only did she fall flat in the bedroom, but she failed to stimulate his mind too. He said mentally and professionally that he would always see her as his inferior and deserved more than that.

After a month of tears, she found the courage to scrape the remains of her ego from the floor and attend a few top-secret counseling sessions. She learned that her relationship with Andrew mirrored her relationship with her mother. Toxic and abusive, yet she still craved their approval.

"Get on the table."

Using the scrunchie from her wrist, she pulled her hair into a high bun. She lay face-up on the table and contemplated if Amber could help her overcome the years of heartache, pain, and sadness left behind by her abusers.

She tried her best to steer clear of heavy topics with her friends in California because she wanted to leave her memories behind with the broken version of herself in Ohio.

When she arrived in California, she signed a lease for an apartment, a storefront, and a new life. Mr. Douglas showed her kindness and compassion. She swore she'd never forget how many late nights he spent with her helping to get all her affairs in order. At the grand opening of Carpe Diem, he hugged her tightly and said he was proud of all she had accomplished in such a short time. Her whole life, she wanted her parents to be proud of her. An accomplishment she never achieved, but Mr. Douglas's encouragement gave her the reassurance she needed in a small way.

Amber said, "Alexa play spa music." She lit some incense, dimmed the lights, and grabbed something from her bag. "Close your eyes and try to relax."

The sounds of nature filled the room as Bella closed her eyes. A gentle running stream, the call of a bird, and the chirping of some insect were all she could decipher. She took in a deep breath and exhaled, slow and steady. If a cosmic event blocked her heart, she wanted it to be open, or at least she thought she did.

"In Reiki, I don't always touch my clients. I place my hands above them and read their energy, manipulating that energy to improve the flow and vibration. I want to place this rose quartz in your hand to encourage the connection of universal love," Amber spoke in a low, peaceful tone.

Bella wanted to laugh, but she knew Amber would be upset, so instead, she did as instructed and gripped the stone. She wanted to believe this could work, but her inner skeptic challenged her hopeless romantic and lost. Amber must have picked up on her cynicism because she told her to relax and enjoy the experience.

*Did she abandon me to finish off the popcorn?* She peeked to see Amber holding her hands above Bella's body, wearing a look of deep concentration. She closed her eyes before she could be busted and opted to unwind and enjoy the peaceful experience as Amber had instructed.

An intense heat radiated from her shoulders and gradually moved to her toes. She had to admit, even if she couldn't rationalize it, something was causing the strangest sensation she'd ever experienced. In a low and reassuring tone, Amber said, "Let go and allow the energy to flow through you."

Emotion overwhelmed her. She tried to fight back, but it was too late, her eyes filled with tears as the most powerful feelings she'd ever experienced flooded through her. Embarrassed, she allowed the river to pour from her eyes and down her cheeks, assuming that would be less conspicuous than wiping her face to remove them. Plagued with feelings of failure and a deep desire to be good enough for her parents made the waterworks increasingly challenging to restrain. Bella wasn't sure if this outburst was due to Reiki or if she could blame it on the conversation with Mr. Douglas earlier in the day.

She needed to calm down, or Amber would have questions, questions she wasn't prepared to answer. With a focused effort, the heat that once raged in her body mellowed to a warm simmer. Finally able to relax, her mind settled into a dream-like peaceful state. What seemed like a few minutes later, Amber interrupted her tranquility by whispering, "You can open your eyes when you're ready."

"Are we done?"

Amber snickered and nodded in confirmation.

"I have to admit Reiki felt weird, but it was painless and strangely relaxing."

Amber rolled her eyes. "I told you so. I don't know why you were so resistant in the first place."

Grateful the evidence of her tears had disappeared, Bella floated from the table, feeling weightless for the first time in what felt like her entire life. "Thank you, I don't know if it opened any chakras, but I feel amazing."

"I hate to say I told you so, but …."

"Yeah, yeah." Bella changed the subject. "Guess what I saw today?"

"What?"

"Jack and Chelsea." Amber knew that Bella had a schoolgirl crush on Jack but wouldn't dare act on it. "This morning, I went to throw out the recycling, and he was fighting with her in the parking lot. I hid behind the wall, but he saw me and stormed off mumbling under his breath."

"I wonder what they were fighting about?"

"I'm not sure, but they looked really mad. I did hear her say she was done with his lies and done with him, but the rest was a blur."

"Damn. That is some juicy gossip."

"If he's looking for some hot revenge sex, I'd be happy to help him," Bella said with a wink.

"It's been so long for you. I kind of don't blame you."

"No way, I don't care how yummy he is. Those two hotheads deserve each other."

"I told you, he might be sexy, but he's trouble. That's not the first time someone has caught those two fighting out back." Amber ate a couple more pieces of popcorn. "The last couple times I've seen Chelsea, she hasn't been wearing her engagement ring."

"Sounds like there's trouble in paradise," said Bella, almost holding back a smile.

Amber rolled her eyes, refusing to indulge Bella's curiosity. "Forget about your revenge sex and his washboard abs. You need to stay focused on the hundreds of eligible bachelors walking past your door every day."

"Okay, I'm sorry I brought it up. Pass me the popcorn … please."

Not willing to share, Amber placed a single kernel of popcorn in her mouth while looking sideways at Bella.

"I don't understand how someone so small can be so mean."

"Practice," Amber replied. "There's something else I want to talk to you about from your session."

Wondering what else she could know from holding her hands above her body, she asked, "And what might that be?"

"I felt a blockage in your solar plexus."

She replied, "I don't have solar power," in an awkward attempt to be funny.

"Solar Plexus, not solar power." She tossed a pillow at Bella. "It confirmed a feeling I've had. Are you in trouble?"

*No way. Could Amber pick up on her financial situation from a Reiki session?* "What are you talking about? I'm not in any trouble, you weirdo." And threw the pillow back to the bean bag chair.

Amber restarted the movie and said, "Whatever you say. Don't call me when your world comes crashing down."

The movie checked all the boxes Bella hoped it would, funny, charming, and romantic. Too bad she spent the entire time distracted by Amber's comments. Did she wear her stress so externally Amber could feel it with her hands hovering above her body? Guilt consumed her for not talking to her best friend, but she couldn't bring herself to say the words out loud.

"Can you believe we did a one-hour Reiki session, watched a movie, polished off a bottle of wine, and it's not even eleven yet?"

"The Reiki lasted an hour? It felt like fifteen minutes max."

"Yep, one hour."

Could she have been in a hypnotic trance? Maybe she fell asleep while lying there and talked in her sleep. That would explain how Amber knew about her financial trouble. Doing her best to redirect the conversation, Bella asked, "Any fun dates I need to hear about?"

Hunting for men seemed like a sport to Amber. She would meet people for lunch, dinner, coffee, workouts, and even hikes. It was a wonder she hadn't already dated every available bachelor on the island. Bella understood how most people could see Amber as intimidating. She packed a lot of dynamic qualities into a tiny body; unapologetic, loud, confident, hardworking, and knew exactly what she wanted.

Amber threw herself back in the chair, closed her eyes, and said, "Let me think for a second."

It was comical, Bella hadn't had a date in over a year, and Amber had so many she needed time to think about which ones were worth mentioning.

"Okay, I met with the doctor, you know, the one I met last month. We went to grab some coffee and a take a walk." She paused for a moment. "He reached out to hold my hand, and we had a great conversation. I think this guy is perfect. Maybe he's even, you know," using air quotes "*The one*. Out of nowhere, he asks me if I would consider having a threesome with him and his wife." She grabbed the pillow, placed it over her face, and screamed like a teenage girl.

"And you're telling me about this now?" Bella loved listening to Amber's dating stories. She even tried to talk her into writing a book about it.

"I was so embarrassed. I'm thinking, maybe he is the one and, he's married?"

Emphasizing each word, "Oh my ginger," Bella tried to lighten the mood while referring to the juice of the day.

"I know, I'm sorry. I should have told you sooner."

"So, what did you do?" asked Bella

"I guess you'd say I asked him to get lost in a *much* more colorful way. Funny thing, he seemed shocked by my reaction."

"Are you okay?" Bella asked with genuine concern.

"Me, absolutely, but I don't think the doctor would agree," she replied with a smirk.

"Is there anything else I should know about?"

Amber hung her head low. "There is one more thing."

Eagerly anticipating what she could follow up the doctor's story with, Bella waited.

"Don't be mad, and try to have an open mind," said Amber.

Now, even more curious, she raised her eyebrows and tilted her head.

"I signed us up for speed dating tomorrow night."

Without hesitation, Bella replied, "Nope," simultaneously shutting off the TV. "I'm not going speed dating or slow dating, for that matter."

"No, you owe me. I gave you a free Reiki session."

"One I didn't ask for." Bella shook her head in disbelief.

"Either way, you don't want to leave me to the wolves and doctors all by myself, do you?" asked Amber.

Amber had 100 percent commitment to her marriage plan, and her dedication caused her selection process to suffer. On the other hand, Bella spent her time being entirely too critical. She hadn't given any man, even the good ones a chance, choosing to spend her nights alone. She dated a couple times back in Ohio but quickly realized she could never give her heart away again after the terrible things Andrew said.

"They make the best chicken wings around."

Amber knew where to find Bella's weak spots. "Can I get all flats? Do they charge extra for ranch?"

"Are you serious?" Amber jumped out of her seat. "Are you gonna come with me?"

Surprised by her reaction Bella watched while Amber enjoyed the moment.

"Do you have any idea what this means?" She settled down and made a serious face. She leaned in and declared, "It worked."

Bella realized Amber was referring to the Reiki session. She let out a belly laugh. "It did *not* work."

Serious as a heart attack, Amber looked at her and said, "Bella Roberts are you trying to tell me my Reiki was ineffective?"

"I'm not saying you did anything wrong, only that it's not the reason I decided to go."

"Then why today of all days did you decide to say yes?"

She paused for a beat. *What if it did work?* Amber asked her to go a million times, and a million times she said no, but not today. What made today different? "Did you see dinner tonight, popcorn and wine, maybe I'm hungry, or maybe I'm drunk. Did you consider that?"

"Okay, we'll pretend it didn't work. Will that make you feel better?"

Bella chose silence in response to Amber's snide question. She shut off the lights and walked to the kitchen.

Amber settled in her chair, grinning like the Cheshire Cat. "I'll swing by Carpe Diem when it closes tomorrow." She continued, "Wear something hot, grab me something fun too, in purple."

# CHAPTER THREE

It took ten trips to the dressing room to find the perfect outfit for speed dating. She wanted something to flatter her curvy body and said I'm available but not desperate, even though she was beginning to feel a little desperate. She settled on a beige ruffle mini dress with teal accents, ankle booties, and the cutest pair of dangle earrings with sparkle embellishments.

The idea of speed dating terrified her. She hadn't been on a date in well over a year, and now she had a one-way ticket to the lion's den, courtesy of her best friend. From what she remembered, the first few minutes of a date were always the most awkward, and tonight that process would be stuck on a loop for at least an hour.

Bella did fine on her own for the most part, but she wished she had someone to snuggle with on the couch after a long day. They could talk about their dreams or make plans for the future. Tonight, when fear of rejection or feelings of insufficiency reared their ugly heads, she needed to be prepared.

It couldn't have been more than eleven by nine inches, but the manila envelope Mr. Douglas gave her haunted her from every corner of the store, like one of those paintings that won't stop looking at you. If she opened it, she'd be confirming her worst nightmares. Not only did Bella feel like a complete failure, but she let down Nona, the only person in the world who ever believed in her.

Bella's attitude infuriated her. She was not a failure, at least not yet. She needed to fight, which was exactly what she was prepared to do. The white flag would not be raised today or any other if she could help it.

On the long journey from Ohio, she'd filled the hours dreaming about her new life in Coronado. She knew starting a business required lots of legal paperwork and financial planning because she spent her whole life watching her parents do it.

Now, she spent her evenings developing marketing strategies, and one of them was bound to work. Getting foot traffic into a retail clothing store seemed to be a bigger mountain to climb than she'd anticipated.

She had marketing experience with the Roberts Group, but the activities differed. Her mother's real estate business was well established in the community. She would send birthday and Christmas cards to previous customers. Email them with helpful tips for homeowners and changes in market conditions.

Carpe Diem had customers, but Mr. Douglas told her it wasn't enough. She thought about hiring a consultant, but he explained they were costly and financially irresponsible.

She knew they needed to go digital if they wanted to keep up with the times. He recommended a local web designer who could help her create a website and improve her social media presence, but the store needed to generate more income before spending more money.

The plan she and Mr. Douglas had established was good; she needed to trust the process. She treated the red binder like a Bible, a pathway to achieving everything she wanted. He assured her if she stuck to the budget he provided her, she'd have plenty to cover three years of personal and business expenses, giving the store time to support itself and become profitable.

Finally living her dream, she dedicated herself to doing whatever was necessary to make it work. She gave Mr. Douglas access to her assets and complete control of her finances. Her apartment was only a short walk away from Carpe Diem, so she sold her car and kept her expenses to the bare minimum to prove her dedication. With no plan B, this had to work.

The stress started last month when Mr. Douglas reached out and informed her things weren't going as planned. According to the plan, she should have two years of expenses available, which was now decreased by half. She understood the urgency of the matter and agreed maybe investing in some high yield opportunities was what she needed to get back on track. He told her it was a safe investment, but she had no idea when he said *safe*, his definition was tremendously different from hers. The investment failed terribly and cost her another six months of operating expenses. Now she was faced with a much different reality.

The idea of returning to Ohio and hustling houses to the highest bidder was horrifying, but she wasn't qualified to do anything else. How could she be so negligent with the money it took her nona a lifetime to earn? Face flushing and pulse quickening, she could not catch her breath as panic consumed her.

Her head hung low, and tears streamed from her eyes; she had to call her mother and admit defeat. Would her mother even forgive her for losing the money? Her parents wanted her to take the inheritance and start her own commercial brokerage. They wanted to do residential, and she would sell commercial spaces. They'd be the top-selling real estate group in the Midwest, but that wasn't her dream.

Bella loved fashion; her dream was Carpe Diem. Her nona made it a reality, and she'd let her down. She grasped the guardian angel pendant she wore around her neck, hoping somehow, her nona watched over her. She needed to compose herself before Amber arrived with the juice of the day.

She wiped her face with the sleeve of her shirt and began to refresh her makeup. How was it that emotional stress could make you so physically exhausted? She looked at herself in the dressing room mirror, and her blue eyes glistened, but she and her nona knew when her eyes sparkled like that, she'd been crying.

She breathed a sigh of relief, realizing Tiffany and Addison were scheduled to work tomorrow morning. Two college students she hired when the store first opened, their schedules perfectly complemented what she needed to fill the gaps. Giving her time to do things like grocery shopping or appointments. Tomorrow she would use the time for something entirely different. She wanted to sleep in, read one of Nona's best sellers and feel sorry for herself.

Amber hurried through the door and set a whiteish-colored juice on the counter. "It's Coco Delight. It helps with hydration, but I gotta go."

Bella welcomed the distraction but twisted her body away to hide the evidence of her bloodshot eyes.

"Thanks, Amber," Bella called out to her friend's retreating back.

Bella grabbed the ice-cold juice from the counter and read the label. The ingredients were coconut water and coconut meat. It sounded harmless enough; she liked coconut. She shook the bottle, cracked open the lid, and smelled the milk-like substance. It didn't smell anything like coconut, but she still decided to take a gulp and instantly felt nauseous. *More like Coco Disgusting.*

The day flew by, and Bella sold over two thousand dollars in merchandise, a new record high. A born salesperson, she only needed a person to walk through the door, and she'd be able to find them something they couldn't live without. She had a knack for knowing what clothing and accessories would complement any body type. When a person left Carpe Diem, they looked and felt like a million bucks. She was on a roll and still expecting another hundred from Amber for tonight's new purple dress, sandals, and earrings.

Two more customers entered the store as her cell phone began to ring. She excused herself and grabbed the phone. "Hey Addie, what's up?"

"Is it okay if Tiffany opens in the morning by herself? I'll be right behind her like twenty minutes tops."

"Sure, no problem. Does she already know you'll be in a little late?"

"No, I haven't had a chance to tell her yet."

"No worries, I'll shoot her a text and let her know," replied Bella

"Awesome, thanks."

In the zone, she didn't want to let the last two customers slip through her fingers. She grabbed the first thing she saw, the manila envelope, wrote

Tiffany across the top, then propped it on the register to serve as a reminder to text Tiffany before she left tonight.

"How can I help you," asked Bella.

"She needs something for a first date." The taller girl pointed to her friend.

"I can help with that. Where are you going?"

"We're going to a cool new sushi restaurant near the pier."

"I have some great options for you, let me get you into a dressing room, and we'll see what you like."

"Perfect."

Bella grabbed a few dresses and led the girls to the back. "Here are three different dresses that are going to look dynamite on you." She turned her attention to the friend and said, "I have a couple for you to try on too. Let me know what you think, and I'll grab a couple others." The girls disappeared into their rooms, appearing eager to try on Bella's selections.

Bella swept through the store, finding several more items to keep them entertained. If she could get a person into the clothes, they'd leave as a customer. She made sure every person who came to her store had an outstanding shopping experience using her three-step process. First, treat them like a friend, second get them in a dressing room, and finally, keep the clothes coming until they fell in love.

It wasn't long before both girls found something they needed to have, bringing Bella's grand total to $2350 for the day. "Thank you so much, and I hope to see you again soon." Bella waved before locking the door behind them.

Having preplanned her ensemble, it took only ten minutes to get dressed, re-touch her makeup, and pull her hair into a loose bun. This way, she could show off her neck and new dangle earrings. Amber arrived shortly after, still wearing her yoga clothes, but her hair and makeup were perfect as usual.

"I thought you were backing out on me."

"Fat chance," Amber said, tossing her bag into the corner. "Did you find me a dress?"

Bella held up the eggplant-colored dress. "What do you think?"

Amber snatched it from her hands with wide eyes. "Love it!"

"I thought the color would be perfect for your skin tone."

It took her approximately sixty seconds to change before throwing the curtain doors open with both arms like she had arrived at the academy awards. The stunning V-neck mini dress left her back exposed and cinched her tiny waist with an embellished pattern of flowers. The exaggerated sleeves and flowing skirt gave her an appearance of flirty and fun for their night on the town.

"Girl, you look a-maz-ing."

"I know," Amber said with a wink. "How much do I owe you?"

"Well, the dress is forty-five, but if you want the matching sandals and earrings, it will be one hundred."

"What a deal," said Amber.

Bella's phone pinged with the one-hundred-dollar payment from Amber. "Let's go!"

"Where do you get so much energy?"

"Do you promise not to tell anyone?" Amber leaned in and looked directly into Bella's eyes, "It's the juice."

She should have expected an answer like that. She thought, I drink one juice a day and don't have a fraction of Amber's energy. How many juices is she drinking?

Amber unlocked the doors to her Audi, forcing Bella to realize she was moments away from chatting with more men than she had in the last year. "I'm going to kill you for bringing me here."

"Focus on the chicken wings." For someone so health-conscious, she had no problem using food as leverage to entice Bella, promising all flats and free ranch. "You're going to be fine, and you might even meet someone you like."

Unsure what she even wanted to accomplish at speed dating, Bella immediately had second thoughts. She knew she believed in love, but she didn't have the same hopes as Amber did. She'd read about true love her whole life was hopeful it still existed, but if her parents couldn't love her, how could she expect someone else to? "Sure, maybe I'll get lucky, and Jack will be there. We could spend the night having that revenge sex."

"You're only obsessed with him because you can't have him. He's safe."

"Safe?"

"Yeah, you can't have him, he can't hurt you, there's no chance of rejection or heartbreak. Who hurt you, Bella Roberts?" Amber said with a chuckle.

She smiled at Amber's remark but reflected on her past. Did the constant ridicule from her mother and Andrew make her broken? Was she damaged goods incapable of being in a healthy relationship? This was not the right time to deflate her ego; she needed to change the subject and fast. "How does all this work?"

"Relax, babe, it's all pretty self-explanatory. Besides, I'll be right there with you every step of the way."

When they pulled into valet, it was apparent Amber had been to this establishment before. The attendant knew her by name and gave her a once over. She handed him the keys and a five-dollar tip before waltzing through the door with her head held high. There were at least a hundred people in the bar.

Bella gulped. *I guess they call it a dating pool because folks are swimming around, hoping not to get taken out by the sharks.*

Amber said, "Relax, Let's grab a drink."

Upbeat music played loud enough to hear easily but still allow for conversation. As they strolled over to the bar, Bella couldn't help but feel that all eyes were on them. She wasn't sure if she was being sized up or ridiculed. She did a quick yet graceful check, ensuring she hadn't accidentally done something ridiculous like tuck her dress into her panties or have toilet paper stuck to her shoe.

Amber ordered two vodka cranberries with lime. The building was gorgeous despite the smell of liquor and desperation in the air masked by the eye-watering scent of overpriced cologne. Industrial brick and exposed wooden beams gave a sharp contrast to the contemporary brushed steel countertop of the bar. High-top oak tables with matching chairs and old fashion fixtures hung from the ceiling, providing the ideal amount of light to flatter the eager faces passing by.

Amber said, "You owe me fifty."

Bella felt her face losing color. "Fifty bucks? For what?"

"Speed dating," said Amber. "The drink's on me."

Bella hadn't realized this sort of thing cost money. Not wanting Amber's solar plexus hunch to be validated, she took out her AMEX and handed it to the bartender, trying not to show the disdain in her face.

Amber pointed to a table straight ahead, "Table sixteen, that's yours. I'll be on the other side but still close. Text me if you need anything." Amber's dress looked incredible on her, and as she walked away, Bella gave herself a pat on the back for making a great selection.

Determined to put her best foot forward, she worried if she should have brushed her teeth. She held her hand in front of her face attempting to smell her breath. Too late now. She rolled her eyes at the obnoxious idea of getting close enough to a stranger for them to smell her breath. Taking a quick glance at her watch, she discovered she had just enough time to buy another glass of liquid courage before facing her first prospective suitor.

Standing at the counter waiting to gain the attention of the overworked bartender, she noticed Jack stroll up beside her holding a plastic bag barely large enough to contain the abundance of food inside. He looked like he walked directly off the page of some cheesy chef of the month calendar. She could see his page layout vividly in her mind. Standing in some industrial steelyard, wearing his slightly worn blue jeans, no shirt, in front of an old school smoker cooking something saucy.

"Hey Bella, I've never seen you here before."

She could barely breathe. How did he know her name? They'd never formally met, but she had seen him many times over the past year. Attempting to be casual, she replied, "Yeah, Amber talked me into it." Jack nodded while glancing around the room. She couldn't tell if he was looking for someone specific or people watching. "I'm guessing you are here on business?"

"Yeah, sometimes I make deliveries for my friends." He waved over the bartender, who came immediately. "I have everything you asked for."

She wondered how the man she saw by the dumpster could be the same person standing in front of her today. He appeared to be laid back and carefree, but she'd seen a different side of him.

"Thanks, man, I'm starving. How much do I owe you?"

"This one's on me, buddy." He dropped a twenty on the bar and said, "Please buy my friend a drink. She seems a little nervous about tonight."

"Absolutely, what will it be?"

Jack peered at Bella, waiting for an answer. "I'll take a Cosmopolitan. Thank you." She needed a drink and wasn't in a position to turn away free alcohol.

The bartender rushed off to stow the food under the counter and start her martini.

"I wanted to apologize for the other day. You really caught us at a bad time. That's not who we are, and I don't want you to think of me that way."

Bella raised her hand and said, "Look, it's not my place to judge. I have no idea what I walked into, and I don't want to know." She lied. She was curious, but she knew it was none of her business.

Jack smiled and said, "Copy. Have a good night, Bella, and don't worry, I'm sure speed dating will be a breeze."

"Thanks, Jack."

Drink in hand, she turned her attention back to the table she'd abandoned to discover a man waiting. She rushed over, careful not to spill her drink. "Hi, my name is Bella."

"Hi, I'm Joe." He reached out to shake her hand.

She glanced around the bar, but Jack had already disappeared. Oddly disappointed, she tried her best to focus on Joe, but his words faded into nothingness as he talked.

Joe cleared his throat. "Bella, are you okay?"

"I'm so sorry. I'm new at this sort of thing, and I was searching for my best friend. She forced me to come, and now I don't see her anywhere. I apologize for being rude."

"I understand. This can feel a little intimidating, but you look gorgeous, and what's the worst that can happen? Maybe you'll find love."

Bella's shoulders dropped, and she felt a sense of relief wash over her. She appreciated Joe's kindness and optimism. "You're too sweet. Would you mind if we start over so you can have my undivided attention?"

He politely smiled, happy to oblige. They continued their conversation, and from that moment on, she paid attention to every word he said.

Bella wasn't sure what she was looking for, but she knew it wasn't Joe. He was gone in five minutes and replaced by the next prospect.

For the next two hours, Bella met a total of twenty different men. After Joe, she met Peter, Eric, Brad, and so on. After a while, she had trouble keeping track of everyone. Fortunately, the hosts provided a small piece of paper to rate each interaction. Ultimately, the facilitator used the personal scorecards to make connections.

Checking the room to find Amber, she spotted her way in the corner waving like a lunatic.

"Over here," Amber shouted. She sat at a table with two other women and one man. Bella acknowledged her in hopes she would stop flailing her arms.

She would have been justifiably annoyed that Amber had left her on her own after promising she'd be there every step of the way, but she wasn't. And although fifty bucks felt like a strain on her budget, the event was the most fun she'd had in a long time. Speed dating boosted her confidence, and it taught her that putting herself out there wasn't as terrible as she thought it would be.

As Bella approached the table, Amber said, "This is Tonia and Nancy, I met them last time I was here, and this is an old friend Marcus. He asked me if I'd join him for a drink." She gave a sideways smile to Bella and shrugged her shoulders, "I'm sorry for skipping speed dating. I told him you were going to be mad at me."

Marcus took his eyes off Amber for only a second to greet Bella, "Nice to meet you." He seemed mesmerized by Amber, but the fact that she'd never mentioned him to Bella didn't bode well for him.

## CHAPTER FOUR

Not quite ready to face the day, she kept her eyes closed a bit longer. She lay still and listened to the birds chirping, wondering if the finch she saw yesterday made a home in the tree outside of her apartment. She enjoyed the sound of birds in the morning; they were the one thing that reminded her of growing up back in the Midwest.

Her California king was lavish; some would even say fit for a queen, with four down pillows, a matching white comforter, and a blue snuggle blanket. Soft and cozy, the way she liked it. She lifted her hands above her head and stiffened her whole body to release an immense stretch, deciding it was time to open her eyes.

Most people didn't sleep well when their worlds crashed down around them, but not Bella. The more stressed she was, the more she wanted to hibernate. Catching some quality shut-eye often helped her gain perspective and feel more optimistic. Today was designated for her, and all she needed was a warm cup of coffee, hazelnut creamer, cheetah print slippers, and the book from her nightstand.

She sank into the comfort of her favorite chair and began to read. *A Smoky Mountain Love Affair*, by Jacqueline Del Mar, her nona, the famous romance author. Her novels were filled with everything Bella needed right now: love, inspiration, but most important, happy endings. Speed dating had been okay. She'd exchanged numbers with two men but didn't have high hopes that either was a love connection.

Lost in fiction, she was startled by her cell phone when it vibrated on the table next to her. She glanced at it, contemplating if she should answer it. It was her mother. "Good morning, Mom."

"Darling, I told you please call me Jackie." Her name was Jacqueline, after her mother, but she preferred Jackie. Bella wasn't sure why she didn't want to be called Mom. Maybe it had something to do with their professional relationship, or she didn't want to be a mom. Either way, the question was more than she wanted to tackle on her lazy day off.

"What's going on?"

"Roger and I will be out soon for a visit; we'd like to see you while we're there." Roger was her dad. Although he didn't mind the title Dad, he followed the direction of whatever Jackie told him to do.

"Sure," Bella replied, "That would be fine."

"Maybe we can go to dinner and meet your boyfriend."

Bella threw her head back and closed her eyes. She completely forgot she'd told her mom she was in a relationship. That was easier than putting up with her mother's obnoxious remarks about her lackluster love life. Without skipping a beat, she replied, "He'd love that." Lying was not something she liked to do, but she was lying more than ever these days. Somehow her mother still made her feel like a complete failure. For the first time today, the gravity of her financial situation came flooding back to her. Would Jackie be able to forgive Bella for losing her mother's inheritance? Overwhelmed with the idea of having to break the news to Jackie, she began to second guess her willingness to allow them to visit. "When did you want to come?"

"In two weeks, darling. We will be staying at the Hotel Del Coronado."

Coronado Island offered a variety of accommodations, from quaint bed and breakfasts to lavish vacation rentals. Her parents were successful but not wealthy, and Hotel Del Coronado was fancy enough to suit their needs. Bella opted not to share the rumors the hotel was haunted.

"Did you already book the trip?"

"Yes, it's all taken care of."

# Carpe Diem

"You'll like it there. It's close to Carpe Diem." Bella needed to make the most of this visit, and in some twisted fantasy, she even hoped, like Mr. Douglas, they would like the store and be proud of all she had accomplished in the last year.

"Excuse me?"

"You know, Carpe Diem, my store."

"Ahh, I always forget about that," replied Jackie.

Why wouldn't she forget about Carpe Diem? Jackie was selfish and always has been. Why would Bella expect anything different from her now? "Sorry, Jackie, I need to go." Another lie.

"Ciao Bella," said Jackie.

How was it possible Nona could be Jackie's mother? They were opposites in every way. Jackie was a cold workaholic who only looked out for herself. Nona was a loving person who put family first and even started a charity foundation to help underprivileged children access books. Nona begged Bella on several occasions to forgive her mother's behavior. But as a child who was only seeking love and understanding, it felt impossible to see past her mother's egotistical actions.

What was she going to do? Stuck in a pickle; she couldn't tell her mother she was a failure or refuse to allow her to visit. She needed to fix this fast! This impromptu visit was the motivation she needed to get off her butt and discover some solutions with Mr. Douglas. She dishonored her grandmother and didn't deserve a day of leisure.

Her entire day changed with a single phone call. She was now a woman on a mission. She pulled her hair into a high ponytail, tossed on a grey cotton romper with sneakers, and headed for Sunshine Tax Pros.

She threw open the door with authority, and a new young lady was standing behind the counter. She was the fifth receptionist in the year she'd used Mr. Douglas as her accountant. A twenty-year-old platinum blonde with gigantic fake breasts and, judging by real-world anatomy, butt implants too. It was apparent Mr. Douglas had a type and was stretching well beyond his reach.

"Welcome to "Sunshine Tax Pros. How can I help you?"

"I'd like to see Mr. Douglas."

The lobby had a large sign featuring a rising sun. The space was immaculate with white walls, a small waiting area with two chairs, a water cooler, with a couple of tall plants in the corners.

"I'm sorry, Mr. Douglas is booked all day."

Bella asked, "When's his next appointment?"

She glanced at the calendar and said, "He can see you in four weeks."

"I'm sorry, four weeks?" Bella closed her eyes for a second and reopened them almost as if she was hoping the receptionist would disappear. "That's not gonna work."

"I'm sorry, that's his next available appointment."

Bella marched down the hall to Mr. Douglas's office and knocked three times on the door. The secretary followed steps behind in protest. After no response, Bella pushed open the large wooden door, determined to get answers. To her surprise, Mr. Douglas was not in a meeting. Instead, he was practicing putting on artificial turf in his office.

"Bella, what a surprise," he said.

"I'm sorry to barge in, but she said it would be a month before I could get an appointment." Bella pointed at the new secretary. "You know my situation is going to require more attention than that."

"No problem, please come sit." He excused his receptionist and turned his attention back to Bella.

He had a huge L-shaped mahogany desk with an attached bookcase containing no books. His office was decorated with sports memorabilia and images of California, no personal items or family photos. He rocked in a leather chair with pursed lips, focused on Bella. Going up and down repeatedly, allowing her to say what was on her mind.

She hesitated. Perhaps she overreacted. One minute she was reading a book and enjoying a beautiful morning, the next she was talking to Jackie, and before you know it, she was blowing through the door of her accountant. She was a little embarrassed by her behavior, but she was already there, and this matter did require urgent attention.

She rested her forearms on the desk and leaned in. "When we talked a month ago, you let me know there was some trouble, but I had no idea it was this bad." She fought the temptation to cry. "Originally, you said if I stuck to my budget, I'd have enough for three years of expenses. That was with no money coming in, and now twelve months later, I only have six? I know the store isn't performing as well as I'd like, but we generate sales. Where is that money?"

She didn't want to come off as rude or disrespectful, but she needed her accountant right now. She needed her friend and trusted advisor to explain how this happened.

He cleared his throat and took a second before answering, "Bella, I know you're upset, and I understand why." Mr. Douglas looked at her with tears in his eyes. "You have to understand as soon as I discovered the severity of the situation, I came to talk to you right away." His shoulders were hunched over and his face void of the joy she once experienced with him. "This is as disappointing for me as it is for you."

She wanted to be calm and rational, but her emotions were bubbling over and impossible to contain. "I can't comprehend how it was possible to lose so much so fast."

"I tried my best to explain that the store sales were struggling. The only chance we had for survival was to invest more assets in the market." He sat back in his chair and rolled his head from one shoulder to the other. "You were on board when I left ... we took a gamble, and unfortunately, we lost almost everything."

Bella knew a little bit about money, but she didn't have the financial aptitude for managing her inheritance.

Her frustration was getting the best of her, and she could see he was visibly shaken. Someone needed to be accountable for this disaster, and she couldn't be solely responsible for everything. She did her due diligence by conducting interviews and reviewing references. Mr. Douglas was professionally sound, and he reminded her of her Uncle Phil. "I'm sorry, Mr. Douglas,

I lost so much money, and I'm kind of freaking out. How did you remove such a large amount of money from my account without my knowledge?"

She may have gone too far because she could see an immediate shift in his response.

"Bella, I've always had access to your accounts. Are you trying to say I didn't explain this to you before I invested? You signed the paperwork. Did you read the report I left for you?"

With those words, time stood still. The report … in the envelope … on the register … with a rather prominent reminder across the top to text Tiffany. "I never texted Tiffany," she said out loud.

Mr. Douglas stared at her. "Who's Tiffany?"

Pale as a ghost, she looked at the ceiling in disbelief for about three seconds before she grabbed her belongings and stormed out. It was clear she wouldn't receive the reassurance she needed.

For the last year, Tiffany had been a loyal employee; Bella didn't want her to find out about her financial troubles like this. She walked to Sunshine Tax Pros this morning, but if she wanted any chance at reaching Tiffany before she discovered the envelope, she would have to run.

The girls were more like family than staff, they'd been at Carpe Diem since the beginning, and she couldn't bear the idea of letting them go; they trusted her. When she arrived exhausted, sweaty, and panting for air, it was already too late. Through the window, she could see Tiffany holding the envelope while talking with Addison.

Bella pushed the front door open, causing the chimes to sing a much happier tune than the mood in the room. Still breathing hard from running the entire way, she could smell the scent of fresh linens and lavender in the air. She glanced at the surfboard in the corner, the very first decoration she purchased for the store, and became overwhelmed with emotions. Denial was no longer an option.

Tiffany was a stunning twenty-two-year-old with poker straight strawberry blonde hair, green eyes, and fair skin kissed by a million tiny freckles. She was intelligent with a brilliant blend of book smarts and common sense.

Although the girls had a lot in common, their differences made their friendship special. Addie was adventurous, boy crazy, expressive, and overflowing with love. She had deep chocolate eyes and dark brown hair that rested in tight spring-like spirals on her shoulders. Addie was five foot two, but her confidence was at least six feet tall. She had no problem strutting around with the perfect hourglass shape. Even at a young age, she was a master at human behavior and understanding what made people tick.

Judging by the jagged edge along the top of the envelope, there was no question they'd seen the report. When Bella's eyes met Tiffany's, a single tear fell. Bella said, "I'm so sorry. I didn't want you to find out this way."

Like a football huddle in the middle of a boutique clothing store, Tiffany and Addison wrapped Bella in a warm embrace. She hadn't realized how alone she felt until that moment. Her whole life, Nona was the only person she had for support, and after she lost her, she assumed she'd be on her own from then on.

Tiffany said, "I didn't know it wasn't for me until it was too late." She began to cry and continued, "Once I realized what it was, I should have put it down."

"This isn't your fault. I should have told you sooner," Bella said.

"When did you find out?" asked Addie.

"About a month ago, I got some bad news, then a couple of days ago, I found out it was worse than I thought." Bella walked over and grabbed the envelope. "To be honest, I haven't even read the report yet, so you two probably know more than I do."

A marketing major at San Diego State University, Tiffany offered, "Maybe we can help you come up with a marketing plan."

Addie agreed.

Bella shook her head, feeling defeated. "I'm afraid we're past that point."

Being the optimist in the room, Addie said, "You can't give up. I'm sure if we work together, we can figure something out."

Learning the company you worked for was going out of business had to be hard enough on the girls. Still, they seemed to take the news much better than Bella anticipated. They were eager to act, and it was hard not to be inspired by their determination. She didn't want the girls to find out but had to admit being free from this secret was like having an enormous boulder lifted from her chest. She finally had people who knew the truth, and the next logical step was to tell Amber.

Bella stayed in the storage room for the rest of the night reviewing the books, trying her best to understand where the problems existed while the girls tended to the store. She looked at every single record starting from month one to month twelve. Each month showed a steady incline of traffic, and although it was slower than expected, it looked profitable. She compared her records to the ones Mr. Douglas provided. She could easily see the basics like rent, utilities, and payroll but the data for investment was where it all fell apart. She couldn't understand the gains, losses, or fees for any of it. She threw the pen on the desk in front of her. "This is useless."

There was no time left to procrastinate, the sunset had been replaced by the moon, and the girls said goodnight. She locked the door and walked over to see Amber at Ex-Squeeze Me.

"Hey girl," Amber said with a smile. "What are you doing here on your day off?" Amber's positivity and energy were infectious, nine o'clock at night, and there she was perky as ever.

"I was hoping we could chat," said Bella.

"Is this like a quick chat or like a spill the tea chat?"

"Tea, I guess," said Bella, biting her bottom lip.

"Give me ten minutes to get this place closed, and we'll get coffee."

Walking side by side with Amber down Orange Avenue provided Bella with a sense of peace and just enough time to contemplate what to say to her. Lying to her mother was one thing, but she hated having a secret from her best friend, and she desperately wanted this opportunity to come clean. The bikers of the morning were replaced by a steady stream of luxury cars that zipped past with windows down to enjoy the night air. She could faintly hear the constant swoosh of the ocean attempting to provide her with its peace. Bella drew her head back, searching the night sky for inspiration.

Not a cloud in sight, only a charcoal landscape featuring the tiniest sliver of the moon. The crescent moon was Nona's favorite. Bella always preferred the low full moon, but maybe that was her grandmother letting her know she wasn't alone. She touched her pendant for courage.

They grabbed a couple of drinks and settled at a table in the corner, avoiding a group of rowdy teenagers. She couldn't wait another second to come clean to Amber. "I'm almost out of money." The words still felt foreign in her mouth. "I'm not sure if I'll have enough to even stay for the next six months."

Amber almost choked on her decaf skinny latte. "What?" Bella knew Amber wasn't going to accept the information without some backlash. "How's that even possible?"

"Mr. Douglas came by like a month ago and said we were struggling. He suggested I invest in something with a higher yield. I thought it was a safe option, but I was wrong." She sat back in her chair and slumped down. "I had no idea I was going to lose everything."

"How much did he invest?"

She said, feeling ashamed, "I'm not sure. Mr. Douglas asked to be a signer on my accounts a while ago. I had no idea he could remove as much money as he wanted without my permission." Mr. Douglas explained to Bella this was only for her convenience. This way, he didn't need to call her every time he wanted a bank statement or to transfer money. It made perfect sense to her at the time; she rarely even looked at her accounts. He explained that he would teach her the ropes one step at a time, then he would step back, and she would move to the forefront. She learned how to use her POS system and input her payables and receivables into the software system, but she still hadn't learned what happened after he retrieved the numbers from the system. She needed to stick to the plan and did exactly that.

Looking like a lioness ready to pounce, Amber leaned in. "This is ridiculous. Your accountant shouldn't be asking you for that much control of your money. We need to go and talk to him."

Not wanting another unnecessary outburst at Sunshine Tax Pros this week, Bella reassured her, "Mr. Douglas has always been very upfront with me. I should have given him some limits around the investment, but I need to trust him right now. He gave me some financial reports he said would explain everything, but I don't understand how to read them." She sighed. "Right now, I have to figure out how to save the store."

Bella knew Amber wouldn't let this go, but she surprisingly didn't protest Bella's plea for trust. Sitting back in her chair, she seemed to relax. "There's no way I'm letting you go that easy. We're going to figure something out."

There were thousands of reasons to love Amber, but the thing Bella loved most was her fighting spirit. Grateful to have Amber on her side, she knew it was only a matter of time before they had a plan.

Amber might have some insight; her business was successful, and all of her neighbors were doing great. The coffee shop, Jack's, but somehow, Carpe Diem was going down like the Titanic.

"Did I mention Jackie and Roger will be here in two weeks?"

"No." Amber's jaw dropped. "You poor thing, this has been a crappy day."

"While I'm busy vomiting all of my issues, I should tell you Jackie thinks I'm in a relationship."

Amber attempted to hold back her laughter.

"Hey, what's so funny about that?"

"To clarify, we need to save the store and get you a boyfriend all by the time Jackie and Roger arrive in two weeks?" She tilted her head slightly to the right.

"Sounds about right unless you want me to move back to Ohio and sell commercial real estate for the Roberts Group."

## CHAPTER FIVE

Carpe Diem looked immaculate, and Bella felt on top of the world. When the weight of a secret no longer burdened you, life automatically felt more optimistic. Although her problems were still there, the sun shone brighter. The birds sang louder, and most importantly, she no longer felt alone.

Everything was a learning process because she had never worked in retail before. She read a few books and talked with a couple business owners, but the only real knowledge she brought with her was from her experience with shopping, and she had plenty of that. Carpe Diem had established processes using an opening and closing checklist. It included some odds and ends and bookkeeping but mainly consisted of cleaning.

Her phone vibrated on the counter ... one new message from Eric. He was one of the two guys she connected with at speed dating. After not getting a text yesterday, she'd assumed that neither one of them was interested. Fondly recalling Eric, she concluded he was attractive, educated, yet down to earth.

Eric: Hey Bella, I hope to see you again soon.

She held the phone for a few seconds wishing Amber were there to help guide her. She didn't know if she should answer right away or if that would appear desperate. She did what she thought was best.

Bella: Sure, what were you thinking?

He immediately responded

Eric: Dinner ... Possibly tonight

She glanced at his response, and her pulse quickened. She felt like tonight was too soon, but maybe the jitters were getting the best of her. It had been over a year since she had been on a date. Andrew was the only real relationship she'd ever had, and after he broke up with her, she felt useless and unloved.

Bella: Sure, what were you thinking?
Eric: Ladies Choice

She wanted to keep it close to home and very public because even though he seemed nice, you could never be too careful.

Bella: Let's do Jack's Brews and BBQs on Orange
Bella: Is seven okay?

She glared at her phone for a solid minute before being pleasantly distracted by customers. It was a young couple needing a new pair of sunglasses because the ocean claimed theirs. They were holding hands, and when he looked at her, his face lit up. That's what Bella wanted more than anything, and she wondered why no one had ever looked at her like that. A romance worthy of writing. Her nona swore it was real, the type of love she had with her husband before he died of a massive heart attack in his early fifties. These were kids, and they hadn't been damaged by the realities of the world yet. As she watched them walk out the front door, she smiled. Maybe they would beat the odds and get the happily ever after she never found.

Without skipping a beat, she pulled her phone out, eager to see if Eric responded, and was excited to see the new message indicator.

Eric: See you then

It was a date; she was going on a date. The reality was sobering and inspired a little dance in the middle of Carpe Diem with an impromptu text to Amber.

Bella: I'm going on a date
Amber: ... With who?
Bella: a guy from speed dating
Amber: Oohh Girl
Amber: You better call me after
Amber: I don't care how late.

She wondered if Jack's was a good idea. He was always there and proved to be a distraction for her. Why would she choose his restaurant for her first date? Maybe she was trying to sabotage herself before giving Eric a shot.

She needed to focus; Eric was an attractive attorney who liked to surf and cook. There was a slim chance that he could fall madly in love with her before her mom and dad arrived. Surprised by her outrageous expectations, she knew better than to appear desperate on her date tonight.

The store buzzed all day with a steady stream of customers and consistent sales. Two ladies mentioned how low the prices were, causing Bella to question whether her profit margins were high enough. She had a fifty percent markup on each item, but she had no idea what the industry standard was. Covering her overhead and finishing the day with a profit was her number one priority.

If she could do it all over again, she would have spent the money to hire someone in the beginning to teach her the basics of retail management, marketing, and accounting. Mr. Douglas convinced her that she would be successful between the books she read and the plan they had in place. Now, it was probably too late.

Addison arrived an hour early for her shift and had Tiffany with her.

"You're here early. I thought you were closing tonight."

"I am," said Addison placing a large-sized poster board off to the side. "Tiffany is joining me because we have a proposition for you."

Bella tilted her head and creased her brow. "Proposition?"

"Yes," replied Tiffany.

Both girls were wearing items from the store. Addison wore a mini boho dress with ankle boots. Tiffany in a Beach Bum T with the cutest pair of gold dangle earrings that peeked from behind her strawberry blonde hair. They were great walking advertisements for Carpe Diem.

"What do you propose?" asked Bella.

Addison said, "Last night, you told us you only have six months of capital left before it's game over." She gave a perfectly timed pause causing Bella to anticipate what she would say next. "So, I was thinking, maybe Tiff and I can pitch you some ideas."

Yesterday when they suggested they could help, Bella assumed they were generally speaking like people do. They wished they could help … if only there were something they could do … but no, they were serious. She found their ambition admirable and was humbled by their concern.

"We want to help," Tiffany said with compassion in her eyes.

"I don't think you understand." She reached for her guardian angel pendant, wishing it were that easy. "I don't have enough money to pay you more than what's in the current budget."

The girls looked at each other and chuckled. "No, Bella," Tiffany added, "I don't think you understand. This isn't about money, you're like our family, and we are marketing majors. We can help."

☙❧

Bella felt a little foolish. Tiffany was right; they were marketing majors. She needed to hear what they had to say. "Let's hear it."

Addison grabbed the poster board and propped it on the counter. "We've created a comprehensive marketing plan that will significantly increase your sales." The display was separated into several sections using vibrant colors, statics, and illustrations. "We would like to focus on the three key areas of foot traffic, social marketing, and adding online sales."

Tiffany jumped on the computer and displayed a mockup website she'd designed on the fly.

"This is amazing. You two put this together overnight?" asked Bella.

"I told you, Bella, you're like our family, and this is something we can do ... if you'll let us," Tiffany replied

They took their time and spelled out every detail of their plan. It was creative, detailed, and concise.

Addison said, "Please don't take this the wrong way, but why don't you have a website or do any online sales?"

"I was supposed to get set up last month, but the budget fell short, and we had to reschedule with the web designer." Bella kicked herself for being so foolish.

Addison said, "Well, that's something we can do for you."

After going into extensive detail regarding each section of their plan, they left Bella with some innovative ideas and a lot to think about.

Tiffany said, "One thing we haven't discussed is your profit margins. They aren't high enough. People are constantly saying how cheap things are. You have the best quality clothes and accessories around, and these people have money to spend. We need to increase the prices across the board."

The corners of Bella's mouth turned up. She was so pleased with their presentation. "You two should be so proud of yourselves." It was hard to process everything. "I can't believe I didn't realize how much you two could teach me." Bella tried her best to suppress her emotions. She knew she loved the girls, but she didn't realize how much they loved her. She said, "I think your plan is wonderful, but I don't think I have enough money to support such an overhaul to my business plan."

Tiffany replied, "Using our resources, we have managed to keep the budget under one month's expenses."

Addison said, "Bella, think about it. If it works, we are genius, and you'll be well off for a long time. If it doesn't, worst case scenario, you'll be forced to close shop one month earlier."

Always with the practical angle, Tiffany added, "Plus, this will give us real-world experience for our resumes." They both sat and looked at Bella with puppy dog eyes.

"What do you think?" Tiffany looked hopeful.

Bella sat quietly and contemplated what she knew should be an easy decision after all the trouble they went through. She needed to allow them the opportunity to shine. Besides, she was fresh out of ideas and needed a Hail Mary. Maybe this was the break she'd been praying for. She said, "Let's do it."

The girls jumped up and down in celebration, revealing a more accurate depiction of their ages than the unbelievable business presentation they'd just slayed.

Bella stopped them and said, "Not so quick. I know I can't afford to pay you what you deserve, but I will give you each five hundred upon completion."

"Deal," said Addison. "When our plan works, you give us each $500.00."

After things settled down, Addison took charge of the store, Tiffany went home to work on the website, and Bella slipped away to the dressing room to prepare for her date with Eric. She found the perfect burnt orange jumpsuit with a low V-neck and a long, layered necklace, giving her the right amount of sexy for a first date. Because Eric was a decent height, she opted for a wedge heel instead of her everyday strappy sandals.

Andrew hated when she wore high shoes. He said they made her look like a giant. She assumed it made him feel insecure about his height, so she accommodated his request. She thought heels made her legs appear longer and slimmer, but still, she worried people would see the same giant Andrew did. A new day, living a new life as a stronger person, there was no room for insecurities brought on by the Andrews of the world. She slipped her foot into the surprisingly comfortable wedge, and a smile forced its way to her face.

While touching up her makeup, she reflected on the conversation with the girls. It was clear her pride convinced her that two young ladies could not save her dream, but perhaps she was wrong. She was almost ashamed she had two intelligent young ladies at her disposal since the store opened and never once asked them for advice. Perhaps it was pride or even plain old ignorance. Either way, she was grateful to now have a glimmer of hope.

There were about ten people in the lobby of Jack's when she arrived, and all eyes were on her. She wasn't a superficial person, but she had to admit it felt good to be noticed. She was greeted from behind the hostess stand by none other than Chelsea, AKA the Dragon Lady, wearing dark blue skinny jeans and a black T-shirt that read "Get your smoke on at Jack's."

Her mouth said, "Welcome to Jack's. Will you be dining in or taking out?" But her face said I'd do anything to get out of here.

"Hi, I'm Bella, your neighbor over at Carpe Diem." This lady was as cold as the Arctic Ocean. They'd been neighbors for an entire year, yet she still treated her like a perfect stranger. What did Jack see in her? There had to be some redeeming quality keeping the relationship alive. "I have a reservation for seven p.m."

"Is it just you?"

"I'm meeting a friend for dinner."

Chelsea grabbed two menus and strolled over to a booth in the corner. "Jodie will be your server."

To an outsider looking in, she had everything. A flawless face with the perfect eyebrows, silky, thick brown hair, engaged to Jack, and they had a thriving business. Amber was right; she wasn't wearing a ring. How could someone so beautiful be so angry all the time? You never saw her with anyone other than Jack. Was it possible that she didn't have any friends after twenty years in California?

Bella had been inside Jack's before, but typically it was to grab and go on the way home from work; she never sat down in the restaurant. Her trained eye could easily see this restaurant was well cared for. The main area featured polished brass accents, custom cabinetry, comfortable seating, and a bar big enough to seat at least twenty guests. Everything was clean, right down to the cap of the ketchup bottle that sat on her table.

If it were a commercial property back in Ohio, this place would have fetched a pretty penny. She couldn't help but wonder if the kitchen shared the same affinity for cleanliness as the front of the house.

Jodie stopped by and asked if she could get an appetizer or drink started. Bella glanced at her watch. Five more minutes before Eric arrived. It was almost time, and she didn't want to let her nerves get the best of her. She ordered them each a water and, at the last second, added a skinny margarita for herself.

She glanced at the menu and laughed about the idea of eating BBQ with a stranger. It wasn't the most lady-like food choice. Done right, there was lots of eating with the hands, finger licking, and gnawing on bones. She didn't usually eat a salad, but that was the smartest choice for today.

She immediately noticed when Eric entered the restaurant. She assumed the enormous smile on his face meant he was happy to see her. It wasn't long before her optimism came to a screeching halt when she realized he hadn't even noticed her. He rushed straight over to the Dragon Lady and wrapped her in a friendly embrace.

Together they stood for a couple of minutes smiling and talking like old friends. She didn't want to stare but was curious how these two knew each other. Finally, the Dragon Lady walked him over to the table where Bella waited. When she smiled at Eric, she didn't look nearly as menacing as she usually did. She almost looked ... friendly, and this left Bella with more questions than ever about her fire-breathing neighbor. How did she know Eric? More importantly, why?

Bella stood to greet Eric as he approached the table, trying not to be distracted by the whole scene that unfolded. "So nice to see you again. I

# Carpe Diem 53

hope you didn't have any trouble finding it."

"Not at all. I'm somewhat of a regular here." The Dragon Lady was still looming, and Eric said, "This is my friend Chelsea. Chelsea, this is Bella."

Eric seemed to tame the dragon and bring out the best in Chelsea, causing Bella to wonder if Jack was the problem.

"It's nice to meet you." Chelsea bobbed her head. "I'll let your server know your whole party has arrived."

Eric scooted into the booth. "You look incredible."

"Thank you," Bella said with a polite smile.

"I hope you weren't waiting too long."

"No, not at all. I work next door. I came by when I finished for the day."

"Are you at the juice bar or the clothing store?" He stopped her before she could answer. "No, wait. Let me guess. I would say, judging by your impeccable fashion sense, you're from the clothing store."

"Thank you, I own the shop." Typically, saying those words gave her a sense of pride, but they left a knot in the pit of her stomach right now. It was her identity, her pride, and joy, and without it, she wasn't even sure who she would be.

Luckily Eric was pleasant to be around, charming, easy on the eyes, and a terrific conversationalist. Clean-shaven with very dark blonde or light brown hair depending on how the light was hitting it. His eyes were a golden brown with honey accents. Fitting right in with the crowd at Jack's, he wore blue jeans, a graphic T-shirt and appeared to be more relaxed than any attorney she'd ever met before. She could see a small tattoo peeking out from under his sleeve, but it seemed to be more of a last-minute decision than a lifestyle choice.

"What type of law do you practice?" she asked.

Eric replied, "I do family law and immigration, but my firm has several different specialties."

She talked to him about Carpe Diem and her move to California from Ohio. It turned out he was originally from St Petersburg, Florida, and even ran a marathon there last year. For most of Eric's life, he lived in the same area as her father's family. It provided them with plenty of things to talk about because she was familiar with the area too.

The evening was effortless, like two old friends enjoying dinner together. On his recommendation, they ended up splitting the BBQ sampler. Even with the bone gnawing and finger-licking, everything felt enjoyable.

She liked Eric, but there were no sparks like she read about in the romance novels. No butterflies in her stomach, no stars in her eyes, and no indications of a happily ever after, but Eric was fantastic. She did allow herself to wonder if maybe he'd be willing to do her a solid and have dinner with good ole Jackie and Roger, but she wasn't going to ask him today. That would be weird, but she was going to keep him on the shortlist of definite possibilities.

"Can I ask you a personal question?"

Eric replied, "Okay," without hesitation.

She admired his sense of adventure, but what if she wanted to know something very personal or embarrassing? Would he still be so eager? "Speed dating? I can't imagine you have trouble finding people ... Why are you single anyway?"

He laughed and said, "Don't forget, I met you at speed dating. I could ask you the same question."

"Great point. I can't argue that logic."

His spontaneous retort was all the proof she needed; he was indeed a clever attorney.

"I probably shouldn't tell you this, but there was a girl, but she wouldn't give me the time of day. I heard she would be at this local bar for speed dating, so I had to see if she was there." He glanced down at the table then back up at Bella. "I couldn't find her, but I believe everything happens for a reason, even if we don't understand it."

Bella leaned back in her chair. "You must have screwed up pretty bad for her to ice you out. Let's face it. You're pretty much the whole package. What the heck did you do?" She felt at ease with Eric, so it didn't feel weird that they were on a date, and he was talking about another woman.

"This is kind of embarrassing." Eric shifted in his seat. "When I asked you out, I had no idea that you worked here because she works at the juice bar."

Bella's jaw dropped, and her eyes popped open. "Amber!" she exclaimed. "Are you talking about Amber?" She didn't realize how loud she was until the surrounding tables turned their attention to their table.

"So, you know her?"

"Um, yeah. Amber's my best friend."

Eric turned away; cheeks flushed with embarrassment. "Well, this is awkward."

"Oh my gosh. You're the attorney, the one that went to the bathroom and never came back." She locked eyes with Eric. "Say it ain't so."

"I'm afraid it is." He rested his head into his palms and wiped them outward. "I loved her energy. We were completely vibing, and then it happened."

"What? She thought you ditched her?"

"I was sick for days. It turns out there were mushrooms in the appetizer we had. I couldn't leave the bathroom. It came out of both ends for days. She wouldn't even let me apologize."

Bella laughed out loud. "My first date in over a year, and he's got the hots for Amber."

She was sympathetic to his situation, and although he was perfect for bringing home to Jackie and Roger, she could see how he'd be a better match for Amber.

## CHAPTER SIX

The large glass windows in the front of her store were the only things Bella refused to maintain on her own. She was grateful when she met Joe, the window ninja. He would come by every other week to clean them for twenty bucks. Watching him clean the windows of Carpe Diem had a hypnotic effect, almost as relaxing as folding T-shirts. Not everyone could produce a streak-free window, but Joe never disappointed.

On window day, the morning typically flew by, but not today. Every minute lasted an eternity. She was chomping at the bit to see Amber and spill the tea on her date last night with Eric. Bella could vividly remember the conversation she had with Amber about *The Attorney*. She said they hit it off right away. He had a killer smile; he loved dogs and ran marathons. Next thing you know, he excused himself from the table and never returned. She was stuck with two drinks, a ton of food, the check, and a shattered ego.

Knowing only half the story, she'd agreed with Amber. *The Attorney* didn't deserve a callback or a second chance. Now that she knew the whole story, she was duty-bound as Amber's best friend to help rectify the situation.

Ironically, the date with Eric last night was the best she'd been on in a long time. She enjoyed the whole process more than she thought she would ... the anticipation, getting ready, even flirting a little bit. More than anything, it was nice to have an escape from her financial problems, even if it was only for a couple of hours.

She sneezed not once but three times. A common occurrence thanks to her allergies. The culprit ... dust. She frequently propped the door open to feel the cool California breeze, but it came with a price. They dusted the store every Friday but only at the ground level. These dust bunnies were living rent-free and needed to be evicted. She grabbed the step ladder from the back and climbed to the top, feather duster in hand. The shelf was high and difficult to reach, but she'd done it before, so she knew it was possible. She pushed her weight to the balls of her feet and extended her arm as far as it could reach. With one swoosh of her wrist, millions of dust particles were thrown in the air, causing a sneezing fit of epic proportions.

She threw her arms out to regain balance, but it became undeniably clear that she was going to fall. She closed her eyes tightly and braced herself for impact. Of all the ways to die, she never thought dust would be the victor.

Backward she went, expecting to crash on the hard cement floor below her. Instead, she found herself cradled in the sculpted arms of her extremely attractive yet very off-limits neighbor, Jack.

"Jack," said Bella, surprised yet grateful he saved her from a nasty spill.

She rarely saw him smile, but the grin that overtook his usually stoic face was undeniable. He laughed out loud while still holding her tight in his embrace.

"What's so funny?" She suddenly felt vulnerable.

"That's the most dramatic fall I've ever witnessed." He said while gently placing her down.

Having suffered only a bruised ego, she straightened her clothes and pulled herself together mentally.

Jack always dressed casually, and today was no different; jeans and a signature Jack's T-shirt with the phrase "I bleed BBQ sauce" across the back.

Several thoughts rushed to her mind. What brought him here? How long was he standing there before she fell? Why did she have to sneeze like a lumberjack?

Bella was determined to get at least one of her questions answered. She smiled and said, "I suppose I owe you a pretty big thank you."

"It's, ahh, no big deal."

"You kind of saved my life or at least my limbs, but if you say so." A curvy girl who loved food, she wasn't the lightest falling object, but Jack caught her with ease. She couldn't remember a time in her life she felt safer than she did at that moment. "What brings you in this morning?"

He reached into his back pocket and pulled out an invitation. "I'm hosting a charity party tomorrow night to benefit homeless veterans. It would be great if you came by." His voice sounded deep and seductive, but maybe Bella was still enchanted by his heroic act.

Despite her best efforts, she couldn't stop her heart from fluttering. Jack went from a Sexy 7 to an I'll Walk Through Fire for You 10 in less than five minutes. She needed to shove those ridiculous thoughts from her mind. This man was in a relationship, a toxic one, but a relationship nonetheless. She kept her emotions in check and replied, "Ah sure, what time?"

"Starts at 5 p.m., there's a hundred-dollar cover, but it includes food, drinks, and a raffle ticket. The winner gets a cruise for two to Catalina Island."

Jack stood tall and exuded masculinity. It was a refreshing change from the slumpy shoulders and sagging pants of the beachgoers she watched all day walking down Orange Ave. He spoke with intent, causing a small rush of goosies to run along her right side. She wanted to be a good neighbor and support the veterans, but deep down, she really wanted to learn more about him. Other than Chelsea, only one thing stood in her way, the cost of admission. The words, one hundred per person, went straight from her ears to the pit of her stomach like a boulder, but she wouldn't let that stop her.

"I'll be there."

He handed her a flier and said, "Great, see you then," offering her a tiny glimpse of the smile she saw earlier.

She would deny it in a court of law, but she was becoming more obsessed with Jack by the minute. Watching him come and go was frequently the highlight of her day, but after she felt the comfort and safety of being in his arms, he became even more alluring. Before, she could at least pretend he was an arrogant jerk. Now it was like he was determined to prove her wrong.

Frustrated by her thoughts, she snapped herself back to reality. Jack was engaged to none other than the gorgeous Chelsea and was unavailable to Bella or anyone else.

Between the great date with Amber's dream guy last night and her encounter with Jack this morning, she should have been in good spirits, but instead, she felt an overwhelming sense of unease. She loved having her friends, but it would be nice to share her life with someone. Damn Amber and her voodoo magic. A week ago, she was fine being alone before her heart chakra was opened up. Now she was faced with all these feelings; she didn't want loneliness, vulnerability, and putting herself out there for rejection.

Public enemy number one waltzed in, holding the juice of the day. "Mornin' Miss Bella," she said while helping herself to a seat on the stool behind the counter. "You never called me last night."

To prolong Amber's curiosity, she replied, "You didn't even tell me about my juice yet."

"It's carrot, ginger, apple blah blah blah. It's good for you. Now tell me about the date," said Amber. She was wearing powder blue yoga pants and a sports bra combination, her usual attire.

Bella walked over and said, "Well, it was interesting, to say the least."

"Interesting? How?"

"He spent half the night talking about another woman, and it was still the best date I've had in a long time." Bella tried her best to withhold her mounting excitement.

"What, does he have kids or something?"

"Nope, just a crush on a woman who won't give him the time of day."

Amber's face made a twisted expression. "What's wrong with him? How could anyone be on a date with you and even think about another woman?"

"Nothing's wrong with him. He's smart, attractive, funny, and down to earth."

"So, what gives? If he's so great, why won't this lady talk to him?"

Bella replied, "I guess there was some kind of misunderstanding when they went out for their first date."

"Like what? I've been on a million first dates. How bad could it have been?"

Amber had no idea.

Bella wanted to burst out laughing, but she needed to hold her composure for a little bit longer. "He said they were having a great time, she had the best smile, a positive attitude, and she was into health and fitness. Then it happened." Bella paused dramatically, taking her time to tell the story, using every opportunity to stretch it out as far as she could without revealing the big ending too soon.

"What?" Amber was on the edge of her stool.

"I guess they were sharing an appetizer, and he didn't realize it had mushrooms in it."

"And?"

"Well, I guess he is allergic to mushrooms. He excused himself from the table and spent the next two hours in the bathroom with it coming out of both ends."

"How embarrassing." Amber wrinkled her nose.

"Well, two hours later, when he made it back out, she was gone. He tried to call her at least fifty times. She refused to take his calls and wouldn't let him explain what happened."

Amber said, "Women can be so stubborn. It's way too hard to find a good guy."

"I agree. He's the total package," Bella said, wondering how long it was going to take Amber to put two and two together. She decided to share a little more. "He said he went to speed dating because he heard she would be there. Hoping with his two minutes, he'd get the chance to explain and win her over."

A sucker for love, Amber hovered on the edge of her seat. "So, was she there?"

"Yeah, she was there, but he didn't see her. It turns out, instead of doing the speed dating with her best friend like she promised, she sat with an old friend named Marcus and spent the entire night in the bar talking to him." Bella paused again, this time hoping she provided enough information for her to take the hint.

Amber wrinkled her brow and said, "Oh shit, was he looking for me?"

Bella sat there with a smug look on her face waiting for Amber to put all the pieces together.

"The Attorney?" exclaimed Amber. "His name was Eric. You've got to be kidding me. Do you remember me telling you about him?"

Bella grinned, no longer able to hold back her enthusiasm. "I do. That's how I figured it out," she said. "Why wouldn't you take his calls?"

"Um, because I thought he ditched me." Amber shot up from the stool. "I liked him, and I was so confused when he didn't come back. I felt like an idiot when he abandoned me with a table full of food."

Bella told Eric she'd convince Amber to see him again, and now she needed to fulfill her promise. "I get it, but as your best friend, I'm telling you, you have to see him again."

Amber was abnormally quiet, and Bella knew the wheels were turning in her head, but she had no idea what Amber would say.

"I've given this a lot of thought, and If you give him another shot, I'll let you set me up with online dating." Bella learned that you must stay silent when negotiating after you make an offer. The first person who speaks after the offer loses. They sat in silence for a minute because she wouldn't say a word if it meant helping Amber reconnect with her true love.

Amber looked at Bella in disbelief. "Really? You detest online dating."

"Really," replied Bella. "That should tell you how important this is to me." Little did Amber know she was willing to try online dating because she felt lonely, and Eric gave her the perfect excuse to ask without revealing maybe the whole chakra thing worked. She was content letting Amber think this was a concession for the sake of Eric.

"I would have called Eric either way." Amber radiated happiness. "He was freakin' awesome. That's why I was so bummed when he ditched me."

Amber was chomping at the bit to leave, and Bella wasn't going to keep her there a second longer, in hopes she was rushing off to call Eric.

This day was off to a terrific start. She'd already seen Jack, got swept off her feet, received an invite to a benefit, saved Amber's love life, and agreed to online dating. Bella had five customers in the morning but a steady stream in the afternoon. If she could get someone to walk through the door, she could sell them something.

She knew the store wasn't earning a ton of money, but she didn't think it was as inadequate as Mr. Douglas said it was. She assumed the investment was the more significant issue, but she didn't understand investments at all. No matter how many times she reviewed the report, all she saw was a bunch of gibberish. How could she decide what to do next if she didn't understand what was happening?

Tiffany and Addison said they would be in this afternoon; they intended to finalize the plans for what they called *Operation Save Carpe Diem*. According to Tiffany, Bella needed to commit one month's expenses to execute the plan. She couldn't afford to lose another penny in supposed high yield stocks. She sent Mr. Douglas a short but sweet email asking him to take all her remaining assets out of the market.

Oddly enough, he responded immediately for a busy man with no availability for weeks.

> Miss Roberts,
> I understand you are concerned about your remaining assets, but I assure you, the last thing you want to do is liquidate your investments. You'll never have what you need to stay open for the next few months if you waste what little is remaining. The best way to recover the lost money is to allocate a little differently in the market. Would you please reconsider your request?
>       Carl Douglas
>       Sunshine Tax Pros

He'd been so patient with her, Bella hated to go against his suggestions, but in the end, she stood firm. She needed every last dollar of her remaining cash to pay her expenses for the next couple of months. If she were going to invest anything, it would be in *Operation Save Carpe Diem*.

Now the only area of stress remaining was the looming visit of her parents. Worst case scenario, she'd have to tell them she lost all of Nona's money, never had a boyfriend, and she'd rather sell strawberries on the side of the road than return to Ohio to sell real estate for the Roberts Group. Even with her current financial pressure, Bella felt happier than she'd ever been. Life in Ohio was unbearable without Nona; at least in California, she was independent and free to live life on her terms. Surrounded by everything she ever wanted, she had Amber, the girls, her apartment, and Carpe Diem. She wasn't going to give up on this dream, not for Mr. Douglas, Jackie, Roger, or anyone else for that matter.

The girls arrived together carrying burgers and fries from the Night & Day Café. The familiar smell of French fries made Bella's stomach let out a rather unladylike growl.

Addie said, "We grabbed fries for you."

She was touched by their thoughtfulness. "You didn't have to do that." The brown paper bag was stained with grease spots and still felt warm to the touch, just the way she liked it.

"No worries. I know they're your favorite." Addie said between bites of the best cheeseburger ever made. The girls updated her on how the plan was developing. They recruited a few friends from San Diego State University to help. Bella could tell Tiffany and Addison were the popular girls at school. Their confidence was contagious, and if she went to school with them, she'd want to be their friend too. Bella went to a private high school, then community college. She was never allowed to go to football games or have sleepovers, and after hearing no a million times, she stopped asking.

Before high school, she spent all her time with Nona. Her parents worked long hours, and as she got older, they brought her into the family business until it was all-consuming. They started her off with small tasks like putting fliers in mailboxes while out on a walk with her father, then advanced her to more involved projects as she grew, like preparing contracts. They were workaholics and determined to have her follow submissively in their footsteps.

# Carpe Diem

The day Nona died; Bella was devastated. She desperately needed her parents to console her or, at a minimum, grieve with her. But as usual, they were too busy to notice her pain. The thought of how they'd allocate the new assets from Nona's estate into their portfolio consumed them. Her parents quickly cremated Nona and held a small private service with only ten guests.

Bella was disappointed with the way Jackie honored her mother, a national treasure loved by many, but Nona had the last laugh.

When they met with the attorney to discuss Nona's estate, he revealed Bella would receive 750K, and her parents were left nothing. The attorney handed Bella a small envelope and offered his deepest sympathy. He explained that Nona dedicated the remainder of the estate to the Jacqueline Del Mar Foundation for Young Writers.

The news caught everyone, including Bella, by surprise. Jackie was furious, insisting there must have been a mistake, but Nona's wishes were as clear as day in black and white leaving no question about her intentions.

Jackie and Roger took an immediate interest in Bella's wellbeing. They wanted to spend the entire evening with her to discuss her best possible course of action. They explained her inheritance needed to stay with the family as an investment in the commercial side of the Roberts Group. She was disgusted by their appalling behavior and excused herself to her room.

Bella sat at the edge of her bed feeling more alone than she'd ever been, holding in her hand the unopened envelope the attorney gave her. Inside, she had the real treasure, the final words Nona left behind for her.

She opened the envelope and pulled out the note. Two words written in black ink, Carpe Diem. With tears burning her eyes from crying all day, she crumpled the paper and threw it across the room. The very last words her nona left for her, the ones to remember her by, and she didn't even know what they meant. Praying for peace and wisdom, she cried herself to sleep. When she awoke, she searched the phrase Carpe Diem and learned its meaning.

She knew what Nona was trying to say to her. That morning she packed her bags, no explanation, no regrets, and left for California, never once looking back.

Now, Bella told the girls, "Great news, I sent a message to my accountant and secured the funding we need. So, I guess we are all systems go."

"That's awesome. I'm going to get moving on the website design and the social media platforms." Tiffany beamed.

"I'm taking pictures of every item in the store to make them available for purchase online," said Addie

"I can write descriptions for everything," replied Bella licking the remaining salt from her fingertips. For the first time in a long time, she felt like she had a plan that could work. The funding was secured, and Carpe Diem had a chance.

## CHAPTER SEVEN

The weather was a perfect seventy-two without a cloud in sight, giving Bella all the reason she needed to walk to Carpe Diem, skipping her usual bike ride. Coronado was a beautiful place to live, and she wanted to slow down and enjoy the scenery. The girls worked well past closing time last night, but they made a ton of caffeine-fueled progress thanks to Coffee A-Go-Go.

Tiffany finished the website, and the online store already had more than half of the inventory added. Soon every item in Carpe Diem would be cataloged and available for sale online, from earrings to wall décor. Tiffany taught her that when an article was sold online or in-store, it was communicated through her POS system, updating the inventory. She had learned the basics of her POS system, but she was embarrassed that she didn't realize its full potential. Determined to make the most of her current resources, Bella called her provider and signed up for an online class to learn more about functionality.

Startled by a noise behind a nearby dumpster, Bella quickly tuned into her surroundings. On the island, it wasn't typical to see critters lurking in dark corners, so when she heard something rustling, she decided to investigate further. With the sole of her shoe, she gently brushed away some debris revealing a furry little face. Debris must have shifted while the puppy was exploring the area, trapping itself inside the rubble. Judging by how her tail was moving her whole backside, she was excited to see Bella. She had the face of a teddy bear and the spirit of a child, running in circles around

Bella's feet. She looked thin, and her hair was matted. Upon investigation, she had no collar.

Bella scooped her from the ground. "Where did you come from, little one?" Bella loved animals but didn't have any pets as a child because of her allergies. Somehow, this little girl didn't seem to bother her at all. "Maybe I can help you find your family." She glanced around, looking for any possible clues of where this stray belonged.

The pup's heartbeat fiercely thumped in her tiny body, and Bella couldn't help but feel protective of her while cradling her in her arms. She picked up the pace. She couldn't comprehend how this tiny creature had been left to fend for itself, and she was determined to do everything in her power to help. It was approaching nine, and Amber should be to Carpe Diem any minute. She'd know what to do. Not only did she have pets as a child, but her parents often volunteered at the animal shelter.

Bella set a cup of water on the floor, and the pup took no time at all slurping every drop. She must have been exhausted because she immediately climbed into a rack of clothing and fell asleep.

Bursting with energy, Amber waltzed in holding a deep green-colored drink and said something about a Green Machine before Bella interrupted her. "Amber, look under the rack." Bella pointed to where the pup was resting.

Amber looked puzzled when she approached the rack. She took a peek between the clothes and asked, "What the hell is that?"

"It's a puppy."

"A puppy?"

"Yes, a puppy. Skinny and matted, but I found her on my way into work this morning." Bella was excited about her newfound friend, but she knew this pup had a family, and more than likely, they were searching for her.

Amber crawled onto the floor and pulled the pup out from under the rack. "She looks thin. She's must have been missing for a little while."

"I know. I looked all over this place, and there's nothing suitable to feed a puppy here unless you think she'll like top ramen or granola bars."

Amber replied, "Don't worry about anything. I'll call my mom and see

# Carpe Diem

if she can swing by with some food."

"Thank you so much," Bella said, feeling relieved to have one less thing on her to-do list.

The matted pup returned under the rack to rest after Amber left, allowing Bella to search for a mobile groomer. Thankfully she found one available for a same-day appointment due to a cancellation.

Bella explained the situation, and they offered to do the bath free of charge. Tonia, the groomer, said she knew Amber's mom Lizzy from their work with the local shelter. She let Bella know the full grooming would take about an hour, and she would bring the pup back after. Grateful for the opportunity to finish her task for the online store, she proceeded to finish writing the clothing descriptions so they'd be ready for Tiffany tonight.

The groomer gave Bella enough time to finish her work before bringing the pup back into the store. She looked so different; her fluffy snow-white hair made her face look like a cuddly toy. She ran right over to Bella, jumping on her leg while wagging her tail. "Aren't you the cutest little thing?" She rubbed the pup's head.

"I can't thank you enough." Bella insisted on tipping the groomer for her hard work.

"Like I said, I love dogs, and this is the least I can do for someone who saved this sweet girl from the streets."

For the first time, Bella considered she might be stuck with the puppy. She couldn't help but panic; she worked long hours and couldn't consistently feed herself, let alone be responsible for another living creature. She weighed every option she could think of, and the logical decision was to take her to a shelter, but she would never forgive herself if this baby ended up in the wrong hands.

After the groomer left, Amber's mom Lizzy came to the rescue carrying a cardboard box overflowing with handy gadgets for dog owners. She was wearing a long flowing kimono with pink and yellow flowers. She had dirty blonde hair made frizzy from the humidity in the air. Lizzy said, "Honey, I came as soon as I heard."

"Thank you, I wasn't sure what to do, and Amber said maybe you could help."

Lizzy replied, "Of course. I love animals, I wish I could keep them all, but John won't let me." She took a glance around the store while Bella rummaged through the assortment of supplies. "Where is the little one?"

"I'm not sure why but she keeps hiding in the clothes racks."

"Dogs are comfortable in small spaces because they make them feel safe." She reached under the rack and pulled the pup out. "Hey, little one, what's your name?"

"She wasn't wearing a collar when I found her."

"Well, honey, you need to give her a name."

Bella's mom never encouraged her to name things like toys or animals as a child. She said once you give something a name, you form an attachment, making separation more difficult. "Can I call her Snowball?"

"You call her whatever you want, honey, at least until we find her owner. I'm sure someone is looking for her," said Lizzy, giving Snowball a thorough once over.

---

"So, what do we do now?"

"First, we need to see if this little one has a microchip. If she doesn't, we will send the word out to local shelters and put some fliers in the area where you found her. I'm sure we'll find the owner soon."

"So where does she stay until then?" asked Bella.

"With you, Doll."

"With me?" Bella chewed her bottom lip. The idea of having a dog, even for a few days, was more responsibility than she wanted.

"You'll be fine. I'll bring her to the shelter and see if she's chipped. Should take about thirty minutes or so," Lizzy said while holding Snowball.

"Sure, let me know what you find out."

"Of course, honey." With Snowball tucked under one arm, Lizzy grabbed her oversized hobo bag from the counter.

"Thank you for all of your help."

"No problem." Lizzy waved before leaving.

Bella rummaged through the cardboard box, and as far as she could tell, it had everything she would need to care for a pup. A collar, food bowls, a brush, shampoo, toys, a leash, a bed, and even a little shirt that said: "happiness is being a fur baby." Suddenly Bella remembered Jack's event tonight. Her first dilemma of being a responsible parent; she couldn't leave Snowball home alone on her first night at the apartment. She decided she was going to do the right thing. If Snowball came back with no microchip and no inquiries from local shelters, she'd skip the event.

Bella tried her best to continue her day and not worry about what Lizzy might discover. She wanted Snowball to find her family but she'd be lying if she said it wasn't kind of nice having the little furball around.

When Tiffany and Addie arrived, Bella boasted, "You will be happy to know I finished my descriptions!"

"Awesome, I'll get 'em uploaded today," Tiffany promised.

"You're not gonna believe this, but Tiffany made some online sales."

"What?" responded Bella with wide eyes and an eager ear.

"I told you not to say anything." Tiffany rolled her eyes.

Addie jumped back in, "She did an advertising promo on Facebook and Instagram using the Beach Babe brand and already sold over a thousand dollars in merch."

"Are you kidding me? I didn't even sell a thousand bucks all day yesterday." Astonished, she needed to know more. "How much did the ad cost?"

Tiffany responded, "I told her the results weren't typical … that's why I didn't want to say anything. But the ad cost five hundred, it will run for a week, and it's only been active twelve hours." She pulled her hair back into a scrunchie and sat at the stool behind the counter. "Please don't get your hopes too high. Some days will be more, and some days will be less."

"It's okay. I'll try not to make any judgments yet," It was hard holding back the sheer excitement from her voice.

Addie said, "We need to discuss the local promo. We have twenty different girls from school coming here Sunday to help get this thing kicked off."

"Did you say twenty?" Bella paused a minute to gather her thoughts. "Where are we going to put twenty people?"

Addie replied, "We need to do this with a bang, and we're going to need twenty people each month to gain and sustain the momentum we need to save Carpe Diem."

Bella took a second to digest Addie's statement, and she was right. If Addie and Tiffany could find twenty people who wanted to help Bella save her business, she needed to figure out how to host them.

Amber didn't have the space at the juice bar, Carpe Diem was way too small, but Jack's could hold everyone with ease. Since he had a fundraiser for the vets, maybe he'd be willing to help with this too.

She practiced a couple of different ways to ask in her head before she gathered the nerve to walk next door to Jack's. Standing guard at the hostess station was none other than the Dragon Lady. Stunning as usual, her hair was pulled into a high bun, and her ears glistened with the sparkle of a single diamond stud in each lobe. The absence of her two-carrot engagement ring left a void on her once sparkling hand, causing Bella to wonder if it had something to do with the incident out back or if this was part of a larger problem. No longer wearing the warm smile she shared in the presence of Eric, Chelsea addressed Bella like a perfect stranger. "Are you here for lunch?"

Chelsea had a knack for making her feel small. Maybe it was because her demeanor reminded Bella of her mother. "No, I was wondering if, um, maybe we could use a small section of the restaurant for a promotion we are doing in two days." Chelsea looked at her with a blank stare. "I'm going to be hosting twenty people for a one-hour meeting at ten in the morning, and I was hoping since you are still closed at ten a.m., maybe you could let us use some space?"

Without even taking a second to consider it, she replied, "No, it won't work."

Bella tried again. "Okay, well, I mean, I could pay you and even clean when we're finished."

"Yeah, sorry, we need to deep clean after an event, so it's a no."

Sure, Chelsea was referring to the event this evening, she wondered if Chelsea knew Jack invited her after saving her from certain disaster. Bella's frustration mounted; even with the party tonight, Jack's had ample space to accommodate a group of twenty, and Bella knew it. Completely shut down to the idea, Chelsea made it clear she was unwilling to help.

"I understand, thank you." *For nothing*, thought Bella.

Chelsea may have wanted to ruin her day, but Bella smiled from ear to ear when she returned to witness Tiffany and Addison sitting on the floor of Carpe Diem playing with Snowball. "I see you met my new friend." Snowball came running to Bella at full speed. She had to admit no one had ever been quite as excited to see her as this little pup.

"She's so cute," said Addison. "When Lizzy dropped her off, she said there was no microchip and no inquires at the shelter. She said she was going to put some fliers up, and she'd let you know if she hears anything."

Tiffany asked, "How did it go at Jack's?"

Bella shook her head. "I blew it, but I'll figure something out. Promise"

It was hard to believe no one came forward to claim Snowball; she seldom barked, she didn't go potty inside, and she always had a happy disposition. Bella knew she couldn't go to Jack's fundraiser tonight if she wanted to; Snowball needed her, and she wanted to do the right thing. She called Amber, "Do you have plans tonight?"

"No, Eric has a thing, so I'm gonna stay home."

"Oh really, already staying home for Eric, huh?" she razzed her friend. "Do you wanna come over? We can create my online dating profile."

"I'll come by after class. I guess Eric's going to some event your neighbor Jack's doing tonight."

"That's ironic. Jack came by yesterday morning and invited me. If you want, I'll give you my ticket, and you can go with Eric."

"No, I can't stand Chelsea. You should go." Amber was the sweetest person Bella had ever met, but she could carry a grudge forever. After Chelsea yelled at her for parking in the public lot, Amber had no tolerance for her.

"No, it's too soon. Snowball can't be left alone."

"Are you kidding me? I'll watch Snowball, and you can keep an eye on Eric for me." Bella knew Snowball would be in good hands with Amber, and despite her better judgment, she desperately wanted a better picture into Jack's world.

## CHAPTER EIGHT

Bella didn't typically attend events and felt uneasy standing at the door of Jack's and observing her surroundings. The lobby looked like business as usual, with several people standing in groups and others seated on benches that outlined the restaurant's perimeter. If she had even a fraction of the business that Jack's entertained, she'd be rolling in the dough. The pleasant young hostess greeted Bella. Wearing a black cocktail dress, she appeared more formal than the usual jeans and T-shirt uniform. She said, "Welcome to Jack's. How can I help you?"

"Hi, I am here for the fundraiser."

"Oh, great! It's upstairs on the rooftop patio."

The hostess directed her to a set of wooden stairs toward the back of the dining room. Bella climbed the twenty-four narrow stairs leading to the rooftop deck, wondering if it was wise to feed your patrons liquor and send them down a rather intense obstacle course. She felt a slight sense of accomplishment when she reached the top and was welcomed by a jaw-dropping view with a stunning sky, offering hues of pink, grey, white, and deep blue. She had never seen Coronado this way before. Each direction offered something spectacular, the bridge, the ocean, and a magnificent skyline. The traffic sounds below disappeared into the night to be replaced by the soft whisper from the ocean. There was no question in her mind; it was worth the risk.

Thanks to rain, frigid temperatures, and unpredictable weather, they didn't have rooftop patios like this in Middleburg Hts., Ohio.

The crowd was an eclectic bunch. Some guests wore business attire, others formal suits and some chose beach gear, but overall, the atmosphere was relaxed and upbeat. Bella was thankful she settled on a sheer raspberry jumpsuit that could be dressy or casual depending on the accessories paired with it. She chose a long, layered necklace and strappy sandals giving her enough flair but still fit in seamlessly.

Searching the deck for a corner to hide, she wondered why she agreed to attend this party. She considered herself an introvert who would rather snuggle up with a book in front of a fire than schmooze with strangers. She felt a rush of relief when she spotted Eric. Grateful to find her new acquaintance, she made a beeline for him.

"Hey, Bella, what brings you here?" Eric was one of the people in business attire, something she would expect from an attorney after work on Friday.

"Jack stopped by my store and invited me yesterday morning." She opted not to share the story of tumbling off the ladder into Jack's arms.

"I can't thank you enough for talking to Amber for me. I'm sorry about the way our date turned out," Eric said while giving her a friendly one-armed hug.

Bella laughed out loud. "Are you kidding me? That was still the best date I've had in a couple of years." She tucked her wavy brown hair behind her ear. "Besides, I love Amber, so her happiness makes me happy."

"I owe you one."

Bella recalled Eric with the Dragon Lady and wondered what their connection was. In the spirit of wasting no time, she went for it. "I don't need a favor, but I was wondering about something, and maybe you could help me with it."

"What might that be."

"How do you know Jack and Chelsea?"

"They're my friends, but I met them through work. I can't give you the details about the work stuff, but they're great people."

Darn, Bella was hoping for something a little more informative, but she had to respect his professional confidentiality.

"I hope you understand," said Eric.

"Oh, yeah, of course." She understood, but now she was more curious than ever. Were they looking for legal advice on the business or perhaps an equitable division of assets? For now, her questions were going to need to wait a little longer. "Should we grab some drinks?"

"Drinks are the best suggestion I've heard all day."

Bella ordered two beers from the bartender and discovered Jack behind the bar washing dishes. He looked dapper wearing his white button-up shirt, dress pants, and sleeves rolled to prevent the water from getting them wet.

Eric hollered, "Jack" from across the bar, catching his attention. "What's going on buddy?"

Jack grabbed a towel to dry off before shaking Eric's hand. "Thanks for coming."

"I wouldn't miss it for the world," Eric said, looking as comfortable as ever in the company of Jack. "Are you still going through with it?"

"Of course, I always keep my promises," Jack said.

"I can't wait to see this." Eric shook his head in disbelief.

Bella enjoyed the interaction between the two men. She had no clue what they were discussing, but it offered her a glimpse of a fun, easy-going Jack she hadn't seen before.

He appeared to be relaxed behind the bar, washing dishes in the middle of a party he was hosting. Maybe he didn't enjoy crowds, but he did seem to appreciate seeing Eric. Jack always looked sexy no matter if he wore board shorts or jeans but seeing him in his formal attire made him more irresistible than usual.

"Bella, I'm glad you could make it."

When he looked at her, she felt his undivided attention like she was the only person in the room. His deep brown eyes rendered her powerless, and she melted into the floor. How could a man she barely knew have such an impact on her emotional and physical state?

"Thanks for the invite." She was trying to be as laid back as possible while butterflies tap-danced in her belly.

Jack turned his attention back to Eric. "Are you here together?"

"No, no," Eric said, waving his hands in protest. "We're friends."

Jack nodded and looked Bella up and down like a hungry panther before slipping his jacket on to rejoin the party. "Got it, well, I hope to see you around."

It was unclear who he was talking to. Was he hoping to see her or Eric? Chelsea was nowhere in sight; you'd think she'd be in attendance for such a big event. Bella watched as Jack walked away.

She needed to learn more, and Eric had the answers she desired, but she didn't want her attorney friend to become suspicious of her behavior. "Of all the causes to raise money for, why did Jack choose to do an event for homeless vets? Nothing against the vets. I'm just curious."

"You must not know Jack very well."

Eric was right. She didn't know Jack anywhere near as much as she wanted to, but now that her stupid heart chakra was open, her spark for Jack burst into a five-alarm fire. "I know he owns Jack's, he's engaged to Chelsea, he likes to surf, and his abs are," She paused, letting the thought bring a smile to her face. "chiseled"

"Anything else?" Eric appeared to be amused by Bella's description.

Bella watched Jack talking to one of the servers. "Well, between you and me, I wondered if he's a nice boss because new employees are in and out of here like a subway turnstile."

Eric snickered, making Bella wonder if maybe she went too far considering Eric and Jack were friends, and she'd only recently met him. "Well, I can tell you this, Jack is a great guy. Things with Chelsea are …" He shrugged. "He's a killer surfer and a great boss despite the revolving turnstile of employees."

Bella could feel Eric's sincerity while talking about Jack; there was more to their bond than business. "Jack served in the military for over twenty years, and he helps vets transition into civilian life. He does an event once a year for homeless vets because it's an increasing problem here in California. These guys come out of the service, and their lives will never be the same. For some, it is harder than others."

While Eric spoke, she focused on the server, a man who looked a little rough around the edges, despite the neatly pressed uniform he wore. "So, is that why there are always new employees?"

"Yes, he helps to get them on their feet, with updated resumes, and they work for him until they can find something in their desired profession."

Embarrassed by her ignorance of the situation, she said, "I had no idea."

Eric replied, "Most people don't. Jack is a very private person and doesn't advertise his good deeds."

Their conversation was interrupted by a man's voice over the loudspeaker. "Can I please have everyone's attention?"

The crowd focused on the stage. There were two prominent speakers, one on each side of the stage and a DJ booth to the left. A young man appearing to be in his twenties walked out to the center of the stage and said, "Thank you for coming out tonight. Please join me in giving Jack a special thank you for hosting this great event for the third year in a row. Ed would be proud of you, man." Everyone raised their glasses and gave collective praise to Jack. "Tonight, we've already raised over ten thousand dollars to help homeless veterans get back on their feet, and we're only getting started."

Music came over the speaker system, and a stunning string of handsome men paraded across the stage. "Do you know what time it is?" asked the MC with enthusiasm.

"I said do you know what time it is?" While hyping up the crowd, he repeated himself with more oomph. "It's time for this year's annual bachelor auction."

The catcalls were obnoxious, but it was a hilarious turn of events, watching the men be objectified. The MC introduced them one by one, reading a script that sounded like an online dating profile. The last man on stage was Jack, leaving Bella confused because Jack wasn't a bachelor. He was engaged to Chelsea. Bella turned her attention to Eric with a look of confusion. She said, "Why is Jack on stage? I thought he was engaged."

"To be fair, you never asked me if Jack is single. You stated Jack was engaged to Chelsea. I didn't correct you." Caught on a technicality by the clever attorney, she resolved to be more careful when talking to Eric.

"Will you be making a bid on this evening's auction?" Eric asked with a raised brow.

"Me, no," Bella replied, feeling a flush in her cheeks. Even if she had the guts to bid on Jack, she did not have the funds.

Eric nudged her shoulder. "It's apparent you have a thing for him. You should go for it."

"It's bad enough my first date in the last year ended up being with a guy who is head over heels for my best friend. I can't bring myself to pay for the second date."

Eric laughed. "True, I can see how that could be a blow to the ego."

The men stood on stage looking like the Chippendales gone wrong, waiting to see who fetched the highest bidder. This had to be how the phrase meat market came about. It was first-class entertainment, watching these guys excite the crowd with their charming smiles and sculpted bodies. Bella wished she had the money available to buy a date with Jack. But on the bright side, this meant he was single, and she didn't need to hate herself for developing feelings for him.

Eric excused himself to say hello to some old friends, and Bella watched in amusement as the auction proceeded. They started the bidding at a one-hundred-dollar minimum, and each stud came with a dinner package donated by a local restaurant. Mostly women, but some men were raising their paddles too. The bidding escalated and resulted in each bachelor fetching a hefty price tag of around five hundred bucks.

It was Jack's turn, and the MC brought him to the front of the stage. The butterflies fluttered in her stomach with the thought of losing her chance with Jack to the highest bidder. "Meet this year's most eligible bachelor, Jack, the owner of Jack's Brews and BBQs. The finest establishment here on Coronado Island. He is a twenty-year veteran of the US Navy, and he's done more for our organization in the last couple years than we could ever repay him for."

The crowd whooped and hollered with cheers of praise, showing their gratitude. "For this prime cut, we are going to start the bidding at five hundred dollars." Several hands shot up around the room, and the bidding jumped past one thousand dollars in less than ten seconds. For the first time since she knew him, Jack looked uneasy. He did a series of awkward poses and pointed shooter fingers into the crowd before finding a place next to the MC. Despite his terrible stage presence Jack proved to be a hot commodity.

The bid topped off at five thousand dollars, and the MC made it official, "Going once, going twice," wrapping up with a final drawn-out, "Sold."

Bella reached an all-time low, envious of an anonymous bidder. Her heart wanted to bid, but her mind said the budget wouldn't tolerate it, and even if she had that kind of dough, her ego would have never allowed it.

It was getting late, and to her surprise, she looked forward to going home and seeing Snowball. She hoped her new pup liked the apartment and adjusted well to her surroundings. She didn't get the guy, but at least she got the dog. The best part of the evening was seeing Jack and learning that he was available, but she blew that too. Instead of asserting herself and making an effort to get noticed, she disappeared into the crowd and let a mystery bidder move in on the only guy she's been attracted to in over a year. The sight of his sexy five o'clock shadow and full lips behind the bar taunted her memory.

Grateful to finally be home after a long day, she stood at her front door, determined to make the most of the rest of her evening with Snowball. She turned the knob and learned why people had dogs. Snowball jumped onto her legs, wagging her tail and peeking at her from under that fluffy white fur. Clean with a full belly, she looked even more spunky and vibrant than she did earlier in the day.

"Thank you so much for your help, Amber."

"She was a good girl. How was the party?"

"Well, I'm glad I went," Bella said as she kicked her sandals off into the corner. "I learned that Chelsea doesn't wear her engagement ring because they aren't engaged anymore. He was in the Navy for twenty years and does lots of volunteer work to help vets."

"I knew Jack had served in the military, but I had no idea he did it for so long." Amber began gathering her things before abruptly stopping in her tracks. "Wait a minute, did you say Jack's single?"

"He participated in a bachelor auction."

"Did you bid on him?"

"No, besides, it's a bit archaic, don't you think?"

"I guess so, but let's face it, I've seen you checking him out on more than one occasion."

Snowball came trotting down the hall carrying Bella's shoe, whipping it back and forth with her teeth.

"Oh no, not my new shoes." Bella ran after her. "Snowball, drop Mommy's shoe right now."

She released the shoe and stared at Bella with those bright brown eyes. Without realizing it, she'd called herself Snowball's mom, and the thought made her heart warm. Now she understood the expression puppy dog eyes. Snowball made her feel a connection she had never experienced before.

Returning her attention to Amber, she said, "Guilty as charged, but I knew he was with Chelsea, so obviously I didn't even consider him as a possibility." She bit her bottom lip and thought about Jack up on the stage, looking vulnerable while still exuding enough pheromones to drop at least half the panties in the audience. "Until now."

"Not to change the subject, but did you see Eric?" Bella loved seeing Amber's face when she mentioned Eric's name. Her eyes lit up, and joy filled her expression.

"Yes, he spent the majority of the evening with me, but toward the end of the night, he went to see some friends. I snuck out after the auction."

## CHAPTER NINE

Crying and scratching at the door, Snowball woke Bella abruptly from her sleep at five a.m. sharp. She released a huge yawn, pulling her hair back into a low ponytail and grabbing her slippers. She never had a dog before but knew these matters were time-sensitive and didn't want to take longer than necessary. Heading down the cement stairs with her new buddy, it dawned on her she had become one of those people. People who leave the house in their pajamas, slippers, and to make matters worse, she hadn't even brushed her teeth yet.

When she reached ground level, she set Snowball on the rocks and said, "Go potty." Snowball sat there looking at her with a tilted head.

Her neighbor from B-12 approached her walking his beagle, and said, "Good morning, I've never seen you out this time of day."

Embarrassed by her lack of hygiene, she said, "Good morning, Snowball is a new addition to the family."

"There is a dog run and a patch of grass over there. She might feel more comfortable."

"Thank you." Embarrassed by her ignorance, she said, "Sorry, I'm new at this." She grabbed Snowball's leash and joined B-12 at the dog run. Fenced in with a large patch of grass, trees for shade, and several benches, it appeared to be a much better place for a dog to take care of business. Snowball seemed to enjoy playing with the beagle. They ran up and down the grass for what seemed like an eternity while she got to know her neighbor a little better.

"What type of work do you do?" asked B-12

"I own Carpe Diem. It's a clothing store on Orange next to Jack's BBQ."

"I know Jack. I'm his accountant." Oddly enough, B-12 didn't look anything like her accountant. He had messy blondish hair, was in his early to mid-twenties, dressed in Chucks, skinny jeans, and a band T-shirt. He asked, "Do you have an accountant?" as he tossed his head back, shaking it to clear the shaggy hair from in front of his eyes.

"Yes, I use Mr. Douglas from Sunshine Tax Pros. I couldn't dream of doing it all on my own; I'm terrible at that sort of thing."

"Awesome, everyone needs a good accountant. How do you like working with him?"

"I mean, I guess it's alright. At first, he was attentive, but now I'm having some financial problems, and things feel different." She regretted her words as fast as she said them, confident B-12 wasn't interested in her problems. "I'm sorry, I don't even know you, and I'm over-sharing."

"That's alright everyone talks to me about their financial stuff. That's what I do." B-12 shrugged.

The sun began to peek over the horizon, and Bella knew she needed to get ready for work. Life would be different with her new pup; morning meditation wasn't going to be possible for the foreseeable future, and she still wasn't sure what she would do with Snowball while she was at work all day. "I have to get going, but it was nice meeting you."

"Nice to meet you too, and I'd be happy to review your financials for you if you'd like."

Little did he know Bella would love nothing more than someone to sit with her and explain the documents contained in the manila envelope. Unfortunately, her pride wouldn't allow her to ask. "Thank you so much. I may take you up on that someday."

Bella put Snowball back on the leash and walked back to the apartment, regretting not asking B-12 for his help immediately. This wasn't his responsibility; it was hers. She needed to step up and figure out the solutions for herself.

Despite rushing to get ready, there was no way she'd make it to open the store on time. She still needed to stop by the coffee shop and ask them about meeting at their location tomorrow. She only had two options left, this or the beach, but she would secure a spot today no matter what.

She pulled together her confidence and opened the glass door to Coffee A-Go-Go. Five people stood in line waiting for their beverages, and three were working behind the counter. She approached a young man standing behind the register and asked, "May I please speak to the manager?"

"Yes, Ma'am, but you can't have dogs in here." Some people got offended when others referred to them as ma'am but not Bella; she knew it was a term of respect and not a reflection of her assumed age.

"What should I do?" asked Bella

"Wait outside, and I'll have her meet you out there."

"Thank you," she replied while stepping outside. Bella stared off into the distance while she considered the best possible way to ask the manager to reserve the space, this was her last option, and she needed it to work out. The fog was thicker than usual this morning, but her weather app said it would dissipate by eleven a.m. Ohio had fog, but it happened much less than in California.

Bella glanced at her watch, and it was already five minutes after nine; it was a pet peeve of hers to be late. This was the first time she'd ever opened the store late, and she was beginning to feel anxious. Every tick of the watch pounded through her veins while waiting for the manager to come outside.

A woman in black dress pants, a blue polo shirt, and sensible black tennis shoes came outside. "How can I help you?" asked the woman Bella assumed to be the manager.

"My name is Bella Roberts. I own the store Carpe Diem down the road. I need a location to meet with twenty college students tomorrow morning for one hour at ten a.m. Would I be able to do it here?"

"Sure, I don't see why not. We're here to support our community, and we'd love to see some new faces."

Bella sighed with relief. "Thank you, you have no idea what this means to me." She picked up Snowball and did a celebratory dance.

"My pleasure, I'll get it in the books now, and they'll be expecting you in the morning."

"I'd like to have coffee and maybe some pastries available if possible."

"Yes, we can set up a coffee station and have pastries on hand at a per-unit price."

"Thank you, that sounds perfect."

She arrived at Carpe Diem fifteen minutes late but tried to forgive herself because she secured the meeting location. Most days, customers came in around ten or eleven, so hopefully, she didn't miss anything. She propped the door open, and Amber waltzed in, holding the juice of the day.

"You're late." Amber handed Bella the juice.

"Only fifteen minutes, I needed to stop by the coffee shop, and now that Snowball lives with me, I need to find a new routine. Besides your early," argued Bella.

"I'm right on time. The juice is grapefruit, aloe, and mint. I call it *House Call* because food is healing, and you need some help."

"Thank you ... I guess."

"Don't take it personally. You look beautiful, but I can tell you're mentally wiped out." Amber reached out and placed her hand on Bella's shoulder. "Your heart chakra is still good, but the rest of you is out of whack, so drink up."

She was in a T-shirt that said, "I run on Jesus and Juice," dry-fit shorts, and running shoes instead of her usual yoga get-up. "Have you considered running?"

Bella responded by rolling her eyes; no way she would allow herself to be suckered into another one of Amber's schemes to make her a better human.

Snowball returned to her new favorite spot under the clothes rack to take her morning nap. Having a new puppy, being forced out of bed early, made late for work, and now, ironically, her pooch needed a siesta. I guess that's why they call it a dog's life, she thought to herself.

"My mom said she's going to put some fliers out this week to see if she can find Snowball's family."

Amber was lucky to have such a thoughtful, loving mother. She'd even brought Amber a care package last month when she felt sick. Tissue, medicine, a blanket, and some vitamins. Even as a child, Bella's mother rarely showed her affection. Jackie said coddling a child only made them weak. She often wondered why her parents even had her; she assumed she was a mistake but never gathered the courage to ask.

"That would be awesome. I like having her around, but I don't think I can take on any additional responsibility right now." Talking about Snowball like a thing instead of a living creature made Bella think she sounded selfish like Jackie and hated that the words even came out of her mouth.

"I get it. Having a pet is a huge deal."

"I almost forgot to tell you. I went to Jack's and asked if I could use the restaurant for the meeting tomorrow, and of course, the fire-breathing bitch said no ... so this morning, I went to Coffee A-Go-Go, and they are going to let us do it there."

"Look at you, solving problems and making things happen."

Bella took out her phone and sent a group text to Addie and Tiffany.

Bella: Great news, I have our location! Coffee A-Go-Go on Orange. Ten a.m.

Tiffany: Awesome
Addison: I'll let Everyone know
Addison: I have someone to watch the store and Snowball so you can be there with us!

Addison's text stopped Bella instantly. The fact that she even considered the store needed to be staffed while they were in the meeting was so far beyond any expectation Bella could ever have. These girls had nothing to gain, and still, they chose to help her. She needed to find a way to repay them even if it took the rest of her life to do it.

Bella: Yay! You guys are the best

"Bella, are you listening to me?" said Amber

"Sorry, I needed to text the girls back before I forgot."

"Keep your schedule clear tonight. Eric and I are coming over for dinner."

"Oh really, Eric huh?" Bella replied, taking a sip of juice. Amber might have thought Bella needed juice or a run, but what she needed more than anything was a quiet night at home. She hoped Amber didn't expect her to cook. She did a mental inventory of the pantry: a cereal box, two different types of cookies, and more popcorn. *Chinese it is*, she thought to herself.

"I like him," said the doe-eyed Amber.

"He's perfect for you."

"I gotta run, but I'll see you tonight. Oh, and I'll bring dinner."

"I won't argue with that," Bella said, feeling grateful she didn't need to figure it out.

Amber popped in her earbuds and took off down the street.

Bella added new inventory to the display Snowball liked to sleep under. When she opened the store, it had about half the stock she held today, and it made her wonder if maybe she grew her supply too quickly, causing undue stress to the budget. Tomorrow would be a make-or-break kind of day for Carpe Diem, and Bella felt more disconnected from the outcome than she was comfortable with.

She had confidence in Tiffany and Addison's ability to explain the contest, but she wished there was something more she could do. The girls were driving *Operation Save Carpe Diem*, and so far, they were already doing a better job marketing the store than she ever did. In the darkest places of her mind, she wondered if she was making a huge mistake. After all, she was placing her baby in the hands of a couple of kids who were great but ultimately had nothing to lose.

Snowball snuggled against her ankle, giving Bella a gentle reminder that she wasn't alone anymore. She was with her chosen family, and they loved her as much as she loved them; they weren't going to let her down.

She agreed to the plan and needed to do her part in the areas she excelled at, even if it wasn't the sexiest items on the list. If item descriptions could help, she would make them exceptional because no one knew the products like she did. Bella prided herself on finding ethical partners who dedicated themselves to quality. She knew every designer, where they produced merchandise and fun tidbits about their companies.

Snowball came trotting out and began running in circles. "Oh no, you need to potty, don't you?" She ran around and around until Bella brought her outside. Thanks to Lizzy, she had the ideal place for her to go. A patch of artificial grass in a box outside of the back door. Bella pushed the silver bar on the door, allowing it to swing open and Snowball ran straight there to relieve herself.

"We're gonna get along fine."

While she waited patiently for Snowball to take care of business, she noticed Jack getting out of his car and heading for the restaurant's back door. This was a perfect chance to talk to him. Should she take it? He was halfway there, and her window of opportunity was rapidly closing when Snowball started barking. Jack quickly turned his head and noticed them tucked off in the corner. He changed course and walked directly toward them. Bella's heart began to beat rapidly, and she didn't know if she wanted to yell at Snowball for causing a scene or give her a treat.

"Hey, Bella, who's this little one?" Jack squatted down and pet Snowball while she wagged her tail. It looked like Snowball liked Jack, and dogs were supposed to be excellent judges of character.

"This is Snowball. I found her a couple days ago, and we are looking for her family. I'm going to keep her until we find them."

Jack glanced in Bella's direction and said, "She's a cutie." She knew he was talking about Snowball but momentarily fantasized it was her capturing his attention. "I gotta run, but I wanted to say thank you for coming to the event. I'm glad you were able to make it."

"Thanks for the invite. I loved watching the auction."

Jack laughed at the mention of the auction. "I'm glad I could entertain you. Have a great day."

She didn't want him to leave already, but she didn't have a reason to keep him there. "You too," she replied as she watched him walk away. Jack had always been attractive, but after learning of his single status, he was magnetic. She wanted to be close to him, feel his touch and know what his lips felt like on hers. She shook her head to get her mind into a better headspace.

It was much easier than Bella anticipated to have Snowball at the store all day. She didn't bark or have any accidents; she was the ideal fur baby for Carpe Diem.

By the time they got home, Amber and Eric were already there, sitting on the steps. They looked as cozy as two peas in a pod snuggled together like they'd been an item for years. To think Amber was almost stubborn enough to let Eric slip through her fingers. Snowball ran ahead and leaped into Amber's waiting arms, her tail wagging with excitement.

"I think she likes her Aunt Amber," Bella said as she approached the lovebirds.

"Well, her Aunt Amber likes her too," Amber said, giving Snowball belly scratches.

They all climbed the cement stairs together and got comfortable around the table in the kitchen. Twenty-twenty vision wasn't necessary to see the chemistry between Amber and Eric. The fluttering lashes, mesmerized stares, and hand-holding. She was more at peace than Bella had ever seen her before.

"You're going to love dinner."

"What's on the menu?" asked Bella while her stomach grumbled with anticipation.

"We're having Pho from Pho Sho."

Bella had seen the restaurant on Orange Ave but never went in. She had to admit the aroma of fresh herbs smelled great, but she wasn't an adventurous eater.

Amber pulled everything from the bags and placed each item into glass bowls. She gave Bella a fork with her soup but opted for chopsticks in her bowl.

Once they were settled into their seats with steaming bowls of soup in front of them, Amber gawked at Eric. "Can I tell her?"

They just started dating, and now they had secrets together. Bella wanted to know ... she needed to know. Did she learn something about the demise of Jack and Chelsea, or was it something different?

Eric sat back in his chair and looked to the ceiling as if it held the answer to life's difficult questions. Dressed for a round of golf, he wore an olive-green shirt and khaki shorts that flaunted his toned legs. Eric remained even-tempered, and without his fancy suit, it was hard to tell he spent his days working as a lawyer. He replied to Amber's inquiry with a simple nod of the head.

Amber leaned in to the table with a gigantic smile stretching across her entire face and paused.

Bella couldn't stand waiting another second. "Come on already."

"You know how you insisted I give Eric another chance?"

Bella tilted her head, confused and unsure where Amber was going with this.

"Well, at the fundraiser, Eric decided to repay you for your kindness."

Bella's mind raced, trying to recall every minute she'd spent with Eric at the fundraiser. She scrunched her eyes as if to brace herself for impact. "What did you do?"

"Before Jack went up for auction at the event, Eric called me. He thought maybe you had feelings for Jack, and he wanted to confirm before he put in a bid on him." Bouncing up and down in her chair, she squealed. "He bought you a date with Jack at the auction."

Bella popped out of her seat and began to pace back and forth in her tiny kitchen. "You did what?" Maybe she didn't hear Amber correctly. "Did you say Eric bought me a date with Jack?"

"Um yeah," Amber said, not appearing as eager as before.

"The winning bid was over five grand." She was no expert in reading people but sensed Eric and Amber were hoping for a different reaction. "Why did you do that?"

Eric said, "I'm sorry, it wasn't my intention to upset you." His entire posture changed, no longer the laid back and relaxed man he appeared to be only moments earlier. "You did something wonderful for me, and I thought this might be a nice way to return the favor." His tone and sincerity did help her feel better, but she wasn't ready to forgive him yet.

The room went stone cold silent, and Bella sat back in her chair, cradling her face in her hands. She knew Eric was trying to be nice, but this was humiliating for her. How could she show up for a date with Jack knowing she needed Eric to pay for it? "I'm going to kill you."

"Jack doesn't know yet. I could give the date to someone in my firm," Eric said. "The last thing I want to do is upset you. Please tell me, would you like to get to know Jack better or not?" His tone conveyed confidence, no doubt a trait he learned in the courtroom. "If you don't want to go on a date, I can give it to someone else. There are lots of women who would jump at the chance."

Bella listened to Eric's defense; he made a valid point. She'd been admiring Jack at a distance for a year now, assuming he was engaged to Chelsea. With nothing standing in her way, why did she remain hesitant? She recalled being at the event and wishing she had the money to bid. Eric had nothing but the best intentions. He gave her a thoughtful gift; maybe she should think twice before rejecting it.

"I've watched you ogle Jack since you moved here. What do you have to lose?"

Amber made a great point; she needed to get back in the game. Bella wanted to get to know Jack better, and now her wish was coming true. "I'll do it." Her words even surprised her as she said them. "When is this alleged date supposed to take place?"

Amber said, "It's official, my Reiki works! Don't even try and deny it."

Bella shook her head in disbelief. "You are crazy."

Looking smug, Amber counted off on her fingers. "You tried speed dating, you went to the fundraiser by yourself, and now you are going on a date with Jack. All since the Reiki session." She threw both hands in the air to celebrate her victory. "I'm expecting a review on my website within the next twenty-four hours."

Bella hated to admit it, but there was a chance ... a small one, that Amber's Reiki worked. She was more open to the idea of love than she'd been in a very long time.

"Jack works most nights, so the date should be in the morning," Eric said between mouthfuls of food.

She glanced at the calendar on her phone, trying to pick a date that would be the most accommodating for everyone.

"You should know. He's not expecting you."

"Why not?" asked Bella.

"That's my way of having a little fun at my buddy's expense," Eric replied with a devious smile. "I want to make him sweat it out."

Amber chuckled. "Think of the stories Jack will tell your grandchildren one day ... Your grandma paid five thousand dollars to have a date with me in a bachelor auction."

Bella rolled her eyes at Amber. She was correct; it would be a funny story to share when people asked how they met.

She couldn't pass up this opportunity, and even though she was terrified, she was going for it. When she moved to California, she was determined to leave behind the timid girl who had no friends and needed to be told what to do by her boyfriend or parents. She was going on a date with Jack. Maybe it cost five large, but she wasn't going to let this chance pass her by. "Now, we need to figure out where to go."

"Leave it to me," said Eric. "I have an idea."

## CHAPTER TEN

Addie and Tiffany seemed to know everyone. Bella dressed them from head to toe before the meeting as a thank you for all their hard work on the website. Addison in a fun, flirty mini dress that accentuated her curves and bubbly personality. Tiffany wore an oversized opaque white dress that fell off one shoulder, highlighting the beautiful lines in her neck and back. Bella opted for a classic, black, three-quarter length T-shirt dress with a belt to give her an hourglass shape and cropped denim jacket.

Babbling voices filled the meeting space of Coffee A-Go-Go. Clutching a mug, Bella observed the people in the room. The future of Carpe Diem rested in the hands of these twenty college kids and their influence on social media. Bella thought to herself, no pressure, letting go of a slow breath.

She wished she could have been like these girls when she went to college. They were the cool kids, the ones everyone invited to parties, knew all the boys, and seemed to be having all the fun.

By the time she started college, she had worked full-time for the family business. She obtained her real estate license as soon as she turned eighteen and spent most of her nights and weekends at open houses or making marketing calls for her parents.

Considered a late bloomer, Bella wore braces and dressed like a middle-aged school teacher due to the stringent dress code her father enforced. A caged bird trapped in a life she never wanted, making the day she took her freedom the best day of her life.

Addie rallied the group, getting their attention with her commanding voice and captivating presence. Bella stayed close, admiring her poise. Not only could Addison capture the interest of her peers, but she looked fantastic doing it.

She explained the promotion in detail, letting the girls know each of them would receive a complimentary one-hour photoshoot wearing pre-selected outfits and accessories from Carpe Diem. The photos obtained would be used in the retail store, advertising, and the social media contest. They'd each get one entire month to gather as many likes, shares, and followers to the Carpe Diem page as possible. The person with the most activity would receive a thousand-dollar shopping spree, their pictures featured in an advertising campaign, and a framed print declaring them the winner on the dressing room wall of fame. She opened the room for questions, and several girls raised their hands.

The first stood and asked, "Are hair and makeup included in the photoshoot?"

"No, you should arrive shoot ready. We will only be providing the photographer, accessories, and clothing for the shoot." Addie responded with certainty and moved through each question with ease.

"How many outfits are we allowed to model?"

"Each model will have the opportunity to take photos in three full outfits."

"Do we get to keep the outfit we model?"

"No, but you will have the option to buy with a 20 percent discount on the day of your shoot, or if you win, you can purchase the clothes using your winnings."

"Can we participate every month?" asked a girl in plaid.

"You have to wait at least six months before you'll be eligible to sign up again." Addie glanced around the room and called on the next question.

"When will we be notified of the winner?" Another girl called from the back of the room.

"The winner will be announced by social media on the fifth of the following month. You will be able to use your thousand-dollar store credit any time after." There were only eight questions in total, and she handled them with ease. Before letting everyone go, she called Bella and Tiffany to the front to join her. "This is Bella, and she is the owner of Carpe Diem. She can answer any questions about the store, featured designers, or products. Most of you already know Tiffany. She'll get you scheduled for your shoots and help with any questions regarding the website or social media. Please stop over and say hello."

Bella placed her hand on Addison's shoulder. "That was unbelievable. Where did you learn to communicate so well?"

A huge smile graced Addison's face. "Thank you, I've been a part of the debate team since high school, so I know how to get the attention of a room."

Beaming with pride for Tiffany and Addison, Bella could learn something from their organization and professionalism. The meeting had a great turnout, and coffee and snacks only set her back one hundred fifty dollars. Knowing she'd need these numbers for future marketing campaigns, she'd been keeping a notebook to log expenses.

She took the last remaining swig of the lukewarm beverage before gathering the confidence to introduce herself to a few of the students.

"Hello, I'm Bella," she said to a group of three girls that were gathering toward the back. "Did you get your shoot scheduled with Tiffany yet?"

One of the girls responded, "I want to, but I don't think I stand a chance against girls as popular as Trina or Emma."

The timid girl wore skinny jeans with flip-flops and an oversized T-shirt. She had an annoying habit of gnawing on her cuticles based on the blood-stained tares surrounding her nail beds, and her posture needed improvement, but her lack of self-esteem took Bella instantly back to her high school days.

She reminded Bella of a young version of herself, and the last thing she wanted to do was alienate her people. The awkward ones, the ones who were only popular with books and grandmothers. Bella said, "You have to! It will be fun. Think, I'll be there to help you every step of the way. I will choose outfits that accentuate your best features like those beautiful green eyes and long legs."

After a short consideration, the girl agreed, "I'm gonna do it!" She locked arms with her two friends and approached Tiffany, ready to book their appointment.

Overwhelmed with gratitude that she could help encourage the girls to participate in the contest, she wished someone would have taken the time to encourage her when she backed out of important events. She missed her choir solo, the field trip to Washington DC, and her senior prom because fear got the best of her.

The crowd was beginning to disperse, and eager to find out how many people had signed up, Bella headed directly to Tiffany. The projections estimated they needed a minimum of ten people to make it work, but fifteen to twenty would be ideal for a successful launch. After the last person left, Bella asked, "How did we do?"

Tiffany looked at her laptop with a somber face then returned her eyes to meet Bella's. With hesitation in her voice Tiffany said, "Well, twenty girls came. Let's see … there was one, two …" She looked into the air and counted on her fingers three, four, and five without speaking the words. Then a smile overwhelmed her face, and she said, "Twenty, we got all twenty."

Bella could barely believe her ears. She spoke in a delicate voice, "Twenty?"

Tiffany gave her a nod of confirmation.

Bella wasn't the type to cause a scene, but she was bursting at the seams with excitement. The meeting was a huge success, and if nothing else, it meant she'd be having increased foot traffic in the store. She high-fived Tiffany. "Thank you so much. You did a great job."

Tiffany replied, "It's an awesome contest. If I didn't work for you, I'd enter." She carried her confidence with more maturity than most college students. Bella wished she'd had that when she was younger.

Bella replied, "I'd vote for you in that outfit."

Addie and Tiffany were remarkable young ladies, and their commitment to Carpe Diem impressed Bella. They had nothing to gain, yet they

# Carpe Diem

were still willing to go the extra mile for her. Like the three musketeers, they walked to Carpe Diem together, discussing the meeting and the next phase of the plan.

Bella had stayed up late the night before, thinking of ways she could add value. "I was thinking about more ways to bring in business, and I came up with a selfie station, actually several of them. For it to work, our backdrops need to be dope. We need everyone in Coronado to walk through the door because they want a selfie."

"Those are popping up everywhere, and people love them. What's the move?" Tiffany asked while pulling out her phone to show Bella a location she and Addie recently took a picture.

"We need to dedicate a few locations in the store to be picture perfect. The lighting has to be on point. It needs to be extra, you know, over the top and fun." Bella replied, feeling proud of her contribution.

She described her vision in detail and had a plan to cover the cost without cutting into the budget the girls required. Tiffany jumped in and explained that using hashtags at the selfie stations would drive traffic to social media and ultimately reduce the cost of paid advertisements like the one they used for the Beach Bum promotion.

The website and online store were progressing well. Bella suggested she research shipping options to find who could deliver the fastest for the best price.

"Without you two, I'd be sunk." Bella shook her head in disbelief. "I'm so grateful for you both … I don't know how I can ever repay you."

When they arrived at Carpe Diem, the door was propped open, customers were browsing the store, and music could be heard from the sidewalk. It felt alive. Snowball darted out from underneath her favorite rack of clothes to greet Bella, running in circles around her feet. "Were you a good girl while I was gone?" Bella knelt to the floor, and the dog rolled over for belly scratches. She knew they were still looking for Snowball's mom, but she couldn't help herself; that little furball was bringing her a joy she'd never experienced before.

"Thank you for watching the store," Bella said to Addie's friend. "I hope it wasn't too much of a bother."

The guy looked more like a linebacker than someone who worked at a boutique or watched tiny dogs, but everything appeared to be in order. She handed him forty dollars for the two hours of work and said, "It's cool having a man behind the counter for a change. Could we call you again if we need coverage?"

"I'd do anything for Addie," He replied with stars in his eyes, obviously smitten. Addie was a dynamo, a classic combination of brains and beauty.

Addison shook her head and began to blush. "Shut up," she said to her doe-eyed friend before turning her attention back to Bella. "This is Ken. He's in my English Lit class."

"Nice to meet you, Ken."

Addison glanced at Ken. "If it's okay, I'm gonna head to breakfast with this guy. I'll come back after to finish helping."

"Sure thing, have fun." Bella realized forty bucks was only a bonus. Ken would have likely paid Bella to be at Carpe Diem if it meant he could spend time with Addison. "How cute are they?"

Tiffany laughed. "He's been trying to get her to go out with him all semester. I guess he finally got his chance."

"She looks happy," said Bella.

"She hasn't dated much. She stays focused on school, so she must like him."

Tiffany folded shirts on the center table, ensuring each pile was perfect while they chatted.

Bella suggested, "How about we start to get the store ready for the selfie station?"

"That's a great idea. Where should we start?"

"For right now, let's work on clearing out the sections we're going to use and redistributing the products to other areas," Bella said while directing Tiffany's attention toward the chosen spaces. "We're going to use one dressing room, the corner near the register, and the wall on the right. We need to focus on the merchandise, but the attractions will help get people to every corner of the store. The longer they're here, the greater the chance they'll buy."

"Sounds good. We need to be ready since the photoshoots are going to start soon. Addie and I can go shopping this afternoon. We'll get everything we need, some cool backdrops, ring lights, props—stuff like that."

"Perfect. Make sure to give me the receipts so I can pay you back." The girls were the perfect choice to execute the shopping list, and it would get them out of the store for a few hours.

Tiffany gave her a cheeky salute. "Yes, boss."

After only an hour of rearranging, they saw progress. Bella was concerned the store would look crowded, but the merchandise quickly absorbed into the existing displays making the floor appear like it had a fabulous selection. They came up with an idea to incorporate jewelry throughout the store instead of having a designated table. Adding it to existing displays brought a pleasant pop of sparkle and the hope for increased revenue due to improved visibility.

Amber arrived at noon with a radiant glow in her matching lilac and grey tie-dye yoga pants with sports bra combo, carrying the juice of the day. "Hi there. You've been working hard."

"Do you like it?" Bella thought it looked great but was curious what others would think. Amber was the perfect person to ask because she never held back her opinions.

Amber took a quick walk around the store. "It looks good, but what are you going to do with the extra space?"

Bella glanced at her watch. "It's a surprise. I didn't think I'd be seeing you today. It's twelve o'clock."

"You went to Coffee A-Go-Go this morning, so I knew you'd need something healthy. I brought you carrot, apple, and lemon juice." Bella hated whole carrots but for some reason enjoyed them in juice.

"Thanks. You look chipper. Let me guess… does it have something to do with Eric?"

Amber glanced sideways at Bella, trying but failing to suppress her smile. "Is it that obvious?"

"I'm so happy for you," Bella said while continuing to work on the display in front of her. "Operation save my ass is in full swing. These girls have come up with an unbelievable marketing plan. I don't know if it is going to work, but it's a solid plan, and I'm excited about it."

"It's gonna work. Besides, you can't leave me, so it has to." Out of all the things Bella loved about California, Amber was right at the top of the list. She had never had a best friend before, and more than anything else, she didn't want to lose that. "By the way, Eric set up that thing."

It took Bella a moment to realize Amber was talking about the date with Jack. Her heart stopped for a second then her body spiked with adrenaline like she'd been nearly hit by a car. She stopped what she was doing and gave Amber her undivided attention.

"He called Jack and let him know he'll be going on a mystery date. Can you be available tomorrow at six am?" asked Amber.

"Six, why so early?"

"Eric has something planned. I don't have all the details, but it's impossible between the two of your schedules. We thought of everything, and the girls work in the morning. We'll keep Snowball tonight and bring her back tomorrow."

Bella couldn't think of one single reason she should say no. "Okay, six am. I'm in."

"Drink your juice. I'll send you the details later."

## CHAPTER ELEVEN

Waking up while it's still dark outside wasn't something she wanted to do, but a date with Jack made it worth it, or at least she hoped it did. A date with Jack … even the thought felt naughty. What was he going to say when he found out she was his mystery date? Did he see her in the same way she saw him? She couldn't psyche herself out now, this date cost Eric five large, and she needed to make the best of it.

To think it all started with Reiki. Reiki opened the door to speed dating, leading to Bella meeting Eric and then a date. Their date allowed Bella to reconnect Eric with Amber, resulting in this moment. She didn't believe in chance … this chain of events happened precisely the way it needed to, but she wasn't going to say that to Amber.

The clouds were low, causing a haze and making visibility difficult, an excellent metaphor for her life right now. She couldn't see the finish line but was determined something magical existed on the other side. Since Eric planned everything, she had no idea what the day held in store. She dressed in a sporty beach look that included a flowing teal shirt, matching Converse, and a jean jacket to keep her warm in the early hours. Admittedly, her shorts were short, but she knew her butt was one of her best assets, and she wanted to accentuate it.

Jack stood at the dock, looking out in the distance, wearing navy-blue board shorts and a white T-shirt with a logo on the front. Most people were obsessed with their phones, spending most of their free time with the four-by-six object glued to their palm, but not him. He looked perfectly at ease with nothing at all to entertain him.

She didn't need to be there until six but to Bella being punctual meant being early, by at least ten minutes. She locked her bike to the rusty rack near the sidewalk and strolled toward the pier trying not to let her nerves get the best of her.

Before she left her apartment this morning, she rehearsed three ways to break the ice with Jack. She wanted to say something witty or clever, but that flew out the window once he was directly in front of her. She rubbed her sweaty palms on her shorts and cleared her throat. "Hi Jack, how are you this morning?" She chewed on her bottom lip, wondering if he had already figured out she was his date.

His eyes lit up when he saw her. "Bella. You're out bright and early this morning."

Her soul quivered at the sound of her name in his deep seductive voice. "Yeah, I guess you could say that." Judging by his demeanor, he wasn't expecting her. She wanted to tell him she was his date, but her mouth wouldn't allow the words to come out. "Do you like to stand out here, or are you waiting for something special?"

"Waiting for my date from the charity auction." He didn't fidget or hesitate with his words. If the man had an ounce of nerves, he didn't show it.

She was mortified to tell him she was the charity date he was expecting. "Isn't it weird that someone would pay five grand for a date?"

"I'm happy someone was willing to donate that much cash to the vets, all for a date with me. So, I guess I'm flattered."

This was her chance to confess. "Well, um, I guess that person would be me."

"You?" Jack looked perplexed. "I didn't even see your bid."

"I can't take the credit. This was Eric's doing. He may be a bit of an instigator."

Jack snorted, and the corners of his lips turned up like he was trying to suppress a smile. She couldn't tell if he was happy or flattered, but a slight awkwardness lingered.

"Is that okay?" she asked.

He replied, "That sounds like Eric." He lifted his hand and waved an envelope. "Eric left this for me and said I should open it on the dock after my mystery date arrived."

He used his finger to tear the paper, careful not to rip the contents inside. He removed the handwritten note reading it out loud so she could hear. "I've planned a sunrise cruise on a gondola through the canals of the Coronado Cays. Enjoy." Jack crumpled the paper and tossed it into the green wastebasket fixed to the pole on the first try.

"Sounds like fun," said Bella, waiting for an emotional response of some kind from Jack.

"I prefer speed over paddle boats, but I like the idea of getting to know you better."

Her cheeks started to feel warm, and she wondered if he was speaking in general terms or if he had the same type of feeling toward her as she had for him.

The boat came into sight moments later. She'd never been on a gondola before but had no question this was their ride. Painted all black, the boat sat low in the water. It was big enough to hold four passengers easily, but no one else was around, leading her to believe this was a private cruise.

A man in a striped red and white shirt standing on the back of the boat wearing a straw hat greeted them. "Welcome to your sunrise cruise. I'm Marco, your gondolier."

"Thanks, Marco," said Jack.

Jack stepped onto the boat first then turned to reach for Bella's hand, assisting her aboard. A rush of heat warmed her cool skin. His hands were slightly calloused, and his touch, firm. She could tell he was strong yet gentle. She couldn't help but wonder what those hands would feel like on her body. She shouldn't have such strong feelings for someone she barely knew, but it had been so long since she'd been intimate with someone, she craved the touch of another.

She took her seat in the middle of the boat, assuming Jack would occupy the row behind her but instead, he sat next to her. They sat side by side on the cushioned leather seat in the most romantic setting she'd ever experienced in her life. The fit was tight, but she welcomed the opportunity to be close to him. She considered him rugged, with a low tight beard, tattoos, and deep dark eyes. The ultimate checklist of everything her parents warned her about, making him even more appealing.

While he took them around the bay, Marco told them about moving to the states from Venice, Italy. Determined to live out his version of the American Dream, he settled in Coronado, California, where he started his own business doing tours. "Gondoliers originated in Venice over one thousand years ago, and in the beginning, they mainly worked for wealthy Venetian families." He shared a few random facts about the history of gondoliers and the significance of the uniforms they wore before beginning to sing a beautiful opera song.

A bountiful picnic basket sat in the seat directly in front of them. It contained champagne, orange juice, blueberry muffins, and fresh fruit. The fog dissipated, and the sun rose, leaving behind a breathtaking landscape of pink, purple, and blue pastels accentuated by white puffy clouds and a golden halo. It was still a little chilly, but the warmth radiating from Jack's body kept her warm enough to enjoy the ride.

"How did Eric sucker you into coming here this morning?"

She took a deep breath. "I'd love to say he had some devious master plan, but I guess he could tell I liked you, and you could say he owed me a solid." Andrew did a number on her self-esteem, but Jack made her feel like a lioness. You never get a second chance to make a first impression, and she needed to go for it, or maybe next time it would be someone else out with Jack. Bella loved seeing the look of surprise on his face as she revealed her secret crush. What did she have to lose? Her pride? Being in jeopardy of losing her business and her money somehow made her feel bolder than ever before.

"Really," said Jack.

She wasn't sure what to say next. She had been admiring Jack at a distance for a year. Sitting next to him, listening to a man sing opera on a boat at six o'clock in the morning made her nervous. Bella replied, "Sorry, I didn't mean to make you feel uncomfortable."

"No, you didn't make me feel uncomfortable," said Jack. Marco, the gondolier, finished his song right on time to interrupt the awkwardness of their conversation and offered a Mimosa. Jack quickly responded by popping the cork on the champagne. He filled each flute a little more than halfway before adding orange juice. "I guess you could say I'm shocked." Jack lifted his glass to hers.

"Shocked?" This was a massive leap for Bella, feeling more intimidated by the second. Was being shocked a good thing or a bad thing?

Jack shook his head and creased his brow. "That was the wrong word to describe it. You're so beautiful. I never guessed I'd have a shot."

A ripple of relief washed over her body, but now things were even weirder. Jack seemed equally as bad at this whole dating thing. She took a couple of sips from her drink and made her best attempt to relax. The sun rose higher in the morning sky, and she started to feel warm. She slipped off her jacket and set it to her side.

"I guess maybe I should come clean too," said Jack. "I may have mentioned something to Eric about you." His reassurance provided a sense of relief that pushed the remaining tension from her body, allowing her to relax a little more.

"Oh yeah, and what would that be?"

"After I saw you at the event with him, I asked him how he knew you." He took a sip from his glass and looked out to the ocean. "I told him I thought you were out of his league." Bella smiled because his expression was priceless. Jack, a strong alpha male who led a full life, looked so vulnerable.

They were past the hard stuff, and the awkwardness lifted almost as quickly as the fog did. Over a continental breakfast, they shared about living in California and their businesses. Jack turned his attention to Marco and asked, "Do you have time to keep us out a little longer?"

Marco replied, "I'd love to, but I have back-to-back appointments all day long."

It felt like the date had just started, and it was already over. She wasn't ready to let Jack go. She needed to know more about where he grew up. The story with him and Chelsea and what brought him to Coronado.

When they returned to the dock, Jack helped Bella off the boat and thanked Marco for his time. "Are you in a rush to get back to the store?" Jack's rumbly voice made her ravenous for more.

"No, the girls are working this morning." She may have appeared eager, but she didn't care. She enjoyed herself and wanted to spend as much time with him as possible.

Jack suggested, "We could go for a walk on the beach."

"Sure, a walk sounds good." She took off her Converse and tossed them into her bag; nothing was worse than a shoe full of sand.

The beach appeared to go on for an eternity, and that's how long she wanted to walk next to Jack. "What brought you to California?" Bella asked, hoping to ease into the conversation. She preferred to go straight for the difficult questions but didn't want to scare him away.

He squinted against the sunshine. "I was stationed here for quite some time, but I made it my permanent residence after I retired from the Navy. I was enlisted for twenty years and retired two years ago."

"Does that make you forty? Forty-two?"

"That makes me forty, but I'll be forty-one soon."

She never would have guessed Jack to be older than her, but the slight gap didn't bother her in the least bit.

"What about you?"

"You never ask a woman her age," Bella replied with a smile. "I'm joking. I'm thirty-five."

"Really?" Jack seemed surprised by her age, but she wasn't sure if he expected her to be older or younger.

"What is wrong with thirty-five?" asked Bella.

"Nothing. If I'm being frank, I guess I'm surprised you're not married yet."

"I've never even come close. I had a relationship with this guy, Andrew, but I knew he wasn't right for me. I spent most of my time with our family business, and once I came here to California, I stayed focused on Carpe Diem. In retrospect, I guess that's pretty sad, huh?"

"No, I get it. I've never been married either. I was engaged to Chelsea, but as you know, things didn't work out."

"Is it awkward, always being around her?" Bella asked against her better judgment, but she would have regretted it later if she had avoided the question.

"I wouldn't say awkward, only complicated."

"Complicated can mean a lot of things."

Jack didn't respond, but she hadn't asked a question. Next time she'd have to choose her words more wisely.

They walked in silence for a few minutes. She admired his body; he had several visible tattoos that read more like a resume of his life experience, hieroglyphics telling a story she was eager to learn.

She loved the ocean. It had a calming and tranquil effect yet had the power to take a life or even destroy an entire city with ease. Jack offered a level of peace and comfort, but like the ocean, she could tell there was a mystery to him that made him irresistible in a dangerous way. Perhaps the unknown was what made him so compelling. She glanced at him and wondered what his story was, not the one he told the world but the one he kept locked deep inside.

"Am I going to see you again?"

Jack stopped walking and peered through her eyes directly to her soul. "Do you want to see me again?"

"I do."

"Then you will." His response gave her all the reassurance she needed.

They spent the next hour talking. She told him about Snowball, selling real estate in Ohio, and how much she loved living in California. He was a good listener; he asked curious questions and showed a genuine interest in her answers. He told her about his love of surfing, the military, and visiting different countries. He didn't mention anything about growing up or how he met Chelsea, but this was only a first date, and she didn't want to be too aggressive with her questioning.

He reached over and took her hand. "I've enjoyed spending the morning with you." His touch rendered her speechless.

"I have to go soon." He seemed reluctant to leave.

She closed her eyes for a second before nodding in agreement. "Thanks for sticking around after the gondola. Eric paid a lot of money for this date. I'm glad we maximized his investment."

Jack laughed aloud, and Bella appreciated that her humor was well received. He leaned in without warning and kissed her lips as if to test the waters. Surprised by his assertiveness, she welcomed his advance by stepping into his arms. Her legs felt weak, but his powerful embrace supported her. Her heart pounded so hard she wondered if he could feel it. He placed his lips on hers, this time kissing her more passionately than before.

"This is the best I've felt in a long time."

As she soaked in his words, she thought back to the day she saw Jack arguing with Chelsea in the parking lot. Did he fight for their relationship, or had he given up a long time ago?

"I don't want to leave, but I have to."

"I should go too." Her words said she should go, but she'd stay there forever if he asked her. She never felt more desired or safe than she did in his arms, and she didn't want it to end this quickly.

## CHAPTER TWELVE

As she rode her bike down Orange Avenue, her mind fixated on Jack. His arms around her body and lips on hers, the thoughts made her warm and tingly. She hadn't kissed a guy in over a year, but this was nothing like she'd ever experienced before.

Bella had the day off, but how was she supposed to go home and clean her apartment after all the excitement with Jack? She needed to be at Carpe Diem, where she could be with the girls, focused on saving her business and close to Jack even if walls divided them. To her surprise, she even missed Snowball. The attachment grew stronger with each day she spent with her.

A few people congregated outside the store. Unsure what drew the crowd, she greeted the people waiting. Upon further investigation, Addie was helping a customer, and Tiffany assisted the first contestant with their photoshoot.

She'd never seen the store with this many people before. The selfie stations were open and already attracting people. They were even better than Bella imagined they'd be. The space near the register featured a beach chair, multicolored umbrella, balls, and accessories like sunglasses. The stretch along the wall was all about surfing. There was a stunning ocean backdrop, a fan, and a couple of boards. A person could stand on the platform to make it look like they were surfing. The final space in the dressing room had hundreds of iridescent balls, some on the walls, others hanging from the ceiling, and a big one to sit on.

Contestant number one changed in the dressing room while Bella took advantage of the time to chat with Tiffany. "How is it going so far?"

"It's going great. We already have the first two shots. Now we need the third one. With four appointments scheduled per day, we're making great time."

"You girls are amazing. It looks incredible in here." She was floored by the amount of progress Tiffany and Addison achieved in such a short amount of time. The store had customers, a fully functional website, and the contest was underway. She needed to retrieve her pup before making herself useful at Carpe Diem. "I'm going to run next door, but I'll be right back."

Bella popped into Ex-Squeeze Me on an all-time high. The date with Jack still as fresh as today's pressed juice in her mind, things were improving for Carpe Diem, and for the first time in weeks, she felt on top of the world. "I'm here for Snowball," she said to Amber.

"Hey girl, Snowball went for a walk with Eric, but they'll be back soon." Amber passed a juice over the counter to Bella. "I'm sure you haven't eaten breakfast yet."

"As a matter of fact, I did, with Jack,." said Bella with a grin plastered to her face.

"So, how was the date?" asked Amber.

"Good," said Bella in a poor attempt to be vague and torture Amber a little bit.

"Oh no, you don't. You better give me some details." Amber walked around the counter and sat at a nearby table with Bella.

"We went on a gondola cruise, and after, we took a walk on the beach."

"Did you kiss? Who am I kidding? Of course, you didn't kiss."

"Maybe we did." Bella looked sideways at Amber, who rolled her eyes, obviously not believing her.

"Are you going to see him again?"

"I hope so, but I don't know." It felt good to be on the other end of this conversation for a change.

"Did you get his number?"

"No, should I have done that?"

"Rookie mistake." Amber said, looking sideways at Bella, "Now he can't even text you to say he had a good time or ask you out again without coming over and doing it in person."

She hated to admit that she was right. She couldn't even send him a message to say thank you. Dating was more complicated than she remembered. "I'm leaving before you depress me," Bella said, determined not to let Amber kill her vibe. "The girls are working on a photoshoot. You need to come by and check out the spaces we created. It looks amazing."

"I know. I stopped by for a minute this morning when I saw a few people waiting outside. So creative, I would have never thought to do something like that."

"These girls have given me the push I needed to make it through this." She started to feel like slowly but surely things were coming together, and the date with Jack was the icing on the cake. She felt lighter and more carefree than she had in months. It was remarkable how a good make-out session could increase optimism. She smiled at her friend. "Thank you for watching Snowball."

The girls were finished with the first two shots and took some time to talk to Bella before the next appointment arrived.

"How was your date with the hottie next door?" asked Tiffany.

Bella smiled and looked to the floor. "It was nice."

"Nice, are you kidding me? Jack's a ten. A date with a guy like that is hot, adventurous, or intense, but it can't be described as nice," said Addison.

"We went on a gondola."

"But did you ride on his gondola?" Addison wiggled her eyebrows.

Bella blushed to the roots of her hair. "Ha Ha, very funny."

"Ignore her. I didn't know there was one here," Tiffany said. "I did that when I went to Italy with my family."

"I did one at the Venetian in Las Vegas," Addison chimed in.

"Before I forget, check out these shots from today." Tiffany retrieved the pictures on Bella's laptop behind the counter. Not only was Tiffany great with technology she was also an exceptional photographer. "Thanks to your idea of pre-selecting the outfits, the whole shoot only took about forty-five minutes."

"I'm so glad it was helpful," Bella said as she examined the pictures on the laptop. "These are remarkable, Tiffany."

"I try," She was confident and cocky, but Bella loved that about her. She admired Tiffany's confidence and how she made everything appear effortless.

"When's the next appointment?" asked Bella

"They won't be here until one o'clock," Addison said.

"Why don't you two go and get some lunch," Bella suggested.

"Thanks. Do you want us to bring you back anything?" asked Addison.

"No, I'm good." Bella held the door open for them to escape.

The store felt vibrant; several shoppers stopped to pose at the selfie stations. She checked in with each customer to see if she could help with anything before taking her place at the T-shirt display. As she folded, she recalled the numerous confrontations with her mom as a teenager for leaving her clothes sprawled everywhere. Now she folded clothes to relax, and the irony brought a smile to her face.

Eric walked in with Snowball, and Bella ran over to greet them. It was nice to see Eric, but she missed her little dog. Bella found a comfortable spot on the floor to allow Snowball easy access to her lap. Who would have thought she'd come to love something she found behind a dumpster? Turning her attention to Eric, she said, "Thank you for keeping her last night."

"Glad we could help. Amber's apartment doesn't allow pets, so they both stayed at my place." Eric set the pup's overnight essentials bag on the counter.

Amber was quick to ask about the date with Jack, but she neglected to share the juicy little tidbit about staying at Eric's place. His comment left Bella curious, but she didn't want to jump to conclusions, making a mental note to ask Amber about it later.

"Jack called me," Eric said.

She felt like a giddy schoolgirl.

"He thanked me for my donation and told me he had a great time."

She wondered if Jack said more to Eric than he was letting on? She

# Carpe Diem

knew they were friends but had no idea how close. "I had a great time, too. He seems like a great guy." She was proud of her response, not too needy, desperate, or clingy. "How are things going with Amber?"

"Amber is ..." Eric looked out the window with a twinkle in his eye, then drifted his attention back to Bella. "Everything. The first time I met her, I knew I wanted to spend the rest of my life with her, and now that we've spent some quality time together ... I'm sure of it."

*Oh, my ginger.* Eric sounded needy, desperate, and clingy, but it also made her want to cry. Amber deserved to have someone who'd love her that much, and Eric seamlessly fit into Amber's world.

"I can see myself marrying her."

If he wanted to capture Bella's attention, he did a good job. "Amber is one of a kind."

He reached down and ruffled Snowball's fur. "I think I love your little friend." He looked up at her. "Please don't say anything. I don't want to scare her off."

"Your secret is safe with me." Bella had read hundreds of romance novels in her life, so she believed in love at first sight. Amber deserved that kind of attention. "I may not have thanked you for the date with Jack, but I had a great time. The gondola ride was so creative. Thank you."

"Glad to help. Before I leave, there is one more thing I want to talk to you about." His tone was heavier than before. "Amber mentioned Carl Douglas is your accountant. I would tread lightly with him. I don't have any details right now, but I may have heard some office gossip that got my attention."

"What did they say?" Her pulse picked up. She worked hard to find Mr. Douglas, and maybe he was a little strange, but why would they be talking about him in an attorney's office?

"I can't say yet, but it never hurts to get a second opinion on financial matters. I hate to drop news like this and run, but I gotta go."

After Eric left, Bella called Sunshine Tax Pros to try and set an appointment with Mr. Douglas. Once again, there were no appointments available.

She grabbed the manila envelope and put it in her bag. The denial needed to stop; she had to learn how to read these reports now.

## CHAPTER THIRTEEN

Bella grabbed Snowball's leash from her granite countertop and headed for the dog run. At this point, she'd come to expect everyone wore their pajamas outside at five am, except for B-12. He was sitting on the bench wearing torn blue jeans and a plain white T-shirt, reading the morning paper. He looked more like a rock star than an accountant. "Good morning," he said, peeking out from behind the day's news. "How are you?" He folded the paper and rested it in his lap.

"I'm good. How are you?" She spent half the night researching how to read financial reports and still couldn't make heads or tails of the one Mr. Douglas provided to her. Grateful B-12 offered his assistance; she wanted to come right out and ask for his help but didn't want to appear as desperate as she felt.

"Great, I didn't see you outside yesterday."

"Snowball stayed the night at my friend's house." How long did she have to make small talk before she could jump right into full-on begging for help?

"Rex has never had a slumber party before."

Now she knew his dog's name was Rex, but she still didn't know his name. She couldn't remember if she'd already asked and forgotten, but now it was too late to return to first meeting introductions.

She tried her best to be patient, but she couldn't wait for a second longer to ask B-12 about her reports. Her future was hanging by a thread. Deciding to rip off the Band-Aid, she said, "I brought my financial reports home. Do you think you would mind looking at them? I'd love to understand what they mean."

"Sure, I don't need to be at work for a few more hours. If you want, I can come over now and check it out."

"That would be wonderful." She practically begged her accountant to help her for weeks, and thanks to the kindness of a perfect stranger, she could finally get the help she needed. They called for the dogs and headed to her apartment. Snowball loved playing with Rex, and that would allow her to give B-12 her undivided attention. "You have no idea how much I appreciate your help."

"Some people read mysteries or romance. I read statistical data and financials." He smiled. His enthusiasm for his work showed in his voice. He picked up his black and brown beagle and carried him up the stairs. "I think he's afraid of heights."

Pausing for a second, Bella stood at the landing, trying her best to recall if she picked up before bed last night. She considered herself a tidy person, but it had been a busy couple of days, and she hadn't spent much time cleaning. She couldn't ask B-12 to come back later; she needed his help now. She closed her eyes and opened the door. Snowball took off down the hall, and Rex jumped out of B-12's arms to chase after her.

A sense of relief washed over Bella when she realized it wasn't too bad, only a couple of dishes in the sink, a few leftover Chinese food containers on the counter, and a blanket sprawled on the couch. They sat at the kitchen table, and she handed him the dreaded envelope.

He took a pair of reading glasses from his pocket and began to inspect each report page. Bella asked, "Would you like a cup of coffee?"

"No, thank you," He replied, staying focused on the report in front of him. He squinted, made several grunt-like noises, even scratched his head a couple of times but didn't say any actual words.

Bella wanted to give him time to understand what several hours of research couldn't clarify for her. To provide him with some space, she wiped down the counters in the kitchen and emptied the dishwasher.

There were about fifty pages in the report, and it took B-12 thirty minutes to review it from beginning to end. "Do you have a calculator handy?"

"Yeah, let me go grab it." She remembered leaving the calculator on top of her dresser. She found the dogs in her room and noticed Rex chewing on something. She leaned in to investigate further and discovered her favorite blue panties in the jaws of her neighbor's beagle. The closer she got to Rex, the more he bore down on her britches.

Mortified, she said in her most quiet yet stern voice, "Drop, drop right now."

She chased him to the corner before he darted under the bed. Her shoulders sagged, and she threw her head back. She didn't want to tell B-12, but she also didn't want his beagle to choke on her panties.

Sprawled on the floor, she tried to coax the dog from under the bed. "Come here, come on, do you want a treat?"

Rex dropped the panties and came running. Bella left the bedroom with both dogs and a calculator in hand, closing the door behind her. She handed the calculator to her neighbor and grabbed two treats from the counter. "Can Rex have a treat?"

"Yes, he loves treats, but he is allergic to seafood."

Bella checked the label; everything appeared safe for consumption. She passed out the treats and took a quick walk around the apartment to ensure they wouldn't find any more hidden treasures. All clear, she thought to herself before returning to the kitchen.

"How does it look?" asked Bella.

"Well, come sit down."

Bella sat at the table, thinking no one ever asks you to sit down for good news.

"Did you attempt to read these yet?" He waved the report in front of her.

"I did, but I couldn't understand it. The more I read, the more confused I got."

"I graduated top of my class, and I've been working as an accountant in California for the last three years. I've read more financial reports than I can even count, and this report right here is bullshit. Each document contradicts the next, and none of the numbers add up. It's like someone took financials from several failing companies, complied them, resulting in this mess."

Bella leaned forward in her chair, hoping he could offer her some valuable insight.

He said, "I'm going to be as candid as I possibly can. You need to take these documents and give them to an attorney."

"What are you trying to say?" She peered at B-12 with apprehension, unable to remain in her seat.

"I've never seen anything like this before, but from where I'm sitting, this looks sketchy." He ran his hands over his clean-shaven face. "I'd even go as far as saying it might be embezzlement."

Bella's face lost expression, and her entire body went limp, almost causing her to topple over. Mr. Douglas was the first person she met in California, the first person she trusted to help her with her business. How could he do this to her? "You think I should see an attorney?"

B-12 sat back in his chair and let go a slow breath through his nose. "Listen, I don't know the extent of the damage, but this is bigger than us. We're going to need to get some help. Do you have an attorney? If not, I can put you in contact with one?"

His words echoed in her ears, and her vision closed in like a tunnel. She began to breathe more erratically and felt like she would pass out. She placed both her hands on the sides of her face pressing firmly while rocking back and forth.

B-12 rested his hand on her back and said, "Please try and calm down."

Calm down, calm down, calm down, she thought to herself, focusing on her breathing. She needed to relax, or she'd scare him away, and she couldn't afford to lose him. "I'm sorry, I think I'm in shock right now. I don't know what to make of all this."

"Okay, let's take this one step at a time. First, limit communication with Carl Douglas, second reach out to an attorney and provide them with your financial records, next give them my card, and I'll be happy to assist in any way I can." He handed his card to Bella, and she placed it directly in her pocket.

She tried to remain calm, but she desperately wanted to scream at the top of her lungs like a raving lunatic. "I have to give you something. Would a hundred dollars be enough?"

"Please, Bella, I offered to help, and I'm glad I could."

"I can't thank you enough." She said while trying to process everything. Mr. Douglas was more than her accountant, he was her friend, her trusted advisor, and he deceived her. The words felt foreign to her mouth, and she didn't even want to say them out loud. "I'm going to contact an attorney today. I hope it's not too late."

"I'm going to help you in any way I can, so call if you need anything." B-12 placed the report back in the dreaded manila envelope and called Rex back to the kitchen. "Come on, it's time to go home."

Bella closed the door and locked it behind him. She wanted to cry, but her anger wouldn't allow her. She had responsibilities that needed to be fulfilled. She had to open the store and call Eric. He was an attorney; maybe he could help her. She shot him a text.

Bella: Can we talk soon?
Eric: Sure, what's up?
Bella: I've got some bad news about Mr. Douglas
Eric: Really. I can stop by before taking Amber to lunch.
Bella: Sounds good

Every second of the morning seemed to last an eternity. Between customers, she operated on autopilot, tweaking the window display, dusting, and folding shirts. It was almost time for the girls to arrive, and she was hopeful they'd provide some assistance passing the time. They had two photoshoots scheduled in the morning and two in the afternoon.

The girls were working hard to support Bella, and she couldn't help thinking she had disappointed them. It wasn't only them. She let everyone down, her parents, Amber, herself, and Nona. She didn't deserve Nona's gift. She didn't deserve to have her dreams come true, only to have them ripped away by her own negligence. She was a failure, and she was going to lose everything. That was exactly what she deserved… to lose everything. Her face felt hot, and her pulse quickened. She needed to calm down, but she couldn't. Breathe. Breathe. Breathe, Bella, she commanded herself. She gasped for air. *God help me.*

---

Everything appeared muddled, leaving Bella disoriented and out of focus. She could hear people whisper but had no idea what they were saying. A feeling of horror consumed her when she realized she was flat on her back in the middle of Carpe Diem. She attempted to move, but someone touched her shoulder and urged her to lie still for a few moments. She must have fallen and hit her head, judging by the intense throbbing pain radiating from the base of her neck to her forehead. As objects came into focus, she recognized the worried faces of Amber, Addison, and Tiffany surrounding her.

"Bella, can you hear me?" asked Amber in an echo.

There were three paramedics, and one of them said, "She is going to be okay. Her vitals are good. It looks like she fainted. She is going to need to rest, drink lots of fluids and follow up with her doctor." They helped Bella to a seated position. She was still bewildered but becoming more aware every minute.

Amber sat next to her on the floor and asked, "What happened?"

"I have no idea. I was cleaning, next thing I know, I'm flat on my back, and you're all standing around me." With Amber's assistance, she sat up, still feeling woozy. "Is Eric here yet?"

"Please sit. I should bring you home."

"No, I'm fine. Please bring me a juice." Bella took a seat behind the counter, still feeling unsteady on her feet. She'd reached a new level of humiliation. What kind of drama queen passes out in the middle of the floor? Determined she let the stress of the situation overwhelm her, she attempted to relax as instructed.

Amber came back and handed her a juice. "Are you gonna be okay?"

"Yes, I'm going to be fine," Bella replied.

"Eric and I will bring you with us to lunch."

"Okay," said Bella, waving Amber out the door. Even Snowball was acting ridiculous, sitting at Bella's feet and refusing to budge.

"Hey girl, mom is going to be just fine," she said, bending to give Snowball a belly rub. "I want to forget this ever happened."

Bella took a couple of sips from her juice and vowed to relax for the next thirty minutes. Several areas other than her head were sore from the fall, including her wrist and elbow. She assumed they were sprained or strained but didn't want to say anything.

She saw Addison doing her best to assist a pretentious contestant with her outfit selection. She interjected, "Hello, I'm Bella."

"Hey, I'm Trina, and this is my best friend, Emma. We're looking for something savage for the contest."

"I've pre-selected some styles based on your application. They should be in your fitting room."

Trina rolled her eyes, and Emma said, "They're not really our vibe."

"I'd be happy to help you. We have a couple of new designers over here I'd love to show you."

"We've got it." Emma turned her back on Bella.

She wasn't sure if it was the straw that broke the camel's back or if Trina and Emma just reminded her of the bullies from her high school, but Bella snapped.

"I don't appreciate your attitude because I'm trying to help. We've pre-selected the outfits to expedite the shoots, and there isn't enough time for you to spend another thirty minutes aimlessly wandering around the store."

Addison and Tiffany rushed to Bella's side. "Sorry Bella, we tried to help them, but they refused." Addison appeared frustrated.

"I'm not going to deal with anyone coming in here and treating us poorly," Bella said, resting back on her throne behind the counter.

"If we can't choose what we want, then we're out of here," Emma said, grabbing Trina's hand.

"This contest is bullshit, and we're telling everyone at school not to come here," Trina yelled as they stormed out of the store.

The last thing Bella needed was to have the name of her business tarnished based on the opinion of two snotty college kids. She threw her head back in frustration, and tears streamed from her eyes. She should have been more patient; she should have let them choose whatever they wanted. Now they were down two contestants, and she was on the edge of a total meltdown.

Addison rested her hand on Bella's shoulder. "Don't worry about anything. We've got everything under control."

"Now we're short two contestants."

Tiffany showed Bella the list of people waiting to participate in future events. "We are going to be fine. I'll call the next two names on this list, and we'll be right back to twenty by the end of the day."

"You need to relax. You scared the crap out of us." Addison said while touching Bella's leg. "Are you okay?"

"I am. This is a perfect example of why it's important to take care of yourself and manage your stress in healthy ways." She loved the girls and didn't want them to worry about her. They went above and beyond for her; she didn't want to burden them with new information about her accountant.

Eric and Amber approached the counter, walking hand in hand. "Are you ready for lunch?" asked Amber.

"Yes." Bella was elated to see Eric. She didn't even care they were over an hour early. She needed to tell him what happened with B-12 this morning. She grabbed her bag and headed for the door. "Are you girls going to be okay for a little bit?"

Yes, get out of here." Tiffany waved her off.

Amber held the door open. "Eric's going to drive so you don't have to walk."

Bella wasn't going to argue because a walk was the last thing she wanted or needed right now. They were only going a couple blocks to Eric's favorite Thai restaurant, but she still felt unstable on her feet.

She took careful steps getting from the store to the car while Amber watched her like a hawk. Most likely waiting for her to exhibit signs of weakness. Eric had a BMW X5. It put the Lexus she drove back in Ohio to shame. Pure luxury from the panoramic sunroof to the supple leather seats and embroidered floor mats. Bella wasn't sure what kind of clients Eric had, but judging by his vehicle business was good.

The power as he accelerated drew her back into her seat, making her head throb. She took a deep breath to relieve some of the pain.

"Thanks for taking me to lunch." Bella sank into the contour of her seat.

Eric smiled. "Are you kidding me? I've been waiting all day to hear about Carl."

Unable to wait until they arrived at the restaurant, she said, "I showed the financial reports to my neighbor, and after half an hour reviewing them, he suggested I retain an attorney."

"Did he say why?" asked Eric.

"He said it looked like embezzlement."

"Embezzlement?" Eric let out a low whistle.

"Yeah, he said none of the reports made any sense, and he'd be happy to assist any attorney who took my case. So naturally, I called you."

"No wonder you collapsed at Carpe Diem. You must be livid," Amber said in her most righteous tone. "I had a feeling that accountant was crooked."

Bella wanted to defend Mr. Douglas, but it wasn't looking good for him based on the evidence. How could someone she held in such high regard betray her?

The car pulled up to the restaurant, and Amber helped Bella from the back seat. "I'm so sorry you're going through all this."

She was a great friend, and Bella appreciated having her during such a difficult time in her life.

## CHAPTER FOURTEEN

Thanks to Amber insisting she see a physician; Bella was quarantined to her apartment by doctor's orders for the next two days. She rested on her bean bag chair, staring at the flat white ceiling. If she was honest, she knew this was the right thing to do.

She grabbed her book, but the throbbing in her head made it impossible to focus on the words. Day one had only begun, and it was already torture. She watched three movies and played ten games of solitaire, all from the comfort of her pink footed-pajamas.

A knock on the door jolted her more quickly than her head tolerated. She wasn't expecting anyone and didn't have the patience for a door-to-door salesman. She tiptoed over and peeked through the tiny hole. Those eyes, those lips ... it was Jack. Whatever he was selling she wanted to buy.

She panicked. She didn't want to answer the door in her PJs and tangled hair, but she wasn't going to let him walk away. She closed her eyes and tugged the door open in one swift motion. "Jack, what are you doing here?"

"I came by Carpe Diem to say hello, and Addison told me what happened. I hope you don't mind they gave me your address."

"Of course not, please come in," she said, stepping aside to allow him access to her kitchen. "Please excuse the mess. I wasn't expecting company."

He held a glass vase stuffed with a vibrant assortment of flowers. "I wanted to get you something, but I wasn't sure what to bring."

"This was sweet of you." Since their date, Bella couldn't get Jack out of her mind, and now he was standing in her apartment. Warm fuzzy feelings filled her chest at his thoughtfulness.

"I don't know how I missed the EMS arriving."

"It was in the morning, so you were probably getting prepped for opening. They weren't there long, but I was mortified. What kind of drama queen collapses in the middle of the floor?"

Touching the small of her back, he asked, "Are you feeling alright now?" His tone was sincere, and he appeared concerned.

"Yeah, the doctor asked me to stay home for a couple of days as a precaution."

"I have to get back to work, but if it's alright, maybe I can come by again tomorrow?"

Every bone in her body desired his presence.

"You don't have to do that."

"I want to."

Her heart skipped a beat. Had he been thinking about her like she was obsessing over him. "Well then, who am I to stop you?" Bella replied with a smile.

He planted a single kiss on her forehead before leaving.

She rested her back against the wall and sank to the floor. Snowball jumped in her lap and rested her face on Bella's leg. "Do you like Jack?" she asked as she scratched behind Snowball's ear. "I do too." She glanced at the clock on the wall, and it was only four p.m. What was she going to do for another day and a half? "I promise, girl, we might be stuck inside a little longer, but I need to stop moping around. Your momma is going to get her life together."

After two ibuprofens, her headache had subsided. Jack's surprise visit gave her the fuel she needed to stay optimistic.

Sticking to her convictions, Bella sat in front of her computer, determined to move in the right direction. She searched the term "financial literacy for business owners" and found a study that found only 40 percent of business owners considered themselves financially literate, but 80 percent did most of their own accounting. She thought she did the right thing by hiring an accountant and trusting him to lead her down the right path, but in retrospect, she shouldn't have given anyone that much authority over her life.

She read a couple articles that led her to the Small Business Administration in her area. They had several free programs available for business owners like her. A few minutes turned into several hours and resulted in a scheduled visit to her new community partner.

Snowball started barking at the door, and before Bella could investigate, Amber walked in with Eric close behind her. Holding a juice in one hand and keys in the other, she wrapped Bella in a one-armed hug.

"Honey, you look like shit."

"Ahh thanks." She wondered what Amber thought the appropriate outfit was for being sequestered. "I only have one more day, and I'll be back to the store."

"Make sure to take a shower first."

Eric looked handsome, dressed in a blue power suit with a black and white striped tie. He got straight to business. "My firm is taking your case under serious consideration. Do you have any other records to provide us?"

"No, I think I gave you everything."

"I spoke to Dwayne, He's going testify as an expert witness, but Douglas can't hear a word about this until our case is airtight and we present it to law enforcement."

"Who's Dwayne?"

"You know, Dwayne, your neighbor."

Bella's eyes widened in understanding. "B-12, How did you know his name?"

"The business card you gave me," Eric said with a look of confusion. "Maybe you hit your head harder than we thought."

While they talked, Amber walked around the apartment, tidying up a bit. She filled Snowball's food bowls, threw away the empty containers on the counter, and even loaded the dishwasher. Already things were looking better. First, an impromptu visit from Jack, her online research, Amber helping her clean a little bit, and Eric's firm taking her case. "I've been wracking my brain, trying to figure out what I should do next."

Eric wrapped an arm around her shoulders. "I know it's not the answer you want to hear, but there's nothing you can do right now. We're going to do a little more investigating. Once the partners see enough evidence of foul play, we'll provide you with all the documentation you need to file a formal complaint with the police department. They'll assign a detective to your case and proceed from there. This is a lengthy process and can take an extended period before you see any justice served."

"Thank you for your help." She was surrounded by so many thoughtful people, and after years of feeling alone, she wasn't sure they understood the difference their kindness made in her life. "Would I be able to pay you once the case settles? I'm kind of broke right now."

"The partners said we can take the case pro-bono."

Bella wasn't an attorney, but she knew the word pro-bono from watching *Law and Order* in high school. Relief flooded through her. "That's amazing. Thank you so much."

"I'm glad we could help. When I spoke to you about Carl Douglas, it was because I heard some office gossip that he pushed the envelope with his clients' taxes and had been caught cheating on his wife with his receptionist, but nothing like embezzlement. That's like federal prison kind of trouble." Eric looked oddly relaxed while discussing such sensitive topics.

Bella was heartbroken about Mr. Douglas but that sorrow quickly gave way to anger. Despite her annoyance, she couldn't imagine him spending his life rotting away in prison. In her heart, she hoped the attorneys would discover this was a terrible misunderstanding.

"There are a couple things before we go. You don't want to send up any red flags with this guy until we're finished with our fact-finding. You need to protect your remaining assets. Stop all future investment activity and open a new account immediately."

She tried her best to take in everything Eric had to say, but her headache returned, making it extremely difficult.

"One more thing I want to warn you about." Bella wasn't sure how much more she could take, but she had an ally in Eric and couldn't risk offending him. "Once the assets are frozen, you won't have access to any of the money under his management. Is he a signer on any of your business accounts?"

"Yes, I gave him access to all my banking." The more Bella confessed how much control she gave to Mr. Douglas, the more ashamed she felt.

"Do you have any credit cards you can use?"

Bella chewed her bottom lip. "I do, but there's not much available credit."

"It's going to get worse before it gets better, but it will get better. Open the new account and once the existing accounts are frozen, use your credit cards. Every dollar you bring in from today forward needs to go directly into the new account."

"I'll call the bank first thing tomorrow morning. Maybe they can give me some insight on what to say to Mr. Douglas."

"Good thinking," Eric said, still looking as carefree as ever. "We don't want him to be suspicious of an abrupt change."

After sleeping for fourteen consecutive hours, Bella felt like a million bucks. No headache or body aches and stood stable on her feet. She couldn't think of a single reason why she couldn't go to work on day two of her doctor-prescribed vacation until she remembered Jack's promised visit. He worked seven days a week from eleven a.m. to eleven p.m., so she imagined it would be early.

She looked through her entire wardrobe twice, wanting to be cute without looking like a try-hard; nothing seemed to fit the occasion. She opted for a sensible floor-length skirt that stretched to contour her body with an off-the-shoulder shirt and flip-flops.

Looking and feeling better than she could have hoped for, she decided to reach out to her bank. Her business banker at Coronado Credit Union was Nadine. When she set up the account, Nadine insisted that Bella program her direct number in her phone. She said if Bella needed anything, she would always know who to reach out to. Grateful for Nadine's persistence, she called fifteen minutes after they opened, and her banker answered on the second ring.

"Good morning, and thank you for calling Coronado Credit Union."

"Hello Nadine, my name is Bella Roberts, and I'm a business customer. I was hoping I could set up a time to discuss a sensitive matter with you regarding a signer on my account."

"Yes, I can help you with that. When would you like to come in?"

She had a meeting to visit the Small Business Administration on Thursday, so it made sense to knock this out the same day if possible. "How is Thursday at 10 a.m.?"

"Perfect, I have you on my calendar. Don't forget to bring in your business documents in the event we need to make any changes."

After thanking Nadine for her time, Bella set down her phone, feeling proud of making progress in the right direction.

She grabbed the closest book she could find and headed out to the balcony for a small dose of romance while she waited for her prince to arrive. The scent of roses wafted through the air from the bushes below. The birds sang a sweet melody, and the morning sun brought with it a sense of joy.

Bella loved the feel of a paperback book in her hands, the way the pages smelled, and an adventure in the world of fiction. She melted into the comfort of her porch swing while enjoying a steamy new romance. Startled by a pebble clinking against the glass door, she almost dropped her book.

She glanced toward the parking lot, and there stood Jack. She knew running outside would appear desperate, so she intentionally slowed herself down. "Good morning, Jack."

"Are you feeling any better today?"

"I am. I wanted to go back to Carpe Diem, but they won't let me until tomorrow."

"I'm happy to hear that. Maybe, I can take you hostage?"

His choice of words enticed her. If a hostage is what he wanted, then she was game.

"Sure, give me a minute."

The moment's excitement caused a rush of adrenaline, making her feel lightheaded upon standing so abruptly. She stopped to consider if maybe she wasn't as recovered as she initially thought. Locking the deadbolt on her door, she carefully navigated the stairs not wanting another mishap on her record.

Jack had his hair pushed back like he did the night of the charity event. He wore jeans and a military-themed T-shirt with "Freedom or Death" on the back. He motioned to a blacked-out Harley parked in front of her building. "Have you ever ridden on a bike before?"

"A motorcycle?" Bella's eyes almost bulged from her head at the thought.

He smirked. "Yes."

Panic set in instantly, and her palms became clammy. "No, I've never been on a motorcycle. I'm a little afraid of them."

"You don't have to be afraid. I'll take it easy."

She scrambled for a reason not to get on the back of his bike. "What about my skirt?"

"That skirt does look hot on you, but you live here … you could change … or hike it up if you prefer." He smiled, and her heart melted right there in the parking lot.

She liked seeing this fun, flirty side of Jack. She trusted him, but motorcycles were a no-no for her growing up. Jackie forbade it, but Jackie wasn't here, was she? "I'll do it. Give me a second. I'm going to change."

He licked his lips before smiling so big she could see it in his eyes, making him even more irresistible. "I'll wait."

Within five minutes she was back downstairs in a pair of skinny jeans, cropped T-shirt, and Converse, ready for her first-ever motorcycle ride. She wasn't sure this was what the doctor recommended when he ordered her home for two days, but Jack was worth the risk. If anything could lift her spirits, it would be him.

He started the engine, and the bike roared like a lion. After a few instructions, she hopped on the back of his motorcycle while making the sign of the cross.

Before accelerating, he said, "Hold on."

Exhilarated by the powerful hum of the engine beneath her, Bella felt a freedom she had never experienced. She pulled her body into his, closing her eyes to say a little prayer for additional insurance. "Dear God, please keep us safe." She wasn't sure where they were going, nor did she care.

The fresh air, the power of the bike, relinquishing control, and the proximity to Jack made this the most thrilling moment of her life. Almost like climbing the hill of the tallest roller coaster, sitting at the top for a second before flying down at lightning speed. She didn't say a word because the bike demanded her undivided attention.

She wasn't sure how long they rode, but it seemed like thirty minutes before they arrived at the beach. Jack helped her from the back of the bike. She removed her helmet and couldn't stop the excitement bubbling in her body from flowing over to her face. "Amazing."

"I knew you'd like it." He reached for her hand and led her toward the stone wall. "I'm not sure what you have going on, but I hope you feel better soon."

"I'm okay, I have a lot on my plate right now, but I'll be fine." She didn't say that to appease him. She said it because she believed it. When a situation was at its worst, there was only one place to go … up.

They sat on a picnic table staring out into the ocean. "If I have to be a hostage, I sure picked the right captor."

"Oh yeah, maybe I shouldn't be so nice to you. I've learned a thing or two about torturing a prisoner." He caressed the side of her face before leaning in to kiss her.

Batting her long lashes at him, she said, "If you're trying to be mean, you're going to need to try a little harder." This was one of those perfect moments she'd read about in books. The air felt warm with a slight breeze, and the sky was painted a vibrant blue. Not a cloud in sight, the gentle crash of the waves and Jack by her side. Right now, nothing else mattered, not the money, her parents, or even Mr. Douglas.

"I'm not the smartest choice for you, Bella," Jack said after dropping his eyes to the sand.

"May I ask why?" Thinking he was joking, she studied his face and caught his serious expression. He sincerely thought she'd be better off without him.

"For starters, I work too much."

"Easy, I work a lot too."

"I have a complicated situation with Chelsea. I'm dedicated to serving my brothers, but more importantly, spending a lifetime in the military… it changes a person, forever."

She wanted to pretend that he hadn't just waved a huge red flag in her face, but she needed to stop using denial as a coping tool. She liked Jack, and if this relationship had any shot, she needed to face this head-on. "When you say complicated, what exactly do you mean?"

He didn't respond right away, taking an uncomfortable amount of time before saying another word. "I've made decisions in my life that I'm not proud of, but I'd make them all again even with knowing the consequences. Chelsea loved me, and I broke her heart. When I was a kid, I did whatever it took to survive. I stole food, clothes, and I was even homeless at one point. I did what I had to do, but I won't pretend my decisions haven't taken a toll on me."

"I can't say I understand, but I want to know you better. I'm drawn to you, and that never happens for me." She tucked her hair behind her ears. She wanted to lighten the mood because this conversation felt heavier by the second. "Well, I'm not a walk in the park either."

"Please tell me how dreadful you are?"

She closed her eyes while letting out a slow, steady breath. "Alright, let's go there." She paused for a second. "I managed to let an obnoxious amount of money slip through my fingers because my accountant was embezzling money from me." She forced out a smile. "If that's not shitty enough, I could tell you, I'm convinced my parents hate me, and they'll be in California soon. I'll need to tell them I have lost my inheritance, have no relationship, and I'm pretty much a total failure. Hence my dramatic fainting episode."

"I guess you win … maybe I should take you home."

She shoved his arm and said, "I think you should try." Laughing, she took off down the beach. She jogged along, kicking up the sand. Jack followed footsteps behind before gently capturing her in an embrace. Seconds later, they were in the sand rolling around like a couple of teenagers. Her shoes, hair, and clothes were all covered in sand, and she welcomed it.

He kissed her. This time more deeply than before, forcing away every inhibition she had. She gasped. She didn't care where they were or who was watching. Desperate to feel his touch on her body. Jack was her vice, and she was defenseless against him. She pulled his frame closer to hers and made a soft noise of pleasure in his ear as he kissed her neck. He kneeled on the ground between her open legs and observed her as she lay in the sand. He took in a heavy breath and pushed away, "I'm sorry."

"Sorry for what?"

As unexpected as him leaning in to kiss her, he grabbed her hand to help her up. "I'm usually the master of my actions, but you make it hard to do the right thing," he said in a whisper while tracing her neck with a touch that seemed too gentle for his calloused hand.

Every hair on her body stood on end as his words settled into her heart. He made her feel sexy, intelligent and desired. Andrew was harsh in his words but a sensible man, a wise choice for her and her future, or so she thought. Clean cut, well-educated, a professional. Jackie and Roger loved him, and why wouldn't they? He was like them. Emotionless. Robotic. Judgmental.

With Jack, the sun shone brighter, flowers smelled more fragrant, and she stood on top of the world. It didn't hurt that his body was sculpted by the U.S. Military, a machine built with lean muscle for endurance.

"Thank you for breaking me out of house arrest." She looked up to meet his deep dark gaze. "This is what I needed."

He took her hand, intertwining his fingers with hers. "I'm glad I could help, but after all you've revealed to me, I'm afraid your right. You're damaged goods."

She giggled. "At least I was upfront about it.

## CHAPTER FIFTEEN

Bella couldn't stop thinking about Jack as she walked to Carpe Diem, nor did she want to. A couple of days ago, she was convinced the sunrise cruise on the gondola was the best date ever, but a short ride on the back of Jack's Harley proved her wrong. She stayed home for two days, and he came to see her both days. That had to mean something.

Her mind wandered to the back of his bike. For the first time in her life, she felt like a badass. Her body pressed against his, the roar of the engine as he accelerated, the kiss on the beach. Jack was smooth; she'd only read about men like him.

She missed the curb and boom, back on her rump again. She managed to keep hold of her bag and Snowball's leash. She deserved that for being in la-la land when she should be paying attention to what she was doing. Lucky for her, no one witnessed it, or maybe she'd be back on house arrest for another two days. She picked herself up from the ground and pushed forward for the remaining two blocks.

Her apartment was great, but Carpe Diem was her home. She put her heart and soul into every detail, from the funky teal area rug on the floor to the blown glass wind chime on the door. The upbeat music, vibrant colors, and friendly faces constituted her happy place.

Tiffany and Addison were there early and taking care of business as usual. "Thank you both so much for helping while I was out."

"I'm glad we could help." Tiffany rushed over to greet her.

"I'm happy you are feeling better," said Addison.

They engulfed her in a warm squishy hug, making her feel loved and appreciated.

"What's been going on? I want to hear everything."

The store looked immaculate. The girls had done an excellent job while she recovered at home. They reorganized several displays, the counters were free of clutter, and her allergies weren't bothering her at all, indicating a dust-free environment.

Addison said, "We're almost done with the photoshoots, only four more to go. The online store is working great, we're shipping out new items daily, and the super-hot guy from next door came in looking for you." She turned to Tiffany and said, "That covers everything, right?"

"Except how happy we are that you're back. We've missed you." Addison smiled, showing off her pearly whites.

Jackie always said, "In this life, all you have is yourself, so never trust anyone else to get the job done." Against her mother's counsel, Bella remained what her mother considered to be soft. She wanted to believe the best of people, and if that meant heartache, she would deal with it. These girls were on a mission to prove Jackie wrong. They worked extra hours, invested their free time, and showed her kindness for no apparent reason.

"I've missed you too. Being stuck in the apartment was like torture. Thank God Snowball was there to keep me company." With the mention of her name, the little dog came running out from under the clothes rack, wagging her tail. Bella gave Snowball belly rubs and said, "Did you miss the girls too?"

"Listen, we're happy your back. You can't overdo it. Let us take care of Carpe Diem. We'll get the last photoshoots done, then you can approve the final pictures." Addison said with a shrug of her shoulders.

"Deal." She couldn't argue with these two. If it weren't for them, she'd be in a world of trouble right now.

The girls worked like a well-oiled machine. They each knew what tasks were their responsibility and executed them with precision. For the first time, she felt Carpe Diem was flourishing. Photoshoots, customers browsing the racks, and selfies were posted to social media by the dozens.

Bella focused on helping customers. That's the part of the business she liked the most; assisting people in finding the perfect outfit. She always delivered an exceptional customer experience and knew they'd be back. The day was exhausting. Even with three people there, she hadn't worked that hard in a long time.

Tiffany pulled Bella to the side. "I want to show you the website and social media pages."

"You two are remarkable." The scope of work Tiffany completed in such a short time inspired her.

Addison said, "Tiff, show her the pictures."

Tiffany's face lit up with delight, and when Bella saw the shots, it was clear why. "They look professional." Bella's eyes darted between the screen and Tiffany. "This is unbelievable."

Tiffany blushed and tilted her head toward the ground. Addison shoved her hip into the slender frame of Tiffany, catching her off guard. "I know, my best friend's pretty amazing, isn't she?"

"She is, and so are you. I'll find a way to make this up to both of you."

The girls were ready to go, and who could blame them after the intense day of work they put in. Tiffany said, "We're gonna head out if you don't need anything else."

"No, please, have a great night," said Bella.

She locked the door behind them and flipped the sign to closed. The sweet rhythmic sound of Snowball choked her up. She wanted Snowball to have a good life. She wanted her to be safe and well cared for.

Bella released a sigh of exhaustion. She wasn't sure how much longer she'd have the pleasure of owning this little gem or experience the joy of being Snowball's mom. For the first time in her life, she had something to lose, and she wasn't ready to leave. She needed to sit there, soaking up the smell of lavender, and just be.

Nona always said she'd frequently get lost in her writing. She'd start early in the morning and sometimes create well into the night without taking a break. She loved the time she spent in her stories, like Bella loved the time she spent at Carpe Diem.

In all the years she'd spent working with her parents in their real estate firm, she'd never felt this way. This place was everything she dreamed it would be and more. She loved the vibrant colors, textures, and people she met. Maybe helping someone find the perfect pair of earrings or dress wasn't going to change the world, but perhaps it would help one person feel more confident or even bring a smile to their face.

If being home for a few days taught her anything, her negative thought patterns weren't helping. She'd taken a close look at herself and realized she needed to make some changes. She proclaimed that she would no longer use denial as a coping technique from this day forward. She would stand up for herself and stop letting people like her mother, Andrew, and Mr. Douglas take advantage of her. Last but not least, if somehow a miracle fell into her lap, allowing her dream to live on, she was going to educate herself in all areas of business so that she could make better decisions in the future.

Snowball went from a peaceful sleep to barking like a lunatic at the front door within a matter of seconds. She could see someone peeking in but couldn't tell who it was. She crept closer and closer until she could see Jack knocking.

The all black T-shirt with bold white letters gave it away. He was getting good at pop-in visits. Bella welcomed them, especially when they resulted in her making out like a teenager on the beach.

"Jack, what a surprise?" Biting the bottom of her lip, her eyes rose to meet his gaze.

"I saw someone inside and wanted to make sure the store was secure."

"You're right. We've been closed for like an hour." She opened the door allowing the space for him to step in. She loved that he wanted to be protective over her. "I know it's silly, but I was feeling nostalgic and wanted to sit here."

"If it's alright, I'd like to join you."

"Sure." She needed to get home soon and should have said no, but who was she kidding? His broad chest and sexy smile rendered her powerless. She couldn't say no. "Do you realize this is the fourth time this week I'm seeing you, and I've never asked for your phone number? Amber told me it's a rookie mistake."

His cheeks rose, hinting at a smile. "Are you calling me a rookie?"

"I'm calling myself a rookie too." She escorted him to the back of the store. They took a seat on a bench made of driftwood with barely enough room for two. She enjoyed the close proximity, and the fragrance of smoked brisket permeating from his shirt didn't hurt either.

Jack confessed, "You're not gonna believe this, but I've never been on a legit date before the gondola."

"Never? How's that possible?" Bella didn't have much experience in the relationship department, but she had been on several dates. She never met the one or experienced love at first sight, but how she felt for Jack made her wonder if this was what she had been waiting for.

"I met Chelsea in high school. Her parents wouldn't let us see each other. In retrospect, I don't blame them. We were trying to grow up too fast, but we've been together ever since. Until now."

This felt like a confession. Judging by the look on his face, Jack needed to get something off his chest, but she had no idea why he thought it was necessary.

"You two have been together for a long time. You never know, maybe things will work out." She wished she could swallow the words immediately after they left her mouth.

"That ship's sailed. Now I need to gather the pieces of my life and try to find a way to co-exist."

"I'm sure it's been difficult." Bella wanted to be Jack's friend, a non-biased party, but that wasn't even possible when she wanted him all to herself.

"Difficult is an understatement." He leaned forward in his seat with his jaw clenched.

She needed to get him out of the darkest corners of his mind. She attempted to lighten the mood. "Where are you from?"

"Raleigh, North Carolina."

"I've never been there. What's it like?"

"Beautiful." He shook his head. "Horrible." Looking at the ground, he finished, "I guess it depends on your experience. My life began when I enlisted in the Navy." Bringing his gaze back to hers, he said, "When I left Raleigh, I never looked back."

"Chelsea moved here with you?" Bella asked.

"She did. After I enlisted, she lived on base. Sometimes I was gone for weeks, but often it was months at a time. She never complained about any of it. She spent her time alone. Twenty years away from her family and friends. I know it had to be hard." Tears glazed his eyes, but he didn't allow them to escape.

She rested her hand on top of his. She wanted him to know he wasn't alone. His presence made her problems disappear, but she needed to stay focused on helping him through this painful situation. He needed to talk, and she wanted to learn as much as he was willing to reveal.

"She was pregnant, I thought I was going to be a father, but while I was gone, she lost the baby. It happened not once but twice. I should have been there for her. Maybe I could have helped prevent it. Maybe if she were under less stress, it would have been better. But like everything else, she had to deal with that alone too. She hates me, and I don't blame her."

"Truth be told, I'm surprised that you weren't already married. You two have been together for a lifetime." She was stepping on thin ice. Jack didn't owe her an explanation, but she wanted one. Chelsea moved across the country for him. She waited over twenty years for him and attempted to carry his child twice. If she wasn't worth marrying, then who would be?

"We were supposed to get married a long time ago." Jack leaned back against the wall. "Right after we moved here. I was away on my second leave, and when I got home, we were going to fly back to North Carolina and have a small wedding. I made it a few days early, hoping to surprise her. Instead, she surprised me. She had been cheating." Jack looked straight ahead instead of making eye contact. "She said she was lonely and that he didn't mean anything. She said she still loved me, so I forgave her, but no matter how hard I tried, I couldn't forget."

Bella thought they were having a conversation, but this was more. He needed to let her know his story. He felt guilty. Guilty for the way things went with Chelsea, guilty for leaving her, perhaps even guilty for his time with Bella. It's no wonder he said things were complicated with Chelsea.

"After spending enough time apart, it's like you don't know each other anymore. Things become a habit. You come home on leave because that's where you're supposed to be, even if you're not sure it's where you want to be. I couldn't forgive Chelsea's affair, but I understood it. I was lonely too."

Bella had never been close to someone in the military, but she had a customer not long ago who had a husband in the Navy. She said when he came home, the whole dynamic of the house would shift. And although she loved him, it felt like she was sleeping with a stranger. They'd live that way for a couple of months before he'd leave again, and the whole cycle would repeat itself.

"With retirement came clarity, and I proposed again because I owed it to her. We were going to do better this time, but that didn't last long. The straw that broke the camel's back was when I told her I didn't want to go to North Carolina. I needed to stay in California and take over the restaurant for Eddie. Sometimes in life you have to do what's right for you even if no one else understands it. I knew it would piss her off, but I couldn't go back. North Carolina isn't home to me. It only reminds me of a life I was desperate to escape."

Bella understood exactly how Jack felt. She hated the idea of returning to Ohio.

"I get why she was pissed. I moved forward with the purchase without her consent, but this is my home, and I'm not leaving." He leaned forward in his seat and narrowed his focus. "While I worked my ass off, she enjoyed the life of a stay-at-home wife. She traveled back and forth to North Carolina while working odd jobs here and there. The money we had saved was earned from my efforts, not hers, and now she wants half of everything."

"Is she legally entitled to it?"

"We're working through that now with Eric, but the short answer is I'm not entirely sure. I do owe her something, but she's not being reasonable."

Complicated was a great word to describe their situation. Bella finally understood what turned Chelsea into the Dragon Lady and sympathized with her instead of hating her for it. Chelsea waited all those years, and all she wanted was to go back home. She felt bad for Chelsea, but she understood how Jack felt too. While away, he probably wondered if Chelsea was being faithful. Chelsea had to know going back to North Carolina was difficult for him. Then there was the restaurant … anyone who talked to Jack more than ten minutes would see how much he loved that place.

"If you think I'm an asshole, you're right, but you deserve to know the truth about me … about us. This wasn't her fault. It was mine."

Bella pushed her shoulders back into the wall while releasing a sigh. "You've been with her since you were a kid. A person goes through many changes from the time they're sixteen to forty. Try to cut yourself some slack."

"I wish it were that easy."

"What about your parents. Are they back in Raleigh?"

"We'll tackle them another night. I've kept you here too late. How are you getting home?"

"I'm only a fifteen-minute walk from here." It felt nice to be close to him, to feel the warmth from his body radiating toward hers. His eyes were deep and expressive, giving her the tiniest glimpse of his soul. Jack had been more upfront than she'd ever expected, but it was clear things were more complicated than she thought.

"I can't let you walk home alone this time of night. I'll walk with you."

She smiled. It was sweet that he wanted to walk her home. She'd been on her own for most of her life and she never had someone who wanted to watch over her. "Sure, I mean if you don't mind."

They stood for the first time in an hour. Bella followed the gentle sounds of Snowball snoring to the middle of her favorite rack of clothes. She decided to carry her weary friend instead of making her walk.

They didn't say much on the way back to her place. She thought about her parents and how their marriage mirrored a business agreement. They worked all the time and didn't even sleep in the same room. They rarely kissed or said, I love you. She wondered if it was always that way or if, like Jack and Chelsea, they grew apart. Were her parents happy living like that, or did they long for more?

She peeked up at Jack. "I do have a couple of questions if it's okay?"

Her apartment was close by, but the night air carried a chill. She was grateful to have Snowball in her arms. She radiated just enough heat to keep Bella comfortable. The strand hosted more cars than usual, drowning out any evidence of the nearby ocean.

"Sure, but I've been talking all night. I'd love to hear something about you, then I'll answer anything you want to know."

"I guess that's only fair." Bella wasn't comfortable talking about her feelings or the past, but Jack had been so forthcoming. "What would you like to know?"

"You said you're convinced that your parents hate you. Why would you say that?"

"Geeze, you have no problem jumping right in there." She let out an uneasy chuckle while contemplating how to answer the question. "They had expectations for my life, but they weren't what I wanted for myself. I guess we're the same in that respect. My dream brought me to California, and your dream kept you here. We both had to let down the people we loved to make it possible."

"I'm sure they don't hate you." Jack put his arm around her while walking side by side. "I can't see how anyone could hate you."

His touch made her knees feel weak, but she tried her best to remain steady. "Maybe, but when they find out I lost the money, they will." Jack made her feel good. She didn't want him to leave, not now, not ever.

"Why don't you want to go back to North Carolina?"

"My parents were addicted to drugs and couldn't take care of themselves, let alone a child. I grew up in the foster system. My life consisted of being moved from one place to another until I left. I haven't spoken to my parents in over twenty years, and I don't have any other family. North Carolina isn't home to me."

Jack appeared so strong, despite living a difficult life. Positive he needed love as much as she did, Bella craved him more. She wanted to hold him in her arms and assure him that everything would be okay.

"I get it. Even though our lives were very different, I can relate in a small way. I couldn't wait to get out of Ohio."

"Why did you leave?"

"My parents were workaholics. They involved me in the family business at a very young age. Their dreams were different than mine and after my Nona died, leaving seemed like the only option." She couldn't imagine what life must have been like for Jack, young and alone. At least she'd had Nona. "How did you end up with Jack's?"

"I had a mentor named Eddie when I was in the service. I met him at the VFW. He took me under his wing and helped me transition out of the military by working at Eddie's and teaching me the ropes. I know it sounds stupid but believe it or not, it's hard to return to civilian life." Jack pushed his fingers through his hair.

"He gave me a job and helped me cope with all my shit. After about a year, he told me he was ready to retire for good this time. He wanted to pass the business to someone who would keep traditions alive. I wasn't the only vet Eddie helped, there were hundreds, but he said there was something special about me. He taught us about life and gave us the skills we needed to thrive in this world.

"This tradition goes back over fifty years of ownership. When Eddie offered me the business, I couldn't refuse. I invested every dollar we had into taking over the restaurant. Don't get me wrong, he gave me a screaming deal, but only on my word one day I'd do the same for someone else in my position. Chelsea made the same promise I did. Eddie died last year, and Chelsea wanted me to sell to the highest bidder and move back to North Carolina. I can't leave, and I won't break my word to Eddie. Jack's does a lot for homeless veterans, retired military, and the community in general."

"That's amazing. Eddie sold you the business for less than it's worth?" She never heard a more heartwarming story in all the years she sold real estate. Eddie and Jack were giving everything to support a cause they believed in.

"Way under, but the mission was important to him like it is to me. The restaurant has been renamed and sold this way several times over the last fifty years, and I have every intention of doing the same."

"Can I ask you one more question?" She may have been overstepping her boundaries, but he seemed to welcome her curiosity by giving her the all-clear to move forward with her question. "Do you still love Chelsea?"

The edges of his lips shifted, and he let out a soft laugh like he was flooded with memories of the good times. "I do. I think I always will."

"Do you want to try and work things out with her?" He was quiet for a second, making her wonder if she should have asked the question. Did she even want to know the answer?

"No, we don't want the same things. I want her to sell me her portion of the business and move back to North Carolina, but she is asking for the market value of her half, and I don't know how to come up with the cash. Our friend Eric is trying to help us broker a deal."

Now she understood how Eric knew Chelsea. "On a side note, I met your accountant."

"Dwayne?"

"Yes." It felt weird when people called him Dwayne.

"He's helping me with something."

"You're going to love him. He knows his stuff."

"He lives right over there by the lavender archway." Bella pointed in the direction of B-12's apartment.

"I had no idea."

"Thank you for walking me home," said Bella. "Do you want to come in?" Time stood still while she waited for him to answer. Bella didn't put herself out there very often, and she desperately wanted Jack to come up. She needed to feel him close to her, to put her lips against his and make his pain go away.

"I do," he said as he gazed into her eyes. "But I think it's best if I head back."

She knew he was making the right choice. She needed time to think about everything he told her, and Snowball would be up bright and early. She needed to have a clear mind when she met with Dwayne in the morning.

"It was nice talking to you."

He leaned in and kissed her, causing a rush of goosebumps to trickle over her entire body. "Good night, Bella."

## CHAPTER SIXTEEN

"Good morning, Dwayne." A bright-eyed Bella let Snowball off the leash to play with Rex. "Isn't it a beautiful day?"

"Sure is," said Dwayne. "I spoke to Eric. He's sharp. I think he'll be a big help for you."

"He's a godsend, and you are too. I can't thank you enough." Although things were still in turmoil, she had a lot to be thankful for. If she would eventually be forced out of paradise, she wanted to enjoy every second she had left.

"I told Eric I can help you out until you're back on your feet at no charge."

Bella couldn't believe that Dwayne would be willing to do something so generous for her. It's not like his employer would be paying him, this was his business, and he would be investing his time for nothing in return. "No, I couldn't."

"Too late, I agreed yesterday to be a witness. I told Eric I'd help you get your books in order and get back on track. What Carl Douglas did gives a bad name to everyone in my profession, and I won't stand for it." Dwayne went on, "Besides, once you're back on your feet, I'll have a client for life."

"You're right about that." She couldn't believe Eric had arranged this for her. She wasn't sure why everyone was willing to help her, but she knew she wouldn't be able to do it without them. At this point, she'd be fortunate if she could sustain her life. "Do you think I'll be left with anything?"

"It's hard to say. Sometimes the money's gone. Other times they find it stashed in hidden accounts." He cleared his throat. "For you, I hope they find it."

Dwayne was younger than Bella, but he projected confidence and wisdom far beyond his years. She felt like he had her best interests at heart.

"I hope so too. Even if the money is gone, I will not stop until I find a way to make this work. We've been working our asses off, and everything is headed in the right direction." She gestured at the trees and grass around her. "I like it here in Coronado, and I'm not ready to leave."

"I like your passion." His words gave her reassurance.

---

Bella learned to enjoy morning meditations on the beach but didn't mind sacrificing them to walk to Carpe Diem with Snowball. She never had a dog growing up and never imagined she could love an animal but Snowball changed everything. She never barked at other dogs, never pulled on the leash, and best of all, never stopped during a walk to take a number two. She was a lady.

Lizzy and Amber stood outside the store.

"Hey guys."

At first, she was excited to see her best friend with her mother, until she realized their presence together had to mean they'd found Snowball's family. Her steps slowed as the smile fell from her face.

"Hey Bella."

Amber was always upbeat and overflowing with energy, so her somber tone was enough for Bella to confirm her fear was justified. "What's going on?"

Lizzy jumped in, "I know this is hard. I won't beat around the bush. Snowball's mom came to the shelter last night looking for her. Her name is Molly."

"Molly," Bella repeated, thinking Snowball was more fitting. "Are you sure it's her?"

"Yes, she had several pictures, and she lives near the location you found her. The woman suffered a mild stroke and has been in a rehab facility until now."

"I'm sorry." Amber frowned.

She knew giving back Snowball was the only option, but she didn't want to. Her life wasn't in a great place right now, and she needed her. Bella wanted to be mad at Snowball's family for carelessly losing her, but more than losing her, she was angry they were taking her away.

She would do what she had to, even if it went against everything she wanted. Forcing the tears back, she said, "Can I meet her?"

"Sure, I asked her to meet us here this morning." Lizzy passed Bella an unsolicited tissue from her purse. "We can try and find you a new puppy if you'd like."

She didn't want any puppy. She wanted Snowball. "No, I'll be okay."

Minutes later, the door chimed, and two women entered. One had snow-white hair and a sweet smile. She took each step with caution; it was apparent she'd been going through a difficult time. Her frail voice called out, "Molly."

Bella secretly hoped Snowball wouldn't respond, but she did. She ran in circles jumping up and down.

Bella walked over to greet them. "Hi, my name's Bella. I've been taking care of Snowball. I mean Molly."

"I can't thank you enough. I love her with my whole heart and was afraid I'd never see her again." She said, "My name's Linda, and this is my daughter Sabrina."

Sabrina extended her hand to greet Bella. "Pleased to meet you. My mom is so grateful you found Molly. We want to reward you for returning her."

"That's not necessary." No longer able to suppress her emotions, several tears escaped. Amber came over and handed Bella a tissue. "I'd love to give you my number. Maybe I could see her again." She handed the older woman a paper with her contact information on it.

"I'd love that," said Linda. "I live alone. It can be very isolating. The nurses will stop by while I'm in recovery, but it will only be Molly and me after that."

Sabrina said, "I don't live here, and I'll be leaving in a couple of days, so I'm sure Mom would like the company."

Bella gathered Snowball's things and escorted Linda and Molly to the car.

Bella couldn't hold back; a few tears turned into a river streaming from her eyes. It was time to ugly cry, and she didn't care who witnessed it. "I'm going to miss her so much," she said, attempting to steady her breath.

Linda needed Snowball so she wouldn't be alone. How could Bella fault her for that? She was all too familiar with that feeling, but at least she had Amber and the girls. After her daughter went back to Colorado, Linda would have no one.

"I know how you feel," said Amber as she embraced her friend. "We rescued dogs my entire life. I know how hard it is to get attached to a dog and have it taken away."

Bella wiped her eyes with the already exhausted tissue. "Thank you both." Her eyes were bloodshot and puffy. "I need a minute to be sad right now."

Lizzy said, "I understand, remember we're here if you need anything."

Tiffany and Addison waltzed through the open door, looking carefree and chatting. "What's going on?" asked Addison.

Bella didn't have the strength or the desire to explain what happened. She still felt broken from the pain of losing Snowball.

Thankfully, Amber jumped in to explain, "Snowball's mom came in to pick her up this morning."

Bella blotted her eyes and wiped her nose before placing the crumpled tissue back in her pocket. "I'm going to be alright." She said, "I feel better already."

Bella figured Amber wouldn't believe her, and she'd be right because it wasn't true. She didn't feel better, she felt like going back to her apartment, moping around for a week while crying and eating ice cream, but she had a business to save. Tiffany and Addison were already working harder than she could ever repay them, and she wasn't going to put another ounce of responsibility on them.

"Alright, Hon, I gotta run." Amber gave her another hug. "I have a class in fifteen, but if you need anything at all, please call me."

"Thanks," said Bella before turning her attention to Tiffany and Addison.

"I'm going to be okay. This just caught me by surprise." The girls were quiet. Bella knew it was because they didn't know how to react, but neither did she. "What's on the agenda for today?" She asked, using all her might to force a smile.

"All the shoots are finished. Today we need to choose the final pictures and launch the promotion," Tiffany said while grabbing her laptop from her backpack.

Bella felt terrible she forgot such an important task but forgave herself considering the circumstance. They gathered around the computer and admired Tiffany's photos. Bella took a deep breath attempting to push the pause button on her grief for Snowball and provide the girls the concentration they deserved.

Everything Tiffany touched turned to gold, and Addison was a natural-born leader. This dynamic duo had the ideal combination of beauty and brains.

"These shots are ... gorgeous," said Bella.

"I told her they were on point," Addison said while giving her bestie a wink.

"I can't take all the credit. You two styled them." It was common for Tiffany to deflect attention, but she deserved the kudos.

They went through each contestant's pictures with care, choosing the top three for each. "All contestants signed a release form so that you can use these for social marketing, your website, print ads in-store, or anywhere you want," Addison explained.

"Now that we have selected the pictures, what happens next?"

"Tiffany will upload them on Carpe Diem's page. Then the contestants do the rest. It's their responsibility to promote the images and get likes, shares, and votes on our website. Tiffany will do all the tracking, and we just watch while they promote your business like crazy. After the month is over, Tiffany provides the official tally, and you announce the winner on the fifth of the following month."

Bella needed something to do behind the scenes while the contest ran.

"While we wait, I can reach out to next month's contestants and get them scheduled for their photoshoots. That should give us plenty of time to space them out instead of rushing to get them all done at once."

"That sounds perfect." Addison smiled.

"While you're both here I wanted to let you know between the increased foot traffic in the store, improved profit margins, and the online sales, profits are up thirty percent this month over last."

Tiffany and Addison gave each other a high five. "Does that mean you'll be able to keep the store open?" asked Addison.

Incredibly proud of their accomplishment, Bella didn't want them to feel like what they pulled off could be described as anything short of a miracle. She looked to the ground and said, "I can't be positive yet." Her gaze rose to meet theirs. "But you two should be proud of yourselves. In one month, you managed to do what I couldn't accomplish on my own in the last twelve."

She wasn't blowing smoke; she meant every word. If it weren't for their efforts, she'd be toast. "Thank you, from the bottom of my heart. If there is anything I can do to repay you, please let me know."

"We love you, Bella," Addison said while wrapping her in a warm hug.

"We're happy to help." Tiffany joined in.

Tiffany got straight to work on the contest rollout, Addison started dusting, and Bella made phone calls to book out next month's photoshoots. Staying active kept her from obsessing about Snowball.

A man grasping a large cardboard box came through the door, clutching the edges so hard his fingertips were white. He gave a breathy, "Good morning."

"My favorite delivery fairy," said Bella. "What do you have for us today?"

"Looks like the shipper is Beach Babe."

Merchandise delivery always made her gleeful like a child on Christmas morning. She'd been expecting the new rompers and couldn't wait to tear into the package. Bella rushed over to sign for the delivery.

The young man's hair was plastered to his forehead with sweat. He placed the box on the floor near Bella. "Have a nice day."

Eager to reveal the treasure inside the larger than expected box, she grabbed a pair of scissors and carefully cut the tape along the seams. This box contained way more garments than she expected. At least a few thousand dollars more than she could afford to purchase. She examined each item, admiring the quality and trendiness of the designer. "I should give them a call. I can't afford to pay for a shipment this size."

She grabbed the packing slip and called the 1-800 number on top. Waiting on hold, she listened to nineties pop playing in the background. She hummed along with the familiar tune before Addison captured her attention, directing her toward a gentleman upfront. Mr. Douglas stood near the door fidgeting with a pen. Disregarding the last twenty minutes she'd spent on hold, Bella ended the call, curious what he could possibly want.

Her blood felt like it could boil, but she needed to calm down while Dwayne and Eric investigated her financial documents. Despite her best effort, her voice quivered when she said, "Mr. Douglas, what a surprise. I thought your schedule was booked out for weeks."

He cleared his throat and straightened his tie. "Is there somewhere we can talk in private?"

She needed to remain professional for the good of the investigation. This weasel already stole most of her money. What else could he possibly want? "Of course." Leading him into the stock room, she reminded herself not to beat the shit out of him using the broom within arm's reach.

He got right down to business. "I know things are tight for you right now, but I have some good news. When you reached out to pull your assets out of the market, I had a little something of yours invested with a start-up, and they are booming. You earned a quick ten thousand dollars."

She wanted to be excited, but she already knew her accountant was a crook, and she couldn't trust anything he had to say.

He continued, "In light of your recent success, I wanted to discuss a potential opportunity that could change everything."

She offered him a seat, but he refused. Instead, he paced back and forth across the tiny stock room. "There's another opportunity to buy into the same start-up. You need a sure thing, and this is it. My business has invested, and we're expecting to more than double our investment over the next thirty days. Don't you want to be a part of that?"

Bella listened carefully to every word he said, not because she believed him, she hoped they could use this information in the case against him. Dwayne told her there was no such thing as a sure thing in the world of investments, and for Mr. Douglas to imply any different was negligent. "I'm doing everything I can to keep the doors open as long as possible. I think the best use of this money is to purchase new inventory."

Mr. Douglas's forehead wrinkled, and his gentle gaze narrowed in on her. "That would be irresponsible. Don't you want this business to succeed?"

"Of course I do."

"This is your chance to make things right, but if you drag your feet, it will be too late."

Bella glanced at him with a smile on her face, hate in her heart, and disgust brewing in her stomach. She wanted to scream but knew she needed to keep it together for the greater good.

"Thank you for everything, but I have made my decision. I will like the whole ten thousand to be moved over into my general account, and I will be using it to purchase new inventory." Her whole body felt flush. She knew he would be furious with her decision, but she did it anyway. One more step toward becoming the woman she needed to be.

"This is negligent and irresponsible. You're going to regret making this decision." He slithered his way toward the door without looking back.

She grabbed her phone and called Eric. "You're not going to believe what happened."

"What's up?"

"Mr. Douglas stopped in and asked me for more money to invest."

"What?" Eric sounded surprised.

"Yeah, he said it's a sure thing, and I should get him an answer soon."

She couldn't sit still, and she couldn't leave. She wanted to throw a brick through his window and scream at the top of her lungs outside of Sunshine Tax Pros.

"I'm sorry this happened. I'll let you know what to do, but I want to talk to the partners first," Eric said.

*When life turns to shit, why does it seem to happen all at once?*

Jackie would be arriving in California by broomstick soon, Snowball was gone, and now the snake returned to take one last pass at her rotting carcass.

Bella glanced around the corner from the back storage room. She saw Tiffany hard at work on the computer and Addison helping a customer. She couldn't let them down, they believed in her, and now she needed to believe in herself.

## CHAPTER SEVENTEEN

She hadn't eaten all day, and without his knowledge, Jack had teased her with the smell of smoked hickory BBQ. The alcohol combined with an empty stomach was giving her a warm glow.

While she waited at the bar of Jack's restaurant, she thought about the audacity of her estranged accountant asking her for more money. Even a leech knows when it's sucked something dry. Amber, Eric, and Dwayne were meeting up with her to hear the whole story. They asked her to hang tight, and they'd advise her on the best course of action. She hadn't seen Jack all day, so she arrived early, hoping to catch him during his shift. She waited at the bar with her second glass of white wine, feeling her body release tension while her mind relaxed into warm taffy.

She'd been there for thirty minutes, and there was no sign of Chelsea, which was good because she wouldn't know how to face her. Bella felt guilty for being in love with Jack, craving his attention, and wanting Chelsea to move back to North Carolina. She wondered if Jack had told Chelsea about her. Did Chelsea know that he had been spending time with her, and did she care?

The young girl at the hostess stand was much friendlier and likely a better choice to greet customers. After her last conversation with Jack, Bella sympathized with Chelsea's situation. Chelsea wasn't free from blame, but she was far from the villain. All she wanted was to return home to her friends and family. Twenty years was a long time for her to invest in a life that didn't turn out the way she expected; anyone would be frustrated.

She took another sip from her long stem wineglass, leaving behind a hint of lip gloss. She glanced across the bar, and there he was. She could hardly contain the smile that forced its way to her face as he approached.

"Jack."

"Couldn't stay away?" he asked, lips twitching in an amused smirk.

He wasn't entirely wrong. "I am meeting friends tonight. They should be here any moment."

"You look gorgeous as always." Jack placed his hand on the small of her back. She didn't know if it was Jack or the wine, but a rush of warmth rippled from her shoulders to her toes.

"Thanks. How's your day going?" Grateful he noticed her effort, she wondered what he'd say if he knew she wasn't wearing anything under her dress. The thought brought a devious grin to her face. She wanted to look sexy yet relaxed, and based on his reaction, her dress was worth every penny she spent on it.

"Let's not talk about my day. How's your day?"

She rolled her eyes and let out a long exhale before saying, "Trust me, we shouldn't talk about my day either."

"Let me buy you another drink?"

"Sure," she said before taking the last swig from her glass.

"You'll love this one," he said, pouring her another glass of white wine. "It's one of my favorites."

"Can you join me for a glass?"

"I can't, I never mix business with pleasure, but Chelsea is closing tonight if you're free later."

"Sure, maybe you could walk me home again." Maybe it was the lack of food in her stomach or the speed at which she consumed her last drink, but she added, "Maybe this time you'll come up."

Bella knew Jack's situation, and she didn't care. Perhaps it had been too long; maybe she needed an escape from reality or to feel his body against hers one more time.

Jack chuckled and said, "Don't tempt me with a good time." He placed her glass on a crisp new cocktail napkin.

Bella could hear Amber's voice as soon as she walked through the door. She said to Jack, "I'll find you later." She gave him an awkward wink, making him laugh out loud.

The group walked to the booth where she and Eric had their date. He was holding Amber's hand, and judging by the smiles on their faces, they were on cloud nine.

Dwayne said, "It's nice to see you again."

"Thank you so much for all of your help," Bella said to Dwayne. She slid inside the booth, and Dwayne moved just past the edge maintaining at least a one-foot distance from her.

Dwayne didn't wear a ring, nor did Bella ever see anyone else with him. He was funny, wise in a nerdy hipster kind of way, but his love of the grunge look pushed him over the edge from dorky to adorable. She thought perhaps he'd be a perfect match for Tiffany. They were both thoughtful, intelligent, and weird in an exciting sort of way. She decided she needed to find a way to introduce them when there were fewer pressing matters at hand.

They ordered a family-style meal, giving them four types of meat and four sides. The food tasted delicious as usual, but way more than they could eat. Amber was the only one with the good sense to order a salad and save herself from the inevitable sodium bloat that would follow the feast.

"I've got some good news. Thanks to our friend Dwayne, we have the proof you need to nail your accountant. We need you to bring this to the police." Eric handed her another dreaded manila envelope, except this time, she hoped this one would change her fortune for the better.

Dwayne tilted his head, and the corners of his mouth shifted like he wanted to smile, but he stopped himself. "Glad I could help."

"I read those reports a million times, and none of them made sense to me. What did I miss?" asked Bella.

"Nothing, you didn't miss anything. All the documents were forged, completely made up. None of it was real. Your money never even made it to the stock market. Your accountant shuffled it around like he was playing three-card monte. None of the numbers added up because they didn't need to. He used pieces and parts of reports that consolidated to nothing. All creative writing." It was evident Dwayne was proud of his discovery.

Eric nodded while listening to Dwayne before adding, "After talking with the partners, they suggested you take this information to the police and let them launch an investigation. Typically, this is an extensive process, but the sooner we get started, the better." He grabbed his water glass, and condensation dripped along the side, gathering at the tips of his fingers. "Jack knows the chief. Maybe he could introduce you?"

The thought of going to the police station and filing a report made her uneasy. This entire situation suddenly felt very real. In keeping true to her declaration, she would face this head-on. A much less scary task now because she wasn't alone, and denial was no longer her thing.

Bella found her people, the ones who were there for her through thick and thin. After discussing Mr. Douglas, they laughed way too hard over the next hour. Amber almost choked on her water when Dwayne told a ridiculous dad joke about why the chicken crossed the road. He fit in seamlessly with the group and quickly became one of Bella's favorite people to be around.

She glanced across the table and caught a glimpse of the glowing Amber. Eric was good for her; the way she looked at him gave Bella hope. If Amber could finally find the right guy after dating every eligible bachelor on Coronado Island, then she could too.

For the first time in her life, Bella wanted that. She thought about Jack from when she woke up until she fell asleep. His smile captivated her. He touched her like he might break her if he weren't careful. Most of all, she thought about kissing him on the beach and wanting to live in that moment forever.

Having an open heart to receive love sounded good in theory, but there was a dark side Amber didn't mention. Bella now had this void in her life she desperately wanted to fill. She wanted to love someone and be loved in return. For a short time, Snowball filled that void. Saying goodbye to that little pup was one of the hardest things she ever had to do. She loved

Snowball, and now she was all alone. Bella missed Amber too. There was no time between everything with Mr. Douglas, the doctor-prescribed bed rest, and all the hoopla for the marketing promotion at Carpe Diem. Girl talk, rom-coms, cookies, wine, Reiki, speed dating, it didn't matter what they did so long as they did it together.

Dinner was nice, but Bella didn't hesitate when Amber suggested calling it a night. Jack offered to walk her home, and she couldn't wait.

"Can we give you a ride back to your place?" asked Amber.

"No, I'm going to stay here and talk to Jack about the police chief."

"That sounds like a great idea," said Amber with a wink. " Be sure to let me know how it goes."

Jack met them near the door to say bye to Eric and Dwayne. "Sorry I didn't get a chance to talk with you tonight. I ran around most of the night, and time got away from me."

"No worries, buddy," said Eric as he reached out to shake Jack's hand.

Dwayne said, "I'll see you soon. We need to discuss your quarterly earnings reports."

"I'm sorry. I'll schedule soon, promise." Jack held up a hand.

He turned his attention to Bella after everyone left. "Are you in a rush to get home?"

"No," said Bella. She lied. She was absolutely in a rush to get him home but would follow Jack to the ends of the earth if he asked.

"I have a stop I need to make if you'd like to join me."

"Sure." She didn't ask where because it didn't matter. She waited in the front lobby for him to return.

When he returned, he was carrying several boxes, one stacked on top of the other, barely able to see over the top.

"Can I help you?"

"If you can grab the door, I got this."

After they were seated in his car with the boxes secured in the back, Bella asked, "Where are we going?" She could only assume the boxes contained food because the aroma of BBQ occupied every nook and cranny of the car.

"Somewhere important to me." He focused on the road, not glancing in her direction. They were only in the car a couple of minutes before they pulled up to a small yellow building with brown trim and a sign out front reading Veterans of Foreign Wars. She'd been down Orange Avenue a million times and somehow never realized the simple one-story building existed.

Jack walked around the car and opened her door before removing the boxes from the back seat. If he was trying to make her feel special, it worked. He carried what she could only assume was a catering order for some of his buddies. She tugged the door open, allowing him plenty of room to get inside. Judging by the group's reaction, they were excited to see him. A couple people walked over to take the boxes away. Others shook Jack's hand, making him appear like a local celebrity.

The bar had poor lighting with an old oak countertop, a mismatched group of tables for seating, and hundreds of pictures on the wall. An eclectic group surrounded the bar top ranging from bikers in leather vests to strait-laced business people in professional attire. With a ratio of four men to every woman, she couldn't help but think this place could have been a gold mine for Amber before she reconnected with Eric.

Jack grabbed her hand and led her to a small kitchen area in the back. Someone in a white jacket came from behind the counter and gave Jack a handshake that progressed into a one-armed hug. "Thanks, buddy. The guys look forward to this all week."

"I still can't believe we do this so late." Jack glanced at his watch.

"The Moonlight BBQ keeps people here all night drinking while they wait for the food," said the man in the white chef's jacket. "You go have fun. I'll take care of serving this."

Jack grabbed Bella's hand and led her back to the bar. "Are you okay to hang out for a little while?"

"Yeah, I'd love to." Bella loved seeing Jack in his element. She had never seen him more relaxed than he looked in this very moment. At work, there were responsibilities. Here was where he found his peace. He could be himself among people who understood his struggles like no one else could.

"Do you shoot pool?"

She laughed. "I can, but it doesn't mean I'm any good."

A mix of seventies, eighties, and nineties rock played from a speaker nearby. Jack wore his work clothes, jeans, and a basic black T-shirt with the words "Once you get my meat in your mouth, I guarantee you'll be back for more" on the back. She loved the clever sayings on the back of each shirt. He must have made a fortune from selling merchandise alone.

"I'll rack you break," he said, grabbing the rack.

"Maybe you should break."

"No, Ma'am, I want to see what you're made of."

They were interrupted by an older man with white hair wearing a polo and forest green golf shorts. "This is my friend Henry," Jack said to Bella.

"Hi, Henry, nice to meet you."

Henry appeared to be in his late sixties. He maintained his salt and pepper hair, and his hands were manicured. "Is this guy giving you any trouble?" he asked.

Jack replied, "Henry, you caught me right before I was able to make my move."

"You keep your hands to yourself, Jack. This one's mine," said Henry with a raised brow. His eyes were a grayish blue, and he had a little swagger to his walk.

Jack smiled. "Henry was Eddie's best friend."

He racked the balls and handed her a stick. She went to the head of the table and shot the cue ball into the balls with a short, powerful blast, sending them all over the table in every direction and knocking two in, one striped, one solid.

"Looks like it's lady's choice."

"I'll take solids." Bella couldn't believe how well she did on the break. Tonight, luck was on her side, and she was going to take Jack down. "Would you care to make this game a little more interesting?" she asked, exuding pride and confidence that felt foreign to her.

"Why do I feel like you're hustling me right now?" Jack asked with a smirk.

"Maybe I am, maybe I'm not." Bella shrugged her shoulders. "I guess you'll have to find out for yourself."

Sinking two balls on the break was pure luck. As a child, she spent her time at her nona's house or in libraries. She never even touched a pool stick until her twenty-fourth birthday party. "We could bet for money or something else if you prefer."

He chuckled and looked toward the ground before lifting his eyes back to meet hers with laser focus. "Okay, If I win, you have to go sky diving with me next week."

Dumbfounded, she blinked at him in surprise. Never in a million years did she expect him to say skydiving. Maybe a kiss, something a little kinky like his shirt suggested, or domestic like cooking, cleaning but not skydiving. This guy must be on a death wish. She knew she would lose, but she threw down the gauntlet she couldn't retreat now. She looked him up and down like a snack. "What if I win?"

He laughed out loud. "You're not going to win, but if you do, I'll marry you in Vegas this weekend."

She loved his arrogance; he knew she would lose, and now she couldn't back down. "This bet sounds like you win either way."

"That's the only way to make a bet."

"Alright, let's do it. If I lose, I'll go skydiving with you. If I win, you'll marry me in Las Vegas this weekend. At least when my parents come, I won't need to explain why I'm single." They clinked their beer glasses together, sealing the deal. She went for her next shot—a miss.

"Are you trying to lose?" He knocked in three balls with little effort, followed by a miss.

"I'm beginning to think you don't want to marry me." She failed her next attempt.

"What are you talking about? It's like you're trying to lose."

After a hundred belly laughs and complete annihilation, Jack emerged victorious. She knew he would win all along, but she agreed anyway. Now she would need to jump out of a perfect airplane, and she was terrified. "So, when is this skydiving going to take place?"

Jack enjoyed a couple beers while playing pool, and his normally guarded demeanor was nonexistent. Replaced by an easy-going, fun guy who liked to laugh and have a good time. "No skydiving. I just wanted to have fun with you. Mostly, I wanted to see what you'd say, but you surprised me. What would you have done if I had sunk the eight ball too early? Then we'd be getting married this weekend."

"I knew you would win. For clarification, does this mean I don't have to go skydiving?"

"Not next week, but now you owe me." He grabbed her by the hand and said, "There is someone I'd like you to meet."

Her body reacted each time he touched her or even looked at her, for that matter. This man exercised great restraint. She'd been practically throwing herself at him, and either he was oblivious or flat out not interested. Either way, tonight, she would find out.

"Bella, this is Lucky. He's the president of this Chapter."

"Pleasure to meet you, doll. What are you doing with this troublemaker?" Lucky dressed in jeans with a leather vest that featured patches. He looked to be in his fifties, and he didn't have a single strand of hair on his head. She wondered why they called him lucky but didn't want to pry.

Jack jumped in and said, "Bella helped me bring the food tonight."

"It was delicious as always. Thanks again." He clapped Jack on the shoulder before walking off.

She wasn't sure why Jack felt the need to introduce her to Lucky, and his explanation to Lucky of why she was there only left her with more questions about the status of their relationship. "I had a lot of fun. Thank you for bringing me."

"These guys are my family. I don't know where I'd be without them." His eyes were sincere when he spoke, and she could tell this was more than a local bar. This place was special to him, and so were its people. Now she needed to learn where she fit into his story.

☗

They arrived at her building, and it was the moment of truth. "Are you going to come in?"

"I want to." He sat frozen in place. "I like you, and I want to be around you all the time." He usually kept his cool, but she could tell he was physically anxious. He couldn't stay still and kept fidgeting with his keys. "You're gorgeous, and it's hard to exercise restraint when I'm alone with you."

Bella followed the rules her whole life. That's why this adventure to California was all about letting go and chasing after her dreams. She didn't want to do the responsible thing and exercise restraint. She wanted to give in to her desires and drag Jack upstairs. "I'd like it if you came up and set aside your restraint."

He leaned in and kissed her close enough to her ear to feel his breath trickle down her neck. "This isn't a good idea."

"Jack, get out of the car." Bella's assertion came as a shock to her. It was unlike her to be so forward, but she couldn't control herself.

Jack opened her door, taking her by the hand to help her from her seat. They walked up the stairs, and she fumbled in her purse to find the keys. Her hands shook slightly as she attempted to unlock the door. She didn't want him to see her tremble, so she tried her best to steady herself. Aggressive isn't a word she'd use to describe herself, but today she couldn't deny her primal urge for Jack.

She was getting used to having Snowball greet her every time she entered her apartment but not anymore. She tossed her keys on the table and flicked on the lights under the cabinets to allow Jack to see around but still maintain a mood. He took several steps toward her before pulling her in close. She lifted her hand to run her fingers through his hair, slightly pulling it as he kissed her with an intensity that made her feel like a goddess. He lifted her at the waist and set her on the counter. She wrapped her legs around him to pull him in close, feeling his body against hers.

"You're bad for me," he said with a smirk on his face.

"Maybe, I'm precisely what you need," Bella said as he kissed her along her neck. She groaned in delight while he wrapped his strong arms around her making her feel desired and protected. Jack was a beast, his body exuded power, yet his touch felt like pure compassion.

👓

She grabbed the bottom of his shirt and pulled it over his head. Dropping it to the floor, she ran her fingers down the sculpted side of his body while teasing his lips with gentle kisses. She nibbled on his ear and let out a slow warm breath. "Would you like to come to my room, or do you prefer to stay in the kitchen?"

He replied by helping her from the counter, and for the third time tonight, she held his hand in hers. This time leading him to her room, in moments, she would finally experience what she'd only been able to fantasize about. His hands were huge and rough, making her fingers feel tiny by comparison; evidence this man worked hard for everything he had.

"You look a little over-dressed." In what felt like slow motion, he pulled the tie from the back of her neck. She panicked for a moment, remembering she was nude under her dress. She didn't stop him; instead, she allowed him to pull the string until her dress fell to the floor, fully exposing her.

The heat in the room rose from a cool seventy to what felt like a steamy ninety degrees. He raised a brow. "I like your style."

Jack told her that he'd never been on a date with anyone other than Chelsea. Did that mean he'd only had sex with her too? If he lacked in the experience department, his actions weren't evident. Walking her backward, he gently pushed her onto the bed. He stood before her with a look of ravenous hunger in his eyes, taking a deep breath in through his nose, causing his broad chest to expand while gritting his teeth.

He exhaled in a whoosh. "I need to go."

Caught off guard by the unexpected turn of events, Bella gasped.

"What's wrong?" She grabbed her sheet and pulled it over her body in a feeble attempt to disappear.

"I told you things are complicated with Chelsea. I can't do this in good conscience." Without even looking at her, he grabbed his shirt from the floor. "It's best if we don't see each other for now."

She turned her hands up in confusion. "I don't understand."

But Jack had already closed the door behind him.

She thought they'd had a great time tonight; apparently, Jack didn't feel the same way she did.

Maybe Andrew was right about her. She was alone and unlovable … maybe that was all she would ever be.

## CHAPTER EIGHTEEN

Until today, Bella had never stepped foot into a police station. She gripped the report from Dwayne, wishing she would have talked to Jack about his friend instead of embarrassing herself. The lobby had at least twenty blue plastic chairs lined in rows. An officer sat in a high chair behind an all-white counter labeled Welcome. This place felt anything but welcoming.

She was about to make a colossal accusation that could put a man in prison for a long time, and she wasn't sure she had the courage. Her fingers were freezing, and she shivered before advancing to the counter. She approached the officer and said in a faint voice, "Good morning. I want to report a crime."

"What kind of crime are you referring to?" the officer responded, not appearing to grasp the urgency of the situation.

Positive she would throw up at any second, she forced the words from her mouth, "I believe my accountant is stealing money from me." She placed the report on the counter.

The officer didn't bat an eye, just pointed to a clipboard and pen. "Sign in here, and take a seat. Someone will take a written statement soon."

She signed her name to the list and got comfortable in a nearby chair. The officer didn't seem alarmed by her accusation or look at the report.

While she waited to be called to the back, she grabbed her phone. After last night she needed to talk to Amber.

Bella: I invited Jack back to my place last night

Amber: You did what!

Amber: Is the streak over?

Bella: He took off all my clothes, got me into bed, and said he had to leave ...

Amber: WTF

Bella: I'm so embarrassed. Please don't tell Eric

Bella: I could DIE

Bella: I put myself out there and see what happens

Amber: No

Amber: we're not moving backward

Amber: You are perfect

Amber: Jack's not the right guy but he is out there

Irritated by Amber's reality check, Bella tossed her phone back in her purse. Jack wasn't the right guy. Andrew wasn't the right guy. She had the worst luck with men and would never find a great guy like Eric. She should have known better. Jack didn't feel the same way she did and that wasn't his fault. It was hers. She should have never allowed herself to fall for a man that wasn't in a position to explore a relationship.

"Miss Roberts, we're ready for you."

She shot from her chair and followed the officer to a small conference room in the back. Her heartbeat was erratic, her hands felt clammy, and her whole body was warm all over. She couldn't faint again and needed to calm down right now. Returning to her knowledge of meditation, she took a couple of deep cleansing breaths and found a better mental space.

The officer looked slightly taller than her and didn't have the physique she expected. He had short blondish hair and glasses with rounded frames. He looked unexceptional in every way, but somehow, this average man had enough courage to be a police officer and she applauded his heroic choice.

He pulled out a chair for her and said, "I'm Detective Odeckie. I understand you would like to report a crime?" She wondered if the chair she sat in had been occupied by bad guys in the past, worried their bad juju would leave her tarnished in some way.

"Yes, my accountant is stealing money from me." She pushed the report across the table, placing it directly in front of the detective.

He opened the report and leafed through the pages but didn't appear to be reading any of it. "What makes you think he's stealing money?"

"I have an attorney and an accountant who put this together for me. They said you'll need all of this information for your investigation." She feared the detective wasn't grasping the gravity of the situation. "I'm missing hundreds of thousands of dollars."

"Let's start from the beginning." He asked her a series of questions, starting with her name and address then moving along to the more important details like the name of her accountant. "Can we keep the report you provided?"

"Yes, of course." Bella said, "I can bring you anything you need."

"I'm the detective assigned to your case. I will reach out to you soon, but for now, keep your distance from the accountant," said the officer. "Whatever you do, don't give him any more money."

"What happens next?"

"I'll review the information you provided. I'll issue subpoenas for bank records and possibly seize his accounts if your story checks out. Then once everything is verified, the state will present the case before a grand jury, and if they see fit, they will issue an indictment."

"What is an indictment?"

"That holds him in custody while we create our case against him, but it's possible that he could post bail and be free until his trial." The detective remained calm while explaining the process to Bella. "These things can take a while, so try and relax. Here's my card. Call me if you need anything."

"Will he go to jail for doing this to me?"

"I can't promise that, but if there is foul play, we will do everything in our power to put him in prison for a long time. We're going to do everything we can to make you whole if possible, and sometimes that means striking a deal, but our goal is to ensure that justice prevails."

Bella could tell the officer wanted to wrap up the conversation, but she wanted to take action. "If you need, I can show you to his office, and you can search his stuff."

"I'm afraid we will need to do a thorough investigation before we can search anyone's belongings."

"Okay, but if you need me to identify him in a lineup, I can be here in like an hour."

The officer cracked a smile. "Sounds good, Miss Roberts. I'll let you know if that's necessary."

Bella rose from her seat feeling proud of herself for doing what was necessary, but all in all, the whole event proved to be more anticlimactic than she hoped. She had prepared herself to watch Mr. Douglas be hauled off to the big house, but it was apparent justice would need to wait a little longer.

She texted Eric.

> Bella: Leaving the police station. They said to avoid him, and they'll let me know more information as it's available.
> Eric: Did you see Jack's friend?
> Bella: No I spoke to Detective Odeckie
> Eric: I'm going to call Jack

Bella rolled her eyes with a groan. What if Jack told Eric what happened last night? She was already embarrassed, but if Jack had an in with the police chief, she could use his help.

A ride down the strand on her bike would provide her with the time she needed to relax amid the chaos consuming her life. The overcast sky provided the perfect complement to her defeated attitude.

She needed to make peace with her situation; she couldn't afford another breakdown. The facts were clear, and she needed to accept them and move forward.

While she reflected on her pity party, another bike came to a screeching halt in front of her. Unable to slow her progress, her handlebars shifted to the right, and she toppled off the bike, landing like a ton of bricks on the pavement. She reluctantly accepted the apology of the guy who'd stopped so suddenly, then looked up to see a man sitting on a bench watching her.

It took her a few seconds to regain her bearings when the man from the bench approached.

"Are you okay?" he asked, squatting next to her, curiosity and concern in his expression. He was tall with a lean physique, golden brown hair, and light brown eyes.

It all happened so fast. She took a moment to gather her thoughts before responding. "I suppose," she said, wiping the dirt from her hand and shorts. "Just a little banged up." Wasn't this the icing on the cake? Her wrist was already sore from fainting in the store, and she scraped her leg when she fell. Bella never considered herself a clumsy person, but life was determined to prove her wrong.

"Would you like to sit for a minute?" asked the handsome stranger.

"I can't. I need to get back to work."

"I can walk with you."

His touch was kind, and his tone showed a genuine interest in her wellbeing, but she did need to get back to the store. "I'm okay, maybe a case of bruised ego."

"I'm a doctor, and although you feel good, you took a nasty spill. Let me walk with you and make sure you're up to par."

At least now she understood his angle; he watched her take a dive and now wanted to make sure she was okay. "Sure, I guess that's fine."

"Wonderful," said the doctor. He grabbed a paperback book from the bench and stuffed it into his back pocket.

Reaching out to shake his hand, she introduced herself. "I'm Isabella, but my friends call me Bella, Thanks for helping me."

"Not a problem."

"My store is a few minutes this way," she said, pointing to the right.

He lifted her bike from the ground and supported it using only his right hand.

Peeking out from behind a wayward curl that had fallen in front of her face, she asked, "So do you sit around the strand waiting to help people who wreck their bikes?"

"I don't know if you know this, but I'm sworn to the Hippocratic Oath. It means as a doctor I have to help someone in need, especially someone as pretty as you," he said, grinning ear to ear. She couldn't tell if this was a line he used regularly or if it was something he cooked up on the fly. Either way, it was cute.

"Let me rephrase, do you sit around waiting to Hippocraticly save damsels in distress?"

"Not usually. Today I wanted to enjoy this beautiful day while reading a book. You fell right in front of me, almost like you did it on purpose." He laughed out loud at his joke. It was adorable.

"I didn't realize they gave doctors the day off."

"I worked in the emergency room last night."

Feeling rude, she realized she didn't know the doctor's name. The last thing she needed was another situation like B-12. "What's your name?"

"I'm Elijah Jennings, but you can call me Eli." He seemed too young to be a doctor.

"What are you reading, Eli?" She intentionally called him by his preferred name.

"It's nothing," he said, touching his pocket with his available hand.

"No, I'm a reader. I'd love to know." She raised her brow with curiosity. "You can tell a lot about a person from what they read."

His cheeks turned slightly pink, and she could tell this doctor was embarrassed by his selection.

"What if I told you, it's a romance novel?"

"Well, I'd say you are a hopeless romantic and maybe a little," she hesitated while choosing her words, "lonely." They were getting close to Carpe Diem, and she didn't want her time with Eli to end yet. She walked as slow as she could without causing reason for concern.

"In my defense, I don't always read romance. Usually, I read biographies or suspense, but last night I lost a patient, and this book was on her bedside."

He pulled the book from his pocket and waved it in front of Bella. "The family didn't want it, so I took it with me to read this morning. In the very last hours of her life, this book is what she chose to read."

"That is the saddest yet most beautiful thing I've ever heard." She was having fun with Doctor Eli, but now she felt terrible for harassing him. Sure, she had problems, but this put everything in perspective. She was only down, not out. She still could overcome her situation.

"I may have lost her, but I managed to save you." And with that, her heart melted.

His life wasn't perfect, yet he could still deliver a perfectly timed dad joke. Eli would be the ideal guy to meet her parents. Attractive, charming, confident, and a doctor. What parent wouldn't love a man like this for their daughter?

"Looks like you're right ahead." Eli lifted his chin toward her shop.

She needed to do some damage control and make sure Eli wasn't a throwback from Amber's reject pile. "By chance, have you been to the juice bar next door?"

"No, but perhaps I should start visiting there."

She exhaled a sigh of relief. "Well, this is my stop. Thanks again for walking with me."

"Would you like to go out sometime?"

Eli made an enticing offer. One she didn't want to refuse after last night's rejection. It felt nice to have someone as great as Eli giving her attention.

Without hesitation, she replied, "I'd love to. I'll give you my number." She didn't need another lecture from Amber on rookie mistakes.

"Perfect." Eli had a smile that went on for days. "Give me your phone."

She unlocked her phone and handed it to Eli.

He didn't show her what he was doing, but he handed it back a minute later.

"So, does this mean I'll hear from you soon?"

"Absolutely." He grabbed her hand and placed a single kiss on it before pulling the door open, causing the chimes to sing.

"Have a great day."

She pulled her bike through the door, trying not to lose her cool before he walked away.

"Thank you for everything," she said while looking over her shoulder.

Addie noticed her banged-up body, "Are you okay?"

"Yeah, I'm great. It looks worse than it is." Dr. Hottie told her to take it easy with her wrist and that she'd likely have a few bruises tomorrow. She'd look worse before getting better. She parked her bike in front of the display where it belonged. It had damage, but only on the left side. It still looked great in its usual space.

"Who was the eye candy outside?" asked Tiffany. It didn't surprise Bella that Tiffany naturally gravitated toward Eli and Addison toward Jack. Another sign that Dwayne would be a good match for Tiffany.

"Eli. I met him this morning when I fell off my bike." She wanted to get more excited but did her best to act as casual as possible.

"So, this is how we're meeting men these days?" asked Addie. "You know there are safer ways."

"Did you see him? I'd fall off your bike this afternoon to meet a guy like him." Tiffany sighed.

"Funny." Bella grabbed her wrist, checking the remaining flexibility. "Besides, I've already got dibs. He might have asked me if I wanted to go out sometime."

"What did you say?" asked Tiffany.

"I said yes."

"What about Jack?" asked Addison.

"Jack isn't looking for a commitment." Oddly enough, Bella hadn't thought about Jack in the last hour, and after last night, it seemed to be all she could think about.

"I can think of at least one thing I'd do with Jack that wouldn't require a commitment. If you know what I'm saying," said Addison.

Tiffany giggled, and Bella forced herself to smile. Addison wasn't wrong; she just had no idea Jack had rejected Bella after she'd practically thrown herself at him. Eli, on the other hand, was interested. Who said nice guys had to finish last?

"I appreciate you two opening for me this morning while I filed the charges at the police department, but you need to leave." Bella held her hand in the air in protest to the inevitable dispute. "Don't even try to argue with me. You girls have been working so hard. I want you to get out and enjoy the day."

"Cool, we'll go to the beach and work on our tan," Addison said. "Right before you got here, I told Tiffany she's a pasty shade of white."

"Before we go, I want to give you an update on the contest." Tiffany grabbed a post-it from the counter with some numbers written on it.

"Yes, please." Bella knew things were in full swing because she couldn't stop watching their pages on social. She could see people were liking and commenting, but she wasn't sure if those things translated into any additional revenue.

"The pictures are blowing up on social. We've had over five hundred people go to the website and register to vote for their favorite models."

"Wow!"

"That's not all. Online orders are trickling in, more and more every day. I'll show you how to retrieve them before I leave. This way, you can ship them out."

"You're amazing, Tiffany," Bella said proudly. Not only was she proud of the girls for how hard they were working, but she felt a sense of accomplishment for how much they had changed over the last year from college kids into young women. They were intelligent, kind, professional, and had a killer fashion sense.

A grin overwhelmed Tiffany's face. "I'm pretty happy about it."

After Tiffany showed Bella how to retrieve the online orders, they grabbed their bags and headed for the beach. For the first time that day, Bella was alone, and despite her best efforts to shove the memories of Jack out of her mind, they still came flooding back. Lying in her bed exposed, her heart racing, seeing him stare down at her with lust in his eyes, then a dead stop out of nowhere.

She felt a cocktail of emotions: rejection, shame, fear. Andrew made her feel self-conscious about everything, from her curvy shape to her long fingers. He made her afraid to put herself out there in fear that men would see the same terrible things Andrew did, and Jack proved him correct. She wanted to blame someone, but who could she blame? If space was what Jack wanted, she would give it to him.

Amber threw the door open. "Who was out front with you this morning?"

Bella laughed and shook her head. "That was Eli."

"Who's Eli?" she asked with a raised brow.

"You know I went to the police station this morning, and on my way, I may have fallen off my bike when the jackass in front of me decided to slam on his brakes for no apparent reason."

"Oh my gosh, are you OK?" Amber gave Bella the once over.

"I'm fine. Eli's a doctor, and he walked me here to make sure I was alright."

"He's cute." Determined to give Bella a thorough inspection of her own, Amber grimaced when she examined each of Bella's scrapes.

"I can't believe you were spying on me."

"I wasn't spying. We'll call it being curious …," said Amber.

"He's cute," Bella said with a mischievous smile. "He asked me if I'd like to go out with him sometime."

"Are you going to call him?"

"No," she paused. "He is going to call me."

"That's awesome. Look at you back in the saddle."

"If he calls, I'll see him. If he doesn't, I won't. Either way, I can't worry about it right now."

"You see, one door closes, and another opens," said Amber. Without a doubt, she was referring to last night's shenanigans with Jack then the chance encounter with Eli.

Bella's shoulders slumped. "I don't want to be optimistic right now."

"Why not?" Amber looked on the bright side of everything.

"Well, in case you didn't notice, my life sucks. Maybe you need a recap."

She held up one finger and said, "My accountant robbed me blind, and I'm at risk of losing everything." She extended the next finger and said, "Snowball is gone." She held up the third and said, "I put myself out there with Jack, and now I feel like a complete idiot. Is that enough yet, or do I need to add that Jackie and Roger are going to be here soon?"

❦

"I know it doesn't feel like it right now, but everything is going to be okay. The contest will work, and I'm sorry about Jack, but you need to stay optimistic about love in general. Don't let one bad apple spoil the bunch, even if the apple is hot."

Bella huffed out a sigh. "I need some good news."

"I'm sure it's not the best time to tell you this, but Eric called Jack this morning and asked if he could help get some movement on your case."

"It's okay. He told me he was going to call." The least he could do after the fiasco last night was help her get some attention at the police department.

"I have an idea," Amber said with her usual enthusiasm. "Let's go out tonight. We can get some margaritas and tacos."

"I don't know." Bella wanted a quiet night of crying into her pillow while the gentle light from the television soothed her to sleep.

"Come on, you love tacos. My treat." Amber's offer was becoming more difficult to refuse by the minute. Maybe a night out was what she needed to take her mind off everything. "I'm leaving before you can say no." She headed for the door. "I'll pick you up at nine-fifteen sharp."

She had to admit that some great things were happening, too, despite all the negativity. The store had performed better than ever before, thanks to the marketing efforts of her little geniuses. Sales were up thirty percent in-store, and with the addition of the online store, they had their best month to date. She had a new accountant, a great attorney, and who could forget about the smart, funny, attractive Doctor Eli. Sometimes when things are difficult, it can be challenging to see the blessings directly in front of you. A night out with her best friend was exactly what she needed.

The store had a steady flow of customers to keep her busy for the remainder of the day. She flipped the sign to closed and finished packaging the last couple of online orders. A quick double-tap on the window pulled her attention to the front. It was Jack. She was finally in a better place, and now he was back to disrupt her peace. What did he want? Remembering her declaration about facing things head-on, she threw her shoulders back, propped up her chin, and walked with confidence. She took a deep breath and turned the deadbolt.

Jack pushed the door open and pleaded, "I feel terrible, Bella."

She could see this was difficult for him, but why should she be sympathetic to his needs? Anger made her hands tremble. She shifted her eyes to look at him and chuckled because crying wasn't an option.

"Terrible," said Bella. "You weren't the one left humiliated."

"Trust me, I wanted to stay last night, but until I figure things out with Chelsea, I can't."

"I thought you two were over."

"We are, but it's not that simple, we live together, we have the business together … I won't feel comfortable being romantic with you until she moves out."

"Great, now I can add homewrecker to my list of attributes." She threw her hands in the air in frustration.

Jack let out a humorless laugh. "You're not a homewrecker. I'm trying to work some things out, and I need some time. Trust me, I know you deserve better than this, and I want to be the man you deserve."

"So, what am I supposed to do? Sit here and wait for God only knows how long?" That's exactly what she wanted to do, and if he asked her, she would have waited as long as he wanted her to.

"Of course not. I don't expect you to wait for me to figure my shit out." He dragged his hand through his messy brown hair.

She could tell he was distraught, but it wasn't good enough. She didn't want to wait. She wanted to jump into the mess with him. She never felt this way about a man before, captivated, almost spellbound.

His words hit her like a typhoon. She blamed him for everything, but he'd warned her repeatedly this wasn't a good time. She didn't listen. He told her twice going to her apartment wasn't a good idea, yet she insisted. She ignored him despite his best efforts to warn her. This wasn't Jack's fault. It was hers. The realization hit her like a boulder in her stomach, "I guess I'm sorry too. I shouldn't have pushed the issue."

"Please don't apologize to me." His eyes narrowed and focused on her, "The timing sucks. I have put Chelsea through a lot of shit in the last twenty years. I'm not going to do that to you too."

A tap on the door caused the tempo to shift abruptly.

"It's Amber." Bella shook her head. "We're going out tonight."

She grabbed her purse. "I'm sorry, but I gotta go." She wasn't ready for this to end, but she needed to listen to Jack and honor his wishes even if what he asked for felt impossible.

Closing the door behind them, Jack said quietly, "have a good night."

He nodded at Amber before heading back toward the restaurant.

"I wasn't expecting him to be here," Amber said with judgment dripping from her tone.

"He wanted to apologize."

"What did you say?"

If she talked about it, she'd collapse in tears. She waved off the question. "You know what ... I don't want to talk about it. I'm ready for margaritas and tacos."

◦◦◦

Amber loved to drive with the top down and tonight's sky featured stars as far as the eye could see. The moon sat full and low, its beauty only disrupted by the glow of neon lights that illuminated a hot pink and green sign flashing the words Tacos, Tacos, Tacos when they arrived.

The signature pale pink building greeted hungry patrons through a royal blue door. This place had the best street tacos on the island. Guests danced in the aisles to a live mariachi band, drinking tequila shots, devouring tortilla chips with queso and salsa.

"Do you want to sit at the bar?" Amber asked, barely loud enough for Bella to hear.

"Sure," said Bella. The bar was the heart of the restaurant. They had several flair bartenders wearing bright red vests with a single button on the side that read, "Ask me about our specials."

Amber winked. "If this place doesn't make you happy, nothing will."

They ordered two skinny margaritas with salt on the rim and Baja fish tacos. Maybe it was the tequila, but she felt good. Bella swayed in her seat to a catchy tune while Amber caught her up on how things were progressing with Eric.

"Do you miss dating?" asked Bella.

"Ah … no. Girl, you are getting a taste of what dating is like. Would you miss it?"

"Good point," Bella said with a smack of her glossy lips. "I'm still so embarrassed by what happened with Jack."

"After waiting more than a month, I'd be ripping my clothes off for just about anyone." Amber gave the room a once over while Bella got cozy with the queso.

"You're not going to believe this. Is that Eli, the guy from this morning?"

Squinting against the lights, Bella shifted around, trying not to bring attention to herself. "That's him."

"This is your chance. Go over there and say hi." Amber encouraged her with a shove from her seat.

Two margaritas in, she needed no convincing from Amber to make her move. She wasn't drunk but feeling good for sure. She squeezed between Eli and the bar catching him by surprise, "So, they let doctors have nights off, too?"

"Hey Bella, I'm on call tonight. What brings you here?" asked Eli, a huge smile on his attractive face.

"My friend and I came here for dinner." She pointed across the bar to Amber, who in turn started waving like a maniac. "Would you like to join us for a drink?"

"I'm here picking up to go, but I guess it couldn't hurt."

He left money on the counter and grabbed his already packaged food. The crowd in the bar forced him to stay close to Bella. She wasn't sure if it was the tequila, but Doctor Eli cleaned up well. He looked nothing like Jack. His body appeared lean and athletic. He wore an untucked navy-blue button-up with distressed jeans, a smart watch, and brown leather oxford shoes. Eli had the most compassionate eyes she'd ever seen. It was no wonder he helped people for a living.

"This is my friend, Amber," Bella said.

"Nice to meet you. I'm Eli." He reached out to shake her hand.

"Nice to meet you, Eli. Are you going to join us for dinner?"

"Sure, as long as you have room for one more. I don't want to crash girl's night."

"Please," said Amber. "Oddly enough, my friend and I were talking about you. Do you come here often?"

"I live around the corner and come here all the time for the street tacos."

"I live right around the corner, too," said Bella. She wondered how she'd missed Eli until now.

His phone vibrated, and he excused himself. Amber didn't waste a second before saying, "He's cute," with a mischievous grin.

"He is, but I don't know."

"You don't know what?" Amber nudged her. "Jack said now is not a good time. You can't throw a fish like Eli back in the ocean for no reason."

Bella wasn't sure what to say. Amber made a valid point; Jack said he wasn't ready to move things forward. Eli shouldn't be a second choice.

"Sorry for running out. It was the hospital."

"Would you like a drink?" asked Bella. She had fun flirting with him, and she couldn't resist the urge to spend some time with him.

"When I'm on call, I can't drink, but please don't let me stop you," Eli said.

Amber glanced at her phone and said, "Sorry, I hate to be the bearer of bad news, but Eric misses me." She tossed sixty bucks on the bar. "This should cover the check."

Amber wouldn't win any academy awards for that performance, but Bella appreciated the effort.

Eli smiled. "I can hang out for a bit if you're not in a hurry."

She couldn't help but shake her head at the irony of life, knowing without a shadow of a doubt that everything happened for a reason and this chance encounter with Eli was no mistake.

"Sounds good to me." Bella wondered if being alone with Eli might be a bad idea. If her encounter with Jack taught her anything, it was that lonely, depressed, and desperate for attention weren't her best features.

"Believe it or not, I don't get out much," said Bella after taking another swig from her frosty beverage. "I spend most of my time at Carpe Diem, and when I'm not there, I'm home."

"Are you seeing anyone?" asked Eli.

She wasn't sure how to answer the question. *Does getting naked with Jack last night and being rejected qualify as seeing someone?* She hadn't dated in so long she wasn't sure of the etiquette. "No, not really."

"A vague answer if I've ever heard one."

She admired that Eli not only asked the question he also immediately recognized the red flag when she threw it in the air.

"Sorry, I'm not sure how to answer the question. There is someone, but he made it clear he's not looking for a relationship." The rejection from Jack flooded her memory, but before she could allow it to consume her, Eli threw her a life raft.

"I should say I'm sorry, but if he can't recognize a good thing when it's in front of him, then his loss is my gain." Eli locked his eyes on hers.

"You're making me blush," said Bella. His perfectly timed compliment made her feel less broken.

"Then, it's working."

## CHAPTER NINETEEN

Amber burst through the door at nine-fifteen on the dot. "How did it go with Eli last night?" She handed Bella a yellowish juice.

Bella laughed. "You mean last night when you bailed on me?"

"Sure, when I bailed on you."

"Eli's great." Bella smiled at the recollection. "We closed the bar, he held my hand while walking me back to my apartment, and he kissed me on the cheek before he left. He is very sweet."

"I've never heard you describe Jack as sweet."

Bella didn't need to ask to know Amber represented Team Eli. She made a valid point; Jack wasn't sweet. He was sexy, rugged, mysterious, captivating, nothing like Eli. They were opposite ends of the spectrum but intriguing in their own way. Bella said, "Why are we talking about Jack? He ditched me like you did."

"Ouch, I guess I deserve that," Amber said. "On another note, I saw my first ad for Carpe Diem on social. It looked great."

"Those two are marketing dynamos."

Amber announced, "Tiffany's going to revamp my website sometime this week. Technology changes so quickly I can't keep up with it."

"Before I forget, Jackie and Roger will be here tomorrow." Bella shook her head in disbelief. "I don't even know why they're coming—to torture me, I think."

Amber said, "Oh, No. What are you going to do about," using air quotes, "your boyfriend?"

Bella looked everywhere except at Amber. "I might have asked Eli last night."

"You did not tell him about Jackie and Roger on your first date."

"I did." Bella covered her face with her hands. "I know, it's the damn tequila."

"I can't believe he said yes. See, things are already brighter." Amber looked at her watch. "I gotta fly. I have class in ten minutes," she said, running out the door.

Sunshine poured through the front window. Eli provided the confidence boost she needed, and revenue improved every day. Maybe life wasn't perfect, but Amber had a point; things were definitely brighter. Her phone buzzed with a new message; it was Eli. He stored his number in her phone under The Hot Doctor Who Saved Your Life. She laughed out loud.

> Eli: I had a great time last night. Maybe we can get together tonight. You can brief me on your parents before they get here tomorrow.

Eli had no idea what he signed up for when he agreed to meet her parents. She couldn't throw him to the wolves without first explaining the dynamic better.

> Bella: Do they let doctors off two nights in a row?
> Eli: I'm off tonight, not on call. In case you want more tequila

She wanted to see Eli, but she was a little concerned about being alone with him. No matter how many times she tried to convince herself Jack didn't reject her, the thought still plagued her mind. Righteous anger grew in her belly; she wouldn't let Jack stand in the way of happily ever after with Eli.

> Bella: Would you like to come over for dinner? I'm great at ordering out

Eli: Let me know when and I'll be there
Bella: Let's say seven
Eli: See you then

She helped several customers in the morning, and a few people stopped in to take pictures. They said they saw the store online and wanted to see it in person. She created a display with the new Beach Babe shipment and even managed to justify keeping a romper for herself. She would wear it tonight on her date with Eli. *Note to self, wear panties this time.* There was nothing like going from fully dressed to naked with the pull of a single string.

Between customers, she managed to input the receivables and payables into her accounting software. Dwayne had already taught her so much, and she felt a sense of pride. Mr. Douglas may have tricked her into trusting him but going forward, she would depend on herself to make better decisions.

Dwayne met with his customers once a quarter, but because of her situation, he thought it would be more appropriate to meet twice a month until she was on track. During those meetings, he would review her financials and teach her about payroll, her software program, reading reports, and best of all, investments.

With the opening of the door, the warm air rushed in. She would recognize this woman anywhere. She said, "Hi, I'm—."

Bella interrupted her, "Sabrina."

Her mouth curved into a smile. "Yes, you remembered."

Wondering what could have possibly brought Sabrina back, her heart sank. "Is Snowball okay?" Bella asked.

"Yes, Yes, Molly is fine."

Relieved, she replied, "How can I help you?"

Sabrina sighed. "My mom's not doing well. I need to take her back to Colorado and put her in an assisted care facility. She can't bring Molly there, and I can't keep her at my apartment, so we wanted to see if there's any chance you'd like to have her back."

The words felt like a dream. She never considered getting Snowball back could be an option. "Where is she? I'd love to have her back. I've missed her so much."

"She's in the car now with my mom. Would you like to come and see her?"

"Yes." Bella couldn't contain her excitement. She propped the door open and moved to the car parked out front as fast as her feet could take her. Snowball had her tiny snout out the window, and her tail wagged a hundred miles per hour.

Linda rolled her window down and said, "I thought you were the perfect person to keep Molly for me."

"Thank you so much. I can't even believe this is happening." She'd been missing Snowball, and now she was back. It felt like a dream, and she almost wanted to pinch herself. Except, if she woke and Snowball was gone again, her heart couldn't bear it.

"I didn't want to go to Colorado, but I don't have a choice." Her voice sounded frail, and her body looked weak. Linda's situation had deteriorated since Bella had seen her last. "I know Molly belongs here with you."

"Are you leaving her now, or is she coming back later?" asked Bella.

With a tear in her eye, Linda said, "It might be best if I leave her here now."

Bella knew how hard it was to say goodbye to Snowball, and her heart went out for Linda.

"I'm going to take such good care of her for you." Bella reached through the open window to hug the older woman. She didn't want to let her go; she could feel Linda's pain through their embrace. "I'll never forget this."

Linda unlocked the door allowing Bella to reach Snowball. The little dog jumped from the back seat directly into Bella's arms. Linda used a crumpled tissue to wipe the tears from her eyes.

"I'll send you pictures every day," said Bella.

"I'd like that. I have a box of her things in the trunk with a list of the foods she eats and supplements I give her."

Sabrina said, "I'm so grateful you can keep her. I don't think Mom would have come if we had to take her to the shelter."

The idea of Snowball being locked in a cage at the shelter was terrifying to her.

"If there is nothing else, we are going to go. I don't want to prolong Mom's agony," said Sabrina.

Snowball was back; this alone was enough reason to celebrate. There were three customers in the store, and Bella didn't even care. Her girl came back home, and she felt more optimistic than ever. She carried the box to the supply room, and Snowball followed close behind her.

Bella took a couple of minutes to get her furry friend situated before rushing over to assist the remaining customers. She told everyone who crossed her path about the surprise reunion with her dog.

---

Tiffany came in at five, giving Bella plenty of time to order dinner, clean her apartment, and get primped for her date with Eli. She took one last glance over the tiny one-bedroom apartment to ensure everything looked perfect. The windows were wide open, allowing fresh air and sunlight to fill the room, giving the illusion of being larger than real life. As a self-proclaimed fashionista, Bella had to admit she had no talent as an interior decorator. When it came to home décor, she believed less was more, especially when it came to dust collectors. Spend money on the pieces that count and avoid the bric-a-brac.

She caught a glimpse of Snowball in the corner attacking a stuffed rabbit that made crinkle noises each time she chomped on its ear. Remembering her promise to Linda, she decided to snap a few pictures of the pup and send them over. Days ago, Bella wept, sure she'd never see Snowball again. Linda provided her with the gift of love, and for that, she would be forever grateful.

Maybe her life came crashing to the ground like a house of cards, but now she was rebuilding on a firmer foundation. Instead of meditation, she listened to podcasts on her walk to work every morning. They taught her about business management, marketing, and finance. She felt more competent every day. Thanks to the girls, Carpe Diem was producing record-breaking numbers. Dwayne helped her put a financial system in place that was easy for her to manage. Tonight, she had a date with a handsome, caring man. Things were looking up.

She put on a touch of lip gloss and checked her teeth in the mirror. The jumpsuit from Beach Babe fit her like a dream. She left the top two buttons open and double knotted the waist tie to accentuate her curvy figure without being too provocative.

Knock, knock, knock.

Assuming Eli arrived early, she pulled the door open without hesitation. When she saw Jack standing there, her mouth lost the ability to speak.

"Hey Bella, you look amazing." His tone sounded casual, like he hadn't just ripped her heart out days ago.

Bella wanted to say something, but nothing came out.

"Do you mind if I come in?"

Her body disobeyed her mind by taking two steps backward, allowing him the space he needed to come in.

"Why are you here? You told me you needed space, yet you keep coming back." She needed to keep it together and be strong.

"I'm here because I can't stay away."

She wanted to believe him, but her heart couldn't afford another blow.

She looked to the ground, afraid to make eye contact. After pulling together her confidence, she said, "I think you should leave until you get things figured out."

"I'm so sorry. I haven't felt this way in a long time, and I freaked out."

"Now is not the time to have this conversation," said Bella.

He looked haggard. "Why?"

"I have someone coming over, and you need to leave." She wasn't sure if she wanted him to leave or if she wanted to make him jealous, but either way, she gained a slight sense of satisfaction in saying, "You're the one who said you didn't want to see me." He hurt her, and she wanted him to understand the pain she felt.

Jack didn't react how Bella expected him to. He didn't seem mad or jealous; instead, his head hung low, and his posture deflated. Without saying another word, he turned around and left.

Bella went from excited for her date with Eli to frustrated and confused. Jack controlled her emotions like a puppet master, taking her ever higher before dropping her from the fiftieth floor without a parachute. What did he expect her to do?

Eli arrived minutes later with a vibrant bouquet of wildflowers in hand. Joy filled her when she opened the door, and his eyes lit up like the brightest star in the sky. "It's nice to see you."

"Thanks for having me. It smells great in here."

"Don't get too excited. It's takeout, and I think it's a little cold."

"I'm sure it's fine," Eli said in a reassuring tone. "You look stunning."

"You're too kind," Bella said with a polite smile. "Please make yourself comfortable."

Snowball darted over to greet Eli, running in circles around his feet before giving his pant legs a thorough sniff. "Who is this little one?" asked Eli

"This is my fur baby Snowball."

He knelt to the floor, saying, "Hey buddy, I'm Eli," while giving her belly rubs.

People should be more like dogs; they didn't overthink situations. They lived in the moment and reacted based on their intuition. Snowball wasn't comparing Eli to Jack or trying to decide who she wanted a belly rub from for the rest of her life. She gave herself permission to know them both, which is precisely what Bella needed to do.

"I'm starving," Eli confessed.

"Let's eat." She opened each white paper container, lids still moist with condensation from the once piping hot entrees. "The food feels cold. We'll need to warm it up." Bella ate more Chinese takeout than should be allowed by law. When she called the restaurant, they knew her by name and even included free egg rolls every time she ordered.

---

A smile graced his face, and he said with compassion, "It's okay, I know how to use a microwave." He set the timer for forty-five seconds and pushed Start.

"I can't help but feel that perhaps you are a little distracted?"

What would make him think she was distracted? She paused to think about how to answer the question. "Me, no. I'm great. If anything, maybe, a little nervous about having you over."

He laughed. "I'm the last person you should worry about. I'm easy to please, I clean up after myself, and I'm looking forward to getting to know you."

His answer reflected his actions, sweet like him. Eli was a catch, and she wouldn't let Jack ruin this for her.

"You're too kind." She heated her food and invited Eli out to the patio table. "My apartment isn't much, but this view is incredible."

California's summer nights could be chilly, but the layers of pinks and purples in the sky were breathtaking. The table on the patio provided just enough space for the two of them to have an intimate meal together. "Can I offer you a glass of wine? I have white already chilled."

"That would be great."

She escaped to the kitchen and gave herself a pep talk. *I know it's been a while but let's try not to end the evening naked and rejected.* She buffed the tiny watermarks from the glasses before filling them about one-third of the way.

She walked outside and handed him a drink. "I hope you like it. It's one of my favorites."

"I'm sure it's great." Eli's confidence was infectious. He raised his glass and said, "Here's to making beautiful memories with you."

She needed to know if there was more to Eli than he revealed. "Tell me about yourself."

"What would you like to know?" asked Eli while sitting back in his chair.

"We could start with where you grew up?"

"I was born and raised in California. I went to school at Stanford and currently work at Mercy General on Vine and 4th. Where are you from?"

"I'm from Ohio."

"They say Ohio is a great place to be from." He gave a snarky smile like he was attempting to make a joke. "No, really, I've heard some great things about Ohio. It's the home of the Rock N Roll Hall of fame, Honey Hut Ice Cream, and the Dog Pound. Why would you leave everything you know for California?"

On her drive from Ohio to California, she contemplated this question a million times. Her life in Ohio was safe. She could have lived that life and maybe even found some happiness in it. She could have been successful in her career, had a nice car, a fancy place to live, married someone like Andrew, and had 2.5 kids. She wasn't willing to settle for a life that her parents forced her into. She wanted to chase her fairytale and experience her own happily ever after. She opted to respond with a softer truth. "Who could resist the sunshine and ocean air?"

"Tell me this, Isabella. Why are you looking for a date to take for dinner with your parents? You're a beautiful and intelligent woman. Isn't that enough in today's society?"

Her smile turned upside down, and her entire posture deflated. "I might have told them I had a boyfriend."

"I see, and that's why I'm here. I fit the bill to meet the parents?" He chose his words carefully, and his assumption was correct. She knew her parents would respond well to him. Eli was an all-American heartthrob. Handsome, well-educated, with a good family. Jackie and Roger would have hated everything about Jack.

"Although I admit, I think my parents would love you. That's not the only reason. I happen to think you're pretty okay too."

"Oh yeah ... I'm pretty, okay?" Eli was adorable, and the dimples in his cheeks made her melt every time he smiled. "Why do you feel like your parents would be disappointed if you weren't in a relationship?"

She could have told her parents the truth, but she already felt like a failure and wanted to feel like this one thing was perfect. Either way, it was a lie. "I know it's stupid, but my life is kind of chaos right now, and I didn't want to answer to Jackie and Roger about my love life too."

"You call your parents Jackie and Roger?"

She pursed her lips. "Let's not talk about them. I'd like to get to know you better."

"What if they ask us questions at dinner?"

She didn't anticipate this conversation would be difficult, but a lifetime of harsh criticism and feeling like she wasn't good enough overwhelmed her. She needed to change the subject, "Don't worry, they're much too self-absorbed to care about the details." It may have sounded harsh, but it was true. They didn't care about the details of Bella's life. They barely cared about each other.

Their glasses were almost empty, and so were their plates. She gathered the dishes and brought them back into the kitchen. She applied some lip gloss and studied her hair in the bathroom mirror. Should she let it down or leave it up? If she wore it up, she could show off her neck and shoulders but down, she felt sexy and confident. She opted to let it down and spray a few pumps of her signature scent in case Eli got close enough to enjoy it. She rushed back to the kitchen, grabbed the wine bottle, and returned to the patio.

"Would you like some more?"

"Sure."

She filled his glass halfway this time.

He smiled his thanks. "I appreciate you having me over tonight. Even if it's only to beguile your parents."

"I bet all the ladies are beating on your door. Nurses, patients, all the doctor groupies."

"Just because they chase me doesn't mean I'm eager to date any woman. I'm rather selective."

"Oh yeah, what makes me so special?"

"You're different." After some wine, he appeared relaxed and a bit flirtatious.

Eli intrigued Bella, but she couldn't get Jack off her mind despite her best efforts.

They drank the entire bottle of wine while talking about childhood and their careers. He even shared some previous relationship nightmares. Bella had little to offer in the relationship department but enjoyed hearing Eli's stories. Her dating resume was best described as pathetic; she worked too much to enjoy her life; another reason she held contempt for Jackie and Roger. She never had a chance to get out, be reckless, carefree, adventurous, or promiscuous.

Her parents expected her to be driven and professional. While her peers were at parties and on vacations, she created listings and prepared contracts. Handing out glossy fliers with her parent's pictures displayed was the cherry on the top of any childhood. Their tagline read: If you dream it, you can buy it, and we can help.

It was obnoxious, just like them.

"Now that we've had the chance to get to know each other a little better, have I scared you off yet? Or do I need to keep trying?" asked Bella.

"Quite the contrary, I find you rather magnetic, Miss Roberts."

A smile graced her face the entire evening, thanks to Eli. He behaved like a perfect gentleman, but she wanted to move things forward. "Would you like to come in and sit on the couch? I could make you some coffee or open another bottle of wine?"

"No coffee, I'll be up all night, but we can go inside."

Bella's sofa frequently knocked her out after a long day, but not tonight. Wide awake and curious if Eli had a more assertive side, she thought the couch would be the perfect place for a romantic encounter. The bedroom said, "let's get it on," and the front room said, "let's make out," or at least that was what she hoped it did.

All she wanted was a fun, rejection-free make-out session with a total hottie to revitalize her confidence. He sank into the sofa. She kicked off her sandals and joined him, sitting close enough that she wouldn't be on top of him, but he could easily invade her space if he wanted to. "Would you like me to open another bottle of wine?"

"Not unless you want it. I still need to drive home, and I see what happens firsthand when people drink and drive."

"Sorry, I guess I didn't think about it."

"Don't be sorry." His tone was deep and intoxicating. He touched her face, leaning in slightly, allowing her to meet him halfway. He kissed her with a closed mouth and full soft lips. Then moved slightly back to allow the moment time to breathe like fine wine. He returned, this time more intentionally, loving and romantic, as Nona talked about in her books.

When she kissed Jack, it was different. It felt more passionate and primal. Damn it, she thought, why was she thinking about Jack right now? Determined to resist her thoughts, she kissed Eli again. His hands slid up her body, and he pulled her in closer.

"You smell intoxicating."

His breathing became shallower, and a look of hunger stole the sweetness from his eyes.

This was the man she'd been looking for, but once he arrived, she was left with the aching feeling that he still wasn't Jack. As much as she tried to fight it, she wanted Jack to be the one ripping her clothes off and making love to her.

She touched Eli's hand. "You seem like a great guy, but I want to take things slow." His body radiated contagious energy, giving her no question that she enjoyed being around him, but she wasn't sure if that was enough. He gazed into her eyes, almost like he knew what her thoughts were. She needed more time before she could make any decisions about him.

"I guess that's my cue to go." He stood up from the couch, revealing evidence that he felt the moment, making her feel horrible yet pleasantly validated.

She took his hand and walked him to the door.

"Thank you for coming over." She leaned in and gently kissed his soft lips one last time. Making out with Eli proved to be fun, but at the end of the day, he wasn't Jack and never would be.

## CHAPTER TWENTY

A tiny whimper that quickly escalated to high-pitched yelps woke Bella from a sound sleep. Nature waited for no man or woman to get in their beauty rest. She rolled out of bed, grabbed her slippers, and headed for the door. "Come here baby. Mom's going to take you outside." Snowball shook her tail and licked her face as she carried her down the stairs to the grassy field. "You're such a good girl. I'm so happy your home." Happy would be an understatement. She didn't even care that she ran outside in her slippers, pajamas, and unbrushed hair. Bella set Snowball in the grass and wiped the haze from her eyes.

The voice of her new accountant caught her by surprise. "Bella, Good morning."

"Morning, Dwayne. How are you?" Suddenly concerned about her lack of hygiene, she took a single step backward.

"I'm doing great, and you should be too." After Bella failed to respond, he continued, "You must not have heard what happened."

"No, I'm not sure what you're talking about."

"Carl Douglas. The police took him into custody last night."

"Mr. Douglas, are you sure it's my Mr. Douglas?" Things were so anticlimactic at the station she never thought he could already be in custody.

"Yes. Your Mr. Douglas," he said, almost laughing at her.

"No. I had no idea. How did you hear that?"

"I saw it on the eleven o'clock news last night. I called Eric this morning, and he confirmed. I don't know all the details, but from my understanding,

Jack reached out to his buddy at the station, and he kicked things into hyperdrive."

Just the mention of his name made her heart stop. She should have known this had something to do with Jack, but his mixed signals made her crazy. *One second, he can't get involved because his life is too complicated, and the next, he can't stay away.*

Dwayne continued disrupting her thought pattern, "The detective interviewed the secretary who sang like a canary. He stole money from most of his customers and wanted to make one last push with a Ponzi scheme before leaving for the Maldives. They were able to use the information to get a search warrant and found tons of incriminating documents."

Bella gulped. "Do you know if they found my money?"

"I'm sorry, I don't. Maybe Eric can give you more information."

"Thank you so much. I appreciate you letting me know." Of course, this would all happen the same morning Jackie and Roger were scheduled to arrive. "I hate to run, but I need to call Eric."

"Let me know if I can help with anything."

"You've already done so much."

Snowball had only been outside five minutes, but her playtime with Rex had to be postponed until another day. Bella knelt in the grass. "Come on, Snowball," she said, trying to coax her away." Come on, girl, let's get you a treat." Snowball couldn't resist the offer of Bella's secret weapon.

"I'll talk to you soon," she said to Dwayne as she scurried away, eager to find answers.

Showered, dressed, and at Carpe Diem in less than an hour, Bella rushed Snowball into the store providing food and water before popping into Ex-Squeeze Me. Both Amber and Eric stood leaning against the counter.

"Bella, I'm so glad to see you," said Amber. The aroma of sweet earthy fresh-pressed juice filled the space. Ex-Squeeze Me had tons of natural light, green plants, and relaxing spa music playing overhead but none of that was enough to compensate for Bella's anxiety.

"I spoke to Dwayne at the dog park this morning. I got here as fast as I could."

Eric said, "I'm guessing he told you about Carl?"

"Yes, he said his secretary told the police everything."

"Yes, they searched his office and took him into custody. They set bail, but this guy was stealing money from everyone. I can't see how anyone would be willing to post it for him, including his wife."

"Did they recover any of the money?"

"As of right now, none of the money has been recovered. I hate to tell you this, but it may be gone forever."

Slumping into a chair, Bella took a minute to process what Eric shared with her. She felt happy Mr. Douglas was arrested, but that didn't change her situation. She dropped her shoulders and looked to the ceiling in an attempt to compose herself. "So, what happens next?"

"If he tells them where the money is, they'll confiscate it and give it back to his clients. In turn, he will receive a reduced sentence. If he rides it out, he might only spend ten years in prison get released with good behavior. Then the money is his free and clear. We need to wait and see if he thinks spending some time in the big house is worth the payday." Eric looked at Bella. "I know it's not the news you were hoping for, but trust me, this is a great start."

Amber walked over and placed her hand on Bella's shoulder. "I'm here for you."

"We're here for you," added Eric, reaching out to place his hand on Bella's other shoulder.

Amber provided Bella a sympathetic smile before saying, "We're not going to let anything happen to you.

"Everything is going to work out. Have faith," said Eric.

Although she was disappointed, she did feel an odd sense of peace. Mr. Douglas deserved to be in prison for what he did to her.

"Thank you both. Amber, you have been the best friend anyone could wish for." She hugged Amber before turning her attention to Eric. "If it weren't for you, Mr. Douglas would be off in the Maldives sipping on Mai Tais instead of rotting in prison where he belongs." She sat back in the chair. "You have no idea how grateful I am to both of you." She knew she'd be alright; she needed to rest and process the new information. "I need to make it past this visit with my parents, and I'll come up with a plan."

"When are they getting in?" asked Amber.

"They should be here within the next hour. I need to get next door and make sure everything is ready to go."

"Here, take my keys, so you don't need to rideshare." Amber passed her car keys and a green juice labeled Fearless Greens over the counter. "We're here for you, babe. Let us know if you need anything."

She wanted to give the keys back but knew she'd regret it later if she did. "Thank you," she said, heading out the door, then halted in her tracks.

Not only were her parents early, but they were pressed up against the window, leaving smudge marks everywhere. She'd hoped for a bit of time before their arrival to get the store opened and make herself presentable. Bella said, "Jackie," capturing their attention.

"Isabella darling, we were wondering where you were."

"Sorry, I was next door. How was your flight?"

"We flew coach." Jackie reapplied her pale mauve lipstick using her reflection. "I'll never do that again. A child whined the entire time."

How could the people supposed to love you more than anyone be so cold? It had been over a year since she had seen her parents, and no big hugs, no joyful reunion, only Bella with two people who felt like strangers.

She unlocked the front door, determined to make the most of this experience. "Please come in."

After all, she hadn't asked them to come. They offered. Perhaps they were attempting to be better humans.

Snowball darted out from under the rack, and Jackie screeched like she'd seen an axe murder. Frazzled, she sputtered, "What's that vermin?"

Bella rather enjoyed watching her mother squirm. "This is Snowball. She's my dog." Bella lifted Snowball from the ground and gave her a snuggle.

"A dog? We don't keep pets," Jackie said while clutching her purse like a potential weapon.

"I know you don't, but I do." Bella snuggled her face into Snowball's fluffy soft fur.

Roger chimed in, "The store looks great. Did you decorate yourself?"

"I had the help of some great girls who work here, but we did it together."

"Well, it's clean but a little hippie-dippy for my taste." Jackie only left the house dressed in professional attire, assuming that every person she met was a prospective client.

"The girls will be here soon. Then I'll bring you to your hotel so you can settle in. We can grab something small to eat before dinner if you'd like."

"Sounds good to me," said Roger while aimlessly wandering around the store.

Jackie made herself comfortable on a stool in the corner, surveying every inch of the store. Why couldn't her mother be more nurturing, even a little supportive?

"So, this is what you did with all your grandmother's money?"

The words cut Bella's ears like razor blades. Carpe Diem meant everything to her. Not only did she invest her inheritance there, but she also invested her time, laughs, and tears. Her upbringing demanded respect, so she took a beat and bit her tongue before responding. "Yes, I know Nona would be proud."

"I don't know about that," Jackie muttered.

The door chimed, and Bella knew Tiffany and Addison had once again saved her. "Good morning, girls. These are my parents, Jackie and Roger."

"Nice to meet you. Bella has told us so much about you," said Tiffany.

"If you two are ready, we can go." Bella was desperate to get her toxic parents away from the girls.

Jackie snuck up next to Bella and said in a whisper, "You're going to leave these two kids here? Alone?"

"Ah, yeah. The girls have worked here since the store opened."

"Hmm," grunted Jackie.

"My friend let me borrow her car to drive you two around today. The car's parked out front."

"Where's your car, Isabella?"

Of all the things Bella anticipated worrying about for her parents' visit, her car didn't even make the list. "I got rid of it."

"Why on earth would you get rid of the Lexus? You're not in some sort of trouble, are you? I know drugs are a problem in California," Jackie said in her most obnoxious judgmental tone.

Bella rolled her eyes. "Drugs are a problem everywhere, not only in California." Amid everything else in her life right now, how did she expect herself to also deal with her parents? "I'm not in trouble. I don't ever drive, so the car was a waste of money. I can't believe you said that."

"Well, I'm sorry," her mother snapped. "What am I supposed to think, we arrived, and you're nowhere to be found. You show up looking disheveled, and now I find out you sold your car. This store caters to hippies. Maybe you're smoking marijuana."

Roger jumped in, "The hotel would be great. I need to freshen up and make a couple of calls." It infuriated Bella her dad didn't stand up for her and allowed her mother to belittle her repeatedly.

She pulled the keys out of her pocket. "Please call me if you need anything," Bella said to Tiffany and Addison before making the dramatic exit.

She wanted to cry the entire car ride. This was nothing like a reunion with family should be. In times like this, she missed her nona even more. Bella called Nona when her mother made her mental. Nona always knew exactly what to say to calm her down. She searched her memory, grasping for words of wisdom, and came up with nothing. She took a deep breath, regaining control of her mental state. "What time would you like to have dinner tonight?"

"We have it on the calendar for 5 p.m. Did you not get the invite?" asked Jackie.

"I didn't see anything."

"There's a reservation at the hotel. The reviews were five stars with a top-notch menu." Jackie carried on like she hadn't just insulted her only child and accused her of being on drugs.

The ride only took ten minutes, but it felt like an eternity. She hopped out and grabbed her mother's luggage from the trunk. Roger grabbed his bag and gave her a quick wink that only infuriated her more. Her phone vibrated, indicating a new message had arrived.

> Eric: Can you meet up with Dwayne and me at my office in like 15 minutes?
> Bella: Sure of course

Eric's text came as a welcome surprise, providing an excuse to escape. She hadn't seen her parents in over a year, and the sight of them flooded her with memories of being a child.

"I have to make a quick stop. Would it be okay if I met you at the restaurant tonight?" Grateful for the excuse to leave, she wondered what could be so urgent.

"Sure, but please make sure to do something with yourself. We're going to a nice restaurant, and I don't want you dressed like that." Jackie waved her hand up and down in front of Bella.

Just what Bella needed, one last kick to the gut before she left. "I'll make sure I'm ready when I arrive."

"We'll see you later," said Roger. He'd either grown accustomed to Jackie's insults or become desensitized to them. Either way, he infuriated her almost as much as her mother did.

---

Eric and Dwayne were waiting in the conference room when Bella arrived. The table housed hundreds of papers, and they appeared engrossed in their conversation. Her heart sputtered when she realized this meeting had something to do with her money. She lifted her chin and grasped the doorknob, prepared to face her future no matter the outcome. "Hey, sorry you had to wait for me."

"No, we're glad you could make it on such short notice," said Eric. His demeanor was more serious than the carefree guy she had come to know. "Please take a seat, Bella."

"Hello, Dwayne," Bella said while attempting to get comfortable in the chair.

Dwayne greeted her with a nod and smiled.

"I have some good news to share with you."

He said he had good news, but his facial expression said something different.

"But there is also some bad news. I don't like to sugarcoat things, so I'm going to come right out with it." Dwayne sat back in his chair and tapped his pen three times on the table. "We've confirmed they can't find your money."

Bella heard what he said but opted not to respond immediately; instead, she sat in silence.

"As Dwayne mentioned, they questioned Carl Douglas's secretary, and she sang like a canary. She told the police everything they needed to secure a search warrant for Sunshine Tax Pros and his residence. The evidence is overwhelming, but they can't figure out what he did with the money, the secretary has no idea, and he's not talking. It looks like good ole Mr. Douglas will ride this one out. We'll go to trial, but with the evidence against him, he's going away for a long time since he's unwilling to cooperate."

Bella closed her eyes and cracked them open again, hoping this was all a dream. "So, what does this mean?" Tears flooded her eyes. "Do I have to close the store now?"

Dwayne jumped in. "No, that's the good news, Bella. It appears you took the rest of the money away from that crook in the nick of time. Not only is Carpe Diem supporting itself, but it's also generating a profit. My guess is you'll have no problem maintaining your status. It will take some time to build a nest egg, but we'll work on it together."

Eric sat next to her and took her hand. "Listen, Bella, I know this isn't an ideal situation, but Carl Douglas is going away for a long time, and you are going to be able to stay. Dwayne, Amber, and I are all here for you, and we're going to do everything we can to help see you through this."

She couldn't ask for a better outcome to the worse possible scenario, and as she promised herself, she needed to accept the result. A tear rolled down her cheek as she sat stoically in her chair.

Eric handed her a tissue. "I'm sorry, Bella."

She gave them both a watery smile. "Please don't be sorry. If it weren't for you all, I'd have nothing."

## CHAPTER TWENTY-ONE

Bella opted for a slinky black dress with her only pair of Jimmy Choos, hoping her mother and Eli would approve for very different reasons. He deserved something for suffering through dinner with her parents. The dress highlighted every curve on her body. His appreciative words and look of sheer delight made her feel good. "Thank you. Not many people would be willing to do this for someone they just met."

"Everything's going to be fine. Parents love me."

"I hope so, Eli. I'm not even sure if my parents love me."

Eli snickered; he must have assumed Bella was joking, but soon he'd learn this was no laughing matter. "I must admit I've never met the parents this quickly before."

"I know it's lame that I lied to my parents about having a boyfriend, but sometimes you get tired of feeling like a disappointment."

Eli opened the car door for Bella. "You look radiant."

His hand felt cold to the touch, but Nona always said cold hands, warm heart. Bella could tell that was the case with Eli. He closed the door and jumped in the driver's seat.

"How are you still single? You're smart funny. You have the kind of beauty that makes a guy like me stop dead in his tracks."

Eli deserved a woman who would appreciate him and make him feel like the best man on earth. "We'll see if you're still interested after tonight." She explained the situation to him; he understood and agreed to do it anyway. She couldn't help but feel guilty.

Bella sank into her seat and tried to relax before they arrived at the restaurant. His car was extravagant; the leather seats were supple, luxurious, and contoured to her body like being cradled.

His subtle scent wafted through the car leaving behind hints of wood and spice. Dressed in charcoal grey dress pants, a white button-up shirt, accented with a black belt and shoes, Eli flashed her a sliver Rolex on his wrist. He explained it was a gift from his grandfather when he graduated from medical school. He didn't usually wear it, but he thought it would help impress her parents. Eli wasn't the type to brag, but she could tell his boasting came from a place of pride in his grandfather rather than in the watch itself.

They pulled into the parking lot. Bella's stomach churned, making her nauseous. She grabbed a mint from her purse, hoping it would settle the fire raging inside. Eli walked around to grab her door. "Are you ready?"

"Can I say no?"

"If not going was an option, I don't think we'd be here right now."

Her black stiletto kissed the ground, and she realized why people were willing to break the bank for Jimmy Choos. As they approached the eight-foot-tall plate glass doors, two gentlemen opened them like the gateway to nirvana. A young girl who appeared to be about eighteen years old greeted them wearing a basic black dress. Her hair wound tightly in a bun, she wore red lipstick and had the whitest teeth Bella had ever seen. "Welcome to Le Chateau. Do you have a reservation?"

"Yes, I'm meeting Jackie Roberts." Bella knew the reservation would be in her mother's name instead of her father's, and she was right.

"Right this way," said the hostess.

The walk to the table felt like an eternity giving Bella more than ample time to drive herself nuts with anticipation of how the night would play out. Would her parents even like Eli? Who was she kidding? He was perfect. She studied her environment on the way to the table; several crystal chandeliers, antique-looking furnishings with navy-blue, white, and gold accents everywhere. When her father noticed their arrival, he stood to greet them. "Roger, this is Eli," said Bella

"It's a pleasure to meet you, sir," said Eli.

"Nice to meet you too," said Roger. "This is my wife, Jackie."

Jackie extended her hand to greet Eli.

"Isabella dear," said Jackie. "You're looking more acceptable this evening."

Jackie wore a tweed navy-blue dress accented by a short necklace featuring a single diamond pendant. Bella would never wear the same clothes as her mother did, but she still appreciated her sense of style. Why couldn't Jackie extend her the same courtesy?

"Thank you," Bella replied to Jackie's attempt at a compliment. "I'm glad you are finally meeting Eli."

"I hate to say this, but Bella hasn't told us much of anything about you." Jackie appeared eager to get her digs in.

What mother would say something so callous to her daughter's boyfriend?

Eli absorbed the first blow with ease. "That's okay. I can tell you anything you'd like to know." Bella watched him from across the table. Under the pressure of her mother's scrutiny, he emerged like a diamond.

"Where are you from?" asked Roger.

"I grew up in California, went to school at Stanford, and now practice medicine at Mercy General." He sat tall and confident in his seat without fidgeting or fumbling his words. Maybe he's had experience with fake dating parents before. "Your daughter has been a godsend. No offense Mr. Roberts but I can see where she got her good looks from."

Jackie blushed.

The waiter approached the table to share the daily specials—each item listed at market price, the code for way too expensive. Bella's mind began to race. Were her parents expecting her to treat for this swanky dinner or, even worse, for Eli to pay? She scanned the menu for the lowest cost option. Worst case scenario, her credit cards still worked. She'd be paying off this dinner over the next twelve months at seventeen percent interest. Her mother placed an order for a couple of appetizers and a bottle of white wine.

"We'll have that out shortly for you," the waiter promised before vanishing into the distance.

"Isabella, have you ever eaten here before?" Jackie inquired.

"No, typically I get Chinese from a nearby place, sometimes pizza or tacos but most of the places I go don't have a dress code."

"Bella never did like the finer things," Jackie said, shaking her head in disapproval at her only child.

"I don't know about that," said Eli. "I find Bella has a refined palate and a flair for fashion."

Jackie sniffed. "I guess if you like that hippie look. I find it to be lazy and lackluster."

Bella smiled at Eli, knowing if she had an ally at the table, it was him. The waiter arrived in the nick of time with wine and filled each of their glasses. Relieved to have something other than Eli to lighten the mood, Bella reached for her glass and took a big gulp.

"Dear, while Roger and I were here, I wanted to discuss a business deal with you."

Bella almost choked on her wine. "Me?"

"Yes, of course, you. We've found a magnificent multi-family property, and we wanted to invite you to be an investor. All we would need is one hundred thousand, and you'd receive a handsome return in about six months."

Bella swallowed hard; why did her mother need her money? She didn't have a hundred thousand left, and if she did, she'd use it for Carpe Diem, but she couldn't say that. She reached back for her glass, finishing the rest of the wine in one last swallow.

"Isabella, dear, wine is intended to be enjoyed in smaller doses."

"Yes, mother, I'm sorry. Is it possible we can discuss this tomorrow? Tonight, I'd like you to get to know Eli better, and I'm not sure if an investment in real estate is what I want to do at this time."

"I suppose," said Jackie. Judging by her scowl, she appeared annoyed with Bella's response. "So, is there a future for the two of you?"

Eli didn't even flinch. He proved to be even better with parents than she thought he'd be. "Only if Bella will have me."

"Now, Jackie, let's not rush these kids into something they're not ready for." Finally, her father decided to open his mouth, and it was to save Eli.

"Roger, they're in their thirties, hardly children anymore."

Two appetizers arrived. The waiter announced, "Escargots and duck paté."

"Try some Isabella," said her mother.

"No, thank you."

"Don't worry; it won't bite you." Her father said in a failed attempt to be funny. He could learn something from Eli's flawlessly delivered dad jokes.

"I'll save my appetite for dinner. Thank you," said Bella.

Jackie continued on the topic of the investment. "The multi-family unit is a great opportunity, and I don't want you to miss out, Isabella."

"I'll give it serious consideration, and I'll let you know tomorrow." This was worse than she'd thought it would be. She'd thought her mother's visit was intended to ridicule her life, not borrow money.

"I'm not sure what you have to think about. The money is sitting there. Why not use it to help secure your future?"

Sitting back, she wondered what to say. She could lie, holding her mother off until tomorrow, or she could tell the truth and see what happened. Her entire life, Bella walked on a tightrope with her mother. She was always afraid to disappoint or upset her, yet it was never enough no matter how hard she tried.

"Is that why you came here after all this time? To ask me for money?" Bella was surprised and mortified at the words she used to address her mother, yet she felt a sense of freedom.

"How dare you accuse me of asking you for money. I am offering you the opportunity to invest, but you are too ignorant to understand," said Jackie.

Roger said, "Please, dear. Bella said she would like to think about it. She hasn't made a decision." Her father attempted to neutralize the situation, but they were already irritated.

"I'm afraid I have some rather unfortunate news." Bella took another swig from her freshly refilled glass and leaned forward in her chair. "My money is gone. There's only a small portion left." She took in a deep breath then ripped the bandage off as quickly as she could. "I couldn't give you a hundred thousand dollars if I wanted to."

"What?" Jackie jolted in her chair. "Why not?"

"I guess you could say I fucked things up this time, huh, Jackie?"

Bella assumed Eli would run for the door, but he remained seated, sipping wine while he enjoyed dinner with a show.

Roger asked, "How's this possible?"

"My accountant stole almost everything. The police have him in custody for embezzlement, but the money is missing." Bella figured since she was coming clean, she should let it all go. "By the way, this handsome man, Eli? He's not my boyfriend. He's a friend I begged to do this."

"How could you let this happen, Isabella?" asked Jackie. "You have no idea the situation you've put your father and me in."

Bella turned to her mother with a look of confusion. "Me, how did I put you in a situation?"

"You're selfish and irresponsible," Jackie snarled.

"How could you say that? You've barely even spoken to me over the last year. Don't pretend you care about me."

Jackie stormed off, and Roger chased after her.

Bella cradled her face in her palms, afraid to look and see if Eli remained in his chair. When she gathered the courage, she opened her eyes and peeked through the tiny spaces between her fingers.

He looked at her with a sympathetic smile. "Should I order some more wine to go with these snails, or would you like to get out of here?"

---

California was typically chilly in the morning, warm during the day, then brisk at night. Dinner with her parents had her adrenaline raging, so the little black dress she wore with Eli's jacket kept her warm. "I can't believe this is so close to where I live, and I've never been here before."

"It's a local secret, most people don't know about it, but there's no better view at night. Sometimes I come here when I need a break."

"Are you kidding me? You are always so calm and collected. I can't imagine any part of your life is chaotic."

"You'd be surprised. I haven't always been the man you see. I've made mistakes, I've had heartbreaks, disappointments, failures, but I keep pushing forward, and you will too."

"You're too sweet, Eli." She felt comfortable and relaxed with him.

"I know, my fatal flaw."

"Why would you say that?"

"When you let your guard down, that's when people hurt you." Maybe there was more to Eli than he initially let on. "Would you like my professional opinion?"

"Of course," she said, curious to what his thoughts were.

"You've been through a lot recently, and I think you need to have some fun."

"And how do you suggest I do that?"

His warm eyes twinkled. "Turns out the ocean is therapeutic. They say if you go for a swim under the stars, the waves will wash away your worries."

It sounded cliché, but she needed to have some fun before she had another breakdown. "You do realize my life is falling apart?"

"That may be a little dramatic."

"My parents hate me. I lost hundreds of thousands of dollars and feel like a complete failure."

"Well, I didn't know the last part, but my prescription stays the same."

He pulled off his shirt and ran toward the ocean. His long body lean and defined. This wasn't the type of behavior she expected from a doctor. Eli dropped his pressed designer trousers at the shoreline. She tossed her shoes and followed close behind him. He was right; running toward the waves made her feel better, but the second her toes touched the frigid water, she stopped dead in her tracks.

"Come on, the water's invigorating."

Feeling reckless, she pulled her dress off and tossed it near Eli's pants.

The cold water sent a rush of goosebumps to cover her entire body. She swam toward Eli.

He gazed at her with a smile she couldn't resist. "Are you feeling better yet?"

"As a matter of fact, I am." Feeling like she could breathe for the first time in way too long, she didn't care about the money, Jack, her parents, or anything else for that matter. Eli pulled her toward him and kissed her passionately on the lips.

Floating in the Pacific Ocean, nestled in the arms of Eli wearing only her favorite lacy black panties and the matching bra, which had enough push to give her some volume without being sued for false advertisement, she didn't feel uneasy. She could marry a man like Eli, and she'd be a fool not to recognize it. He could provide her with enough love and stability to last a lifetime.

His arms were warm, but the water was cold. "Can we get out of this water? I'm freezing?" She was barely able to stop her teeth from chattering.

They made it back to the shore. Eli grabbed their clothes and placed his jacket around her shoulders. Her body shivered, and her legs felt stubbly, but she'd do it again in a heartbeat. Eli started a small fire to keep them warm using driftwood, a lighter, and random papers he retrieved from his glovebox. They sat in the sand, snuggled under the night sky while he pointed out several constellations. She assumed he'd want to know more about her parents after their dinner, but he never mentioned them. It was clear he wanted to make her happy.

"I want to know everything about you, Isabella Roberts."

Who was the person she'd become, lying to her parents, being less than forthcoming to the most fantastic guy she'd ever met? The nicer he acted, the more she felt like a jerk. She had to tell him about Jack; unfortunately, she wasn't sure what to say. *There's this guy I like, but he isn't looking for a commitment, so I'm going to ruin things with you for no reason.* It seemed like a bad decision, but she needed to be honest with him even if she wasn't entirely sure what the repercussions would be.

"There is something I think you should know."

"And what might that be?" asked Eli with a smile.

"There's someone else." As soon as the words left her mouth, she immediately regretted her decision.

"Are you referring to the guy you mentioned the other night who was not looking for a commitment? Why didn't you invite him to dinner with your parents tonight?" He wasn't being sarcastic or snide; his comment seemed to come from genuine concern.

"I'm beginning to hate this word, but the best way to describe this situation is … complicated. He was in a relationship, but it's been over for a while now. They own a business together, and they live together. He wants to wait to get involved until she is no longer in the picture." She felt stupid even saying it out loud. She didn't want to throw back a keeper for no reason.

"We're not together or dating. I want to be as upfront as I can with you."

"Believe it or not, I understand exactly how you feel." He could have said anything, yet he chose to empathize with her.

Bella reached over and took his hand. "I think you're great, and I have feelings for you. I'm just not sure how to define them yet."

"For now, maybe we should be friends."

His words were an immediate relief to her. "Yes, for now. I'd love it if we could be friends."

"You're going through a difficult time. Don't overthink this and let everything simmer down a bit."

"I wasn't expecting to meet you, and I certainly didn't expect to develop feelings for you so quick." She leaned in and kissed his lips. "I don't want to confuse you, but I also want to see where this goes with us."

He caressed her face. "I'm not going to give up on us, Bella." His words were genuine, and his touch was tender. This man had the potential to love her forever.

# CHAPTER TWENTY-TWO

After the evening's events, they were silent on the way home. She assumed he needed to think over the evening's shenanigans as much as she did.

Being the consummate gentleman, Eli insisted on walking Bella to her apartment. They walked hand in hand through her small community. Despite her best efforts to remove beach sand from her body, it still plagued every surface. Her hair was tangled from the combination of sand and saltwater.

"Thank you for inviting me to dinner."

"Are you kidding me? I can't believe you're still here after everything."

"I'm no quitter."

They rounded the corner near her apartment, and she could see Jack sitting on the bottom of her stairs. Her pulse quickened, and she hoped this would play out better than the dinner with her parents did. Eli looked at her, most likely curious if the mysterious stranger on her stairs was the man they discussed at the beach.

"Jack, what are you doing here?" asked Bella.

"I needed to talk to you, and it can't wait."

"This is Eli." She could cut the tension with a knife.

After an exchange of territorial nods, Jack said, "Listen, Bella, I can't stop thinking about you, and I'm not going to sit back and lose you to this guy or anyone else for that matter."

Eli quietly stepped back and monitored the situation.

Jack stood and moved toward her. "I want to be with you."

Bella couldn't believe her ears. Jack went for it, right there in front of

God, Eli, and the Plaza Apartment Community with no hesitation.

"What about Chelsea?"

"Chelsea is gone. She went back to North Carolina. I secured a loan and bought her out of the restaurant. She left for North Carolina this morning."

Bella gazed longingly at Jack before her eyes went to the ground. She couldn't even look at Eli. She had given him what had to be the absolute worst date of his entire life.

Eli asked, "Is everything okay?"

"Yes, I'm so sorry about this." She walked back to where he waited.

"You don't have to put up with this, Bella. Just say the word, and I'll ask him to leave."

She wiped a tear from her eye. Eli made a good point. She didn't need to stay on this roller coaster. She could get off at any time. Despite her better judgment, she still wanted Jack. Flaws and all. She wanted the peace, the storm, and all of the complications that came with it.

"Eli, this isn't fair to you. I need to figure things out with Jack before I can move forward with my life."

"It sounds like you've already made your decision." Eli's shoulders dropped, and he shook his head. "I should go."

She could see the frustration in his eyes. He managed to make it through the entire dinner without a smidge of despair, but now he was cloaked in it.

She knew nothing she said would make this moment better. "You deserve so much better than this."

"I do." His gaze moved to Jack. "I take it he's the one you told me about?"

Bella looked to the ground, embarrassed by the spectacle taking place in the courtyard of her apartment building. "Yes."

He shook his head and said, "Goodbye."

Her relationship with Dr. Elijah Jennings was over before it had a chance to develop into something special. She burned that bridge to the ground. She watched him walk through the ashes back to his car.

Bella turned back to her apartment, wondering if Jack had listened to her conversation with Eli. She didn't want to give him the pleasure of knowing they were over.

She felt a mixture of frustration and victory. "Jack, you can't show up uninvited like this."

He stood from the stairs and gazed down at Bella. The mystery and complexity of Jack intrigued and aroused her. "Who is Eli?"

"A great guy who liked me quite a bit.

"From here, it looked like you were on a date."

"It was a date." Why did she feel defensive? Jack didn't have the right to protest her relationships. He pushed her away, not the other way around.

"Why are you covered in sand?"

"None of your damn business."

"I'd like it to be."

The deep rumble of his voice sent shivers up her spine. She'd been waiting for this moment; he fixed everything and came back for her like a hero from one of Nona's novels. She sat next to him on the stair and said, "I suppose I owe you one for talking to your friend at the police department."

"Hopper and I go way back. I'm glad he could help you nail that scumbag."

"Would you like to come up? I can make some coffee." Unwilling to wait for his response, she motioned for him to join her.

Thankfully, Jack followed her despite her weathered appearance. She opened the door, and there was Snowball. As eager as ever to greet her after a long day. She knelt to the floor and played with her for a few minutes before turning her attention back to Jack.

"You make the coffee. I need to change." Bella left Jack and hurried off to her room, showering in record time and emerging in yoga pants and a slouchy sweater.

They sat side by side in the oversized beanbag chair, and even Snowball found a place to claim for her own.

"Is it serious? You know with Eli?" asked Jack.

She reflected on their charming evening under the stars. "I'm not gonna lie, Eli's a great guy, and I've only recently met him."

"Does he know about me?"

"Should he? We're not exactly a thing."

"I know, and it's all my fault."

Jack wasn't the kind of guy you would call a great communicator. It's like you could see the thought go from his mind toward his mouth and get lost along the way.

He sighed. "I tried to fix things, but now it's too late."

"Too late?"

"Yeah, now you have Eli."

"Jack, if Eli is who I wanted, you'd be at home, and he'd be here with me now."

He wrapped his arms around Bella, making her feel frail in his embrace. He leaned in to kiss her deeply, reminding her why she felt so powerless against him.

She pulled back, "I think we should take things slow."

"I can do that."

She smiled. "A girl can only handle so much rejection, and I don't think I can take another blow tonight."

"Trust me, Bella, you'll never feel rejected by me again."

It was all she needed to feel reassured. She caught him up on the day's events and fell asleep in his arms.

Amber rushed in, tossing Bella a light-yellow juice. "You're not going to believe what happened."

It was common for Amber to be excited about everything, so Bella took it with a grain of salt. She smiled at her best friend and provided her undivided attention.

"Eric proposed." She ran over, holding out her hand accented by a two-carat princess-cut diamond.

"This is unbelievable." Bella squeezed Amber, and they jumped up and down like teenagers, elated by the news. Most people would be concerned they rushed, but Bella knew they were a perfect match.

Bella knew things weren't perfect in her world, but she was finally ready to move forward. Sometimes life needed to shake you to your core, to show you what you originally built wasn't strong enough. Thanks to her determination and some great friends, Bella stood on a firm new foundation. One strong enough to stand the test of time. "I miss you so much I feel like we haven't had any time to talk."

"Your right. We haven't Netflixed and chilled in a while." They both laughed, remembering the night that felt like forever ago. "How did dinner go with Jackie and Roger?"

Bella smiled and said, "Here goes nothing … I took Eli to dinner with my parents. My mother asked me to be an investor in a business deal. I told them I lost all Nona's money, and Eli wasn't my boyfriend."

Amber's eyes widened.

"That's not all. After dinner, I went skinny-dipping with Eli, and when we got back to my place, Jack was there. He told me he bought out Chelsea, and she went back to North Carolina." She shook her head in disbelief and finished with, "He said he can't stop thinking about me and ended up staying the night at my place."

"What happened to Eli?"

"He went home." She took a deep breath and smiled at her friend.

"I feel like I haven't supported you properly through any of this." She reached out and hugged Bella tightly. "I hope you know I'm here for you if you need anything."

"Are you kidding me? You've been great. I can't believe you're getting married. You need to tell me about everything."

"Maybe Eric and I can have you over for dinner once things are a little less crazy. I'll show you my vision board, and we can talk about your dress."

Bella laughed. "My dress? Who cares about my dress? I want to see your dress."

"Yes, I'm hoping you'll be my maid of honor."

"Yes, of course." Thanks to her lack of friends growing up, Bella had never been a maid of honor, and Amber's request brought a tear to her eye.

"I gotta get out of here, but we'll talk soon. Love you, Bella." Amber floated out the door. She was in love with Eric, over the moon, and who could blame her.

In the spirit of facing her problems head-on, she texted her dad before she could change her mind.

Bella: I'm sorry last night was such a nightmare. I don't want things to be weird between us... I hope you can forgive me.

She stood behind the register at Carpe Diem, holding her phone, hoping he'd respond, but nothing. She shouldn't have been disappointed, considering Roger's track record with this sort of thing, but she was.

She wouldn't let this derail her; things were on the upswing, and she needed to keep her momentum going. She did a quick sweep of the already tidy store, completed packaging some new online orders, then updated her bookkeeping software before she could scratch the last item off her to-do list. The chimes sang when the door pushed open. She saw the last person on earth she expected. "Dad, what are you doing here?"

"I brought coffee ... a peace offering." He dressed like he intended to golf.

"Does Jackie know you're here?"

"I wanted to come to see you on my own," said Roger.

Bella greeted a couple of wandering customers before turning her attention back to her father.

Walking toward the register, she offered him a seat behind the counter before taking a sip of the iced caramel latte he brought her.

"I wanted to apologize for your mother's behavior at dinner last night, she's been under a lot of stress, and she didn't mean it. She felt terrible all night."

*Jackie felt terrible*? Bella didn't realize Jackie felt emotion. "I'm under a lot of stress too. Someone has stolen around five hundred thousand dollars from me."

"I know," he said. "I'm sorry that happened to you." He sounded sincere when he spoke, but a lifetime of neglect forced her to keep her guard up.

It had been over a year since she'd seen her father, and he appeared older than she remembered. His eyes had a sadness she hadn't noticed before. Had he always looked so sad, and she'd been too self-absorbed to notice? "We made a bad investment, and things haven't been the same since."

"What do you mean?" Bella and her parents were on separate sides of the country, yet their situations were similar. Like her, they were scared and financially strapped thanks to an investment. Dinner would have gone entirely different if her mother had treated her like an equal and told her the truth.

"We bought a building for a downtown revitalization project, and it's been one thing after the next. Someone stole all the copper, the structure was damaged, and after sinking in everything we had available, our original investor backed out. I know this isn't your problem, but we thought since you had the money, we should ask."

It was much easier to feel anger for her parents than it was to feel sympathy for them. They weren't the best, most loving people, but they were going through a hard time too. She needed to be the bigger person right now; it's what her nona would have wanted. "I'm sorry, Dad."

"That's the chance you take when you make an investment like this. Big risks make big rewards, but sometimes you need to work a little harder for the payoff." Dad had been beaten down by life, but even as weathered as he appeared, he kept his head held high. She couldn't help but wonder where she'd be right now without the kindness of Amber, Eric, Jack, the girls, and Dwayne. At least she had her people to lean on. Her parents didn't have anyone but each other. In retrospect, it had to be terrifying for them to ask her for help.

"Is the business secure?"

"Yes." He nodded, seeming confident. "We have lots of connections in Ohio. We'll find another investor one way or another."

"Do you think you'll be able to turn the project around?"

"Once we get the funding we need, this thing will be a cash cow."

Bella laughed aloud at the literal idea of a cow that produced cash. "If I could have helped, I would have."

"I know," he said while touching her shoulder. "Your mother does, too. She needs some time to cool off."

"Thank you for coming here to talk to me." She appreciated her father's gesture.

"Before I go, can you tell me why in the world you told us you had a boyfriend if you didn't?"

She hung her head low, ashamed of her decision to deceive her parents. "I guess I didn't want you to worry about me."

"Well, you know it's a parent's job to worry about their only daughter, and we won't be stopping any time soon." He started toward the door. "I have to get back to the hotel before your mother starts looking for me. I love you, Bella."

He didn't hug her like a normal father would. He didn't look back when he left; that's not the relationship they had. The news of their investment left Bella unsettled, she knew her parents were savvy investors, and if they could make a bad investment, she should be more gracious to herself.

Life wasn't perfect, but things were looking up a little more every day. Roger said he loved her, Chelsea went back to North Carolina, Amber got engaged, Dwayne taught Bella how to understand finances better, and she felt more self-sufficient every day.

She enrolled in an online business management class. When her mother called her ignorant, she had a point, Bella had some learning to do, but she never wanted someone to call her that again.

The foot traffic in Carpe Diem had more than quadrupled since the contest started, but profits did even more due to the online presence and price increase. The waiting list of new contestants stretched out several months. Bella had Tiffany and Addison to thank for all of it. After careful consideration of the revised budget, she determined that she could afford a bonus of a thousand dollars each for the girls. It seemed like a fortune to her right now, but she knew without their sacrifice, she'd be in big trouble. Things might be tight for a while, but Carpe Diem would do better than survive; it would thrive thanks to her friends.

Midday, a gentleman entered the store wearing a shield on his chest and a gun strapped to his hip. She could tell he was in law enforcement but not your typical police officer. He wore a heavily starched white button-up shirt and navy-blue dress slacks.

"Are you Isabella Roberts?"

His commanding voice made her nervous. "Yes, I am. And who may I ask are you?"

"I'm Jack's friend, Chief Hopper with the Coronado Police Department." He carried himself well, broad shoulders, impeccable posture, and a steady tone that oozed confidence.

"Chief Hopper, thank you for all of your help with my investigation."

"I'd like to ask you to take a seat, Miss Roberts. I have some news that may come as somewhat of a surprise." The worst possible scenarios plagued her when people asked her to sit down. "Carl Douglas struck a deal last night for a reduced sentence, and in return, he has disclosed where all the money is."

Her legs turned to noodles, and she felt a tingling sensation all over her body. Thankfully Chief Hopper told her to sit down. She counted down from ten in her mind to steady her anxiety.

"They've identified over five hundred thousand dollars that can be traced back to your business. We are expecting it will be returned within the next seven days. Congratulations, Miss Roberts."

"I can't thank you enough, Mr.—I mean Chief Hopper." Bella shot to her feet and shook the chief's hand before pulling him in for a hug while tears streamed down her face.

He handed her a clean tissue from his pocket. This was not his first time delivering impactful news. "No need to thank me, just doing my job. My department will reach out to you." She had an idea while watching him walk out the door, but she needed to talk to Dwayne first.

---

Jackie and Roger arrived fifteen minutes early. Roger waited near the door while Jackie continued toward Bella. Jackie turned back, briefly making eye contact with Roger. He nodded once, and she continued forward.

"Hello, Isabella."

"Hi, Jackie." It felt uncomfortable to see her mother for the first time since their spat, but she was still her mother, and Bella needed to be the bigger person.

"Please dear, call me mother." Bella could have fallen on the floor. She'd called her mother Jackie her whole adult life, and the sudden shift in formalities was confusing.

"I wanted to say I'm sorry. I still believe your behavior was appalling, but I could have conducted myself better."

For the first time in her life, her mother apologized, a terrible one, but an apology nonetheless. "Thank you," replied Bella.

Roger joined Jackie, and Bella pointed them to their seats.

It took some work, but everyone else arrived at Jack's restaurant by seven p.m. The staff set up a private area with plenty of space to fit them all comfortably. The rooftop patio had a stunning view of the ocean, and they arrived at an ideal time to catch a glimpse of a Coronado sunset. They sat together at an oversized table for eleven, Chief Hopper, his wife, Tiffany, Addison, Amber, Eric, Dwayne, Jackie, Roger, and Jack. Bella made sure to sit Dwayne next to Tiffany in hopes they could fall in love organically, and she wouldn't need to meddle like she did with Amber.

Public speaking terrified her, even with a small group of people she loved. She made her way to the large round table dressed in a floor-length navy-blue jumper that flowed more like a full skirt than pants. She hated to be the center of attention, but she felt honored to have the privilege. Tonight, even if no one else knew it, they were going to celebrate.

She began to speak before fear stole her voice. "I want to thank you all for being here on such short notice. At this table, I have people who gave me life, people who saved my life, and people I can't live without." She took a slow deep breath to steady her nerves. "Today, I had a visit from Chief Hopper, and he informed me Mr. Douglas made a plea deal with them to return the money he stole in exchange for a reduced sentence. Next week five hundred thousand dollars will be transferred into my bank account."

Amber gasped. Everyone looked surprised except for the chief and Dwayne.

"Tonight, I gathered you all together to celebrate with me, celebrate justice, and the engagement of my best friend Amber and her fiancé Eric." The guests clapped in celebration with Bella. "After consulting with my new financial advisor, I've decided to make a couple of investments, starting with a one hundred thousand dollar revitalization project in the heart of downtown Cleveland, overseen by my parents, Jackie and Roger Roberts." Her mother's eyes widened when she stood to make a small curtsy.

"The next thing I need to do is difficult but necessary. Addison and Tiffany, Carpe Diem is doing better than ever before because of you. It might take you by surprise, but I'll be terminating your employment at the end of the month. I want to invest in your start-up marketing company, that is, if you're up to the challenge."

The girls were grinning from ear to ear, and they deserved every bit of the accolades they received.

"I'm going to be your first customer, and I'll need your help finding some new employees, but I believe in you both. I'm confident you have what it takes to be very successful." She walked over and handed each girl an envelope containing a thousand-dollar bonus and the promise they'd meet with Dwayne to create a proper business plan.

The smiles plastered on their faces were all the thanks she needed. If anyone deserved a chance to succeed, it was these two girls.

"Jackie and Roger, I'd like to introduce you to Jack. He's not my boyfriend yet, but with any luck, he will be soon." Jack nodded in agreement. "I may have lost my nona, but in doing so, I found my family and I'm grateful for every one of you."

*The End*

## ABOUT THE AUTHOR

Dawn Ramos is a contemporary romance author focusing on vulnerable, flawed, and dynamic characters who draw you in and hold you captive.

Her books include **Carpe Diem**, **Christmas in Winchester**, and **Storybook Romance**. She is currently working on her fourth novel, **Emma's Gift**.

She is constantly cramming new story ideas into her journal; expect many more to follow.

Living in Las Vegas, Nevada, with her husband and two children, Dawn enjoys the never-ending supply of hot sunny days and beautiful views of the desert, as well as the best entertainment in the country.

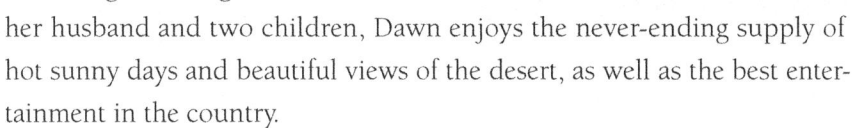

Dawn is a self-described hopeless romantic who believes in happily ever after. She loves to sing her favorite songs at the top of her lungs and spin in her favorite dress like she is starring in her own musical. She is a determined, powerful woman fearlessly charging forward to accomplish her dreams.

Want more? Go to *dawnramos.com*

Made in the USA
Las Vegas, NV
01 March 2022